See Tom Run

A Novel by

Scott Wittenburg

See Tom Run

A novel by

Scott Wittenburg

This is a work of fiction. The characters and events of this book are entirely the product of the author's imagination, and any resemblance to actual events, or to any persons, living or dead, is entirely coincidental.

ISBN 978-0-578-00210-1

Comments concerning this work are encouraged and can be addressed to scott@scottwittenburg.com

For the latest on my novels, please visit www.scottwittenburg.com

In loving memory of my mother and father.

PROLOGUE

Tom Grayson felt a numbing chill in the night air as he and Tracy walked in deliberate silence toward the parking lot. Fumbling absently through his pockets for the car keys, he was still reeling from what had transpired only moments ago when he arrived at her apartment . . .

"I'm pregnant," she announced flatly without so much as a hello.

"You're what?"

"I'm pregnant, Tom, and you are the father."

"No way!"

"Yes, way," Tracy insisted.

"We always used protection—it just isn't possible!"

"Tom, don't do this to me! Have you forgotten that night after Spangler's?"

Tom flashed back to the night they had hit the obscure off-campus nightclub. Damn! That was the one and only time he and the twenty-one-year-old beauty had made love without a condom— too horny after too many drinks and not a rubber in sight—

But surely he couldn't be that unlucky—

Oh yes he could be, he thought, and that was a fact.

"Okay, I believe you. So what are you going to do about it?"

"I'm going to have the child, of course! And I hope you will be its father."

"Whoa, wait a minute! I'm a married man, Tracy! Or have you forgotten? I'm not even supposed to be here!"

His words stung her like a slap in the face, Tom could tell, and he immediately regretted his brashness.

"I'm sorry Tracy, but you have to know it would be impossible for me to be any part of this. Surely you can understand—"

"All I understand is that you are telling me that you won't be a father to our child."

"But couldn't you just have, an uh—"

"An abortion? No, Tom, I will not have an abortion. Besides being Roman Catholic with parents who haven't missed a single mass since the day they were married, I don't believe in murder—"

Suddenly, the piercing screech of skidding tires in the adjacent alley shattered Tom's thoughts. The two turned in unison to see a car's passenger side door fly open and a lifeless body tumble out onto the pavement. A tall, lanky man sprang out from the driver's side and ran over to where the body had come to rest on its side. The man apparently didn't notice the two of them standing just yards away as he kicked the body a couple of times then got back into the car and sped away.

Tom saw the man's face clearly in the glow of the streetlight.

He and Tracy scurried over to the where the body was lying and huddled over it. When he knelt down for a closer look, Tom saw a young black woman bound with rope, gagged, and unconscious. He gingerly removed the duct tape from her mouth, half-expecting the woman to resist or cry out in pain. But except for a slight flinch, she remained unresponsive.

At that moment, Tom was gripped by a sudden wave of paranoia. If he were to get any more involved with this, Peg would almost certainly find out about his affair with Tracy Adams.

And he wasn't about to risk that happening.

"Let's call 911," he told Tracy.

"But shouldn't we get her out of the alley first and make sure she's okay?"

"We shouldn't move her. She's alive and seems to be breathing okay. She needs a paramedic, not us."

"I guess you're right. I'll run inside and call 911."

"Wait! If you call from your apartment, they'll know you made the call!"

"So what?"

"Tracy, I really don't want to get involved in any of this. Nor do I want you to, either."

Her eyes narrowed. "I get it—you're afraid that your wife will know that you were with me and find out about—our child. I think you're horrible, Tom!"

"Give me a break! I just found out about all of this ten minutes ago and it hasn't sunk in yet! At least give me a chance to absorb the whole concept before letting the whole city know! Besides, we can still help out this girl without anyone knowing it was us."

"And how might we do that?"

"I'll run to the phone booth around the corner. I'll call 911 then meet you back here. Then we'll book up to your apartment and make sure that the squad gets here okay. But we need to hurry before the whole neighborhood comes out to see what's happening!"

Tracy thought a moment, and then replied, "All right. But I don't like any of this one bit. I think we should stay right here until the medics arrive."

Tom ignored her. "I'll be back in a flash."

He sprinted around the corner and called 911 from the pay phone. When the dispatcher asked who was calling, he made up a name, reported the incident and promptly hung up on her.

He rejoined Tracy and hastily led the way back up to her second floor apartment. Once inside, they peered out anxiously from the living room window until the squad arrived five minutes later. Tom waited a moment or so then quietly slipped away before the cops arrived.

Peg hadn't suspected a thing when he arrived home. He called Tracy later that night in a lame attempt to downplay the whole incident. He insisted that the assaulted girl most likely knew the man who had dumped her off in the alley so the cops shouldn't have any trouble nabbing him.

But that hadn't quite been the case, as it turned out.

Not by a long shot.

1

Tom stared at his hand and debated whether to call spades trump or pass. He had the right bower, the king and a nine of spades, plus an ace of diamonds. He was also two-suited. Frank, to Tom's left, had dealt and would probably call trump if he didn't—and the way his luck had been going in this game, Frank probably had a loner in hearts or diamonds. The last thing they needed was to give their opponents a possible four points and lose the game.

He peered across the table at Peg, who obviously didn't have squat. His euchre partner and wife of eight years always wore her cards on her sleeve. Funny how he was the only one who ever seemed to notice that.

Frank's wife, Julie, had hesitated a moment before passing. Could be a bluff, but Tom doubted it. She could be holding the left bower for all he knew—or at least a decent stopper hand along with her husband.

Screw it, he thought. He was not feeling lucky at all today.

"Pass."

The moment he looked over and saw Frank's smug grin, Tom knew they were screwed. He literally wanted to bust him in the jaw for a split second.

"I've got a loner in hearts—a frigging *lay-down* loner in hearts!" Frank declared triumphantly.

Tom watched in horror and awe as Frank splayed his cards on the table for all to see: a jack of hearts, a jack of diamonds, an ace and king of hearts and an ace of clubs.

"I believe we just won the game," Frank added, not missing a beat.

Tom groaned, "Screw this! I *knew* I should have called spades!"

"Then why didn't you?" Julie asked.

"Because I'm an idiot."

"No comment," Peg said.

"Oh well, it's just a game," Tom said, with more than a trace of cynicism.

Just then, Kelli entered the room and tugged at Tom's sleeve. "Daddy, can you *please* tell Tyler to quit pulling my hair. He's acting like a little *shit* again!"

Tom tried his best to keep a straight face as he reprimanded his five-year-old daughter, but he didn't have much luck.

"Now you watch your mouth, young lady. Your little brother is not a little—what you just said. And if I hear you swear again like that, I'll take your toys away from you for a whole day!"

"Oh, Daddy, you will not! And if *you* can call him a little shit, why can't I? What's the difference?"

"The difference is," Peg said, "That your father needs to watch his mouth around his kids, that's what. Now don't let me hear you swear like that again Kelli or *I* will take your toys away for a *week!* Now go tell Tyler to come in here right this instant."

"Okay, Mommy," her daughter replied with a frown.

Kelli left the family room and Peg's eyes burned into Tom's like hot pokers.

"You have *got* to quit cursing around the children, Tom! My having to endure that sewer mouth of yours is one thing but I will not let your affliction be passed on to my children!"

"Sorry, dear," Tom replied. "I'm working on it—honest! Kelli must have heard me call Tyler that under my breath earlier today after I saw what he'd done to my iPod headphones. Neither of the kids were in the room when I said it—Kelli must have been eavesdropping."

"Yeah, right."

Tyler came into the room, his head hung down forlornly.

"Do not pull your sister's hair again, Tyler." Peg said.

"I won't, Mommy, I promise. I'm sorry."

"Okay, then. Tell Kelli you're sorry, too."

"I will, Mommy."

Tyler sauntered out of the room

"Anyone need another drink?" Tom asked.

"I could use a Seven-Seven," Julie said.

"New Year's Eve isn't until Wednesday, Jules. Don't you think you're celebrating a bit early?" Frank said to his wife.

"This will be my last one, Frank. I can't help but notice that you're on your third beer already. So what makes *you* so special?"

"I can handle my booze—you can't."

Julie scowled. "That's a crock."

"Whatever."

Tom got up and headed out of the room. Frank followed behind and paused for a moment in the living room.

"How's it going, pumpkin?" Frank asked his four-year-old daughter, Brittany. "Are you and Kelli having a good time?"

"Yes, Daddy. Guess what! We just decided that we're going to be *fashion models* when we grow up!" she gushed. The two girls then commenced to sashay around the room as if they were doing a runway show.

"Perish the thought," Frank sighed as he followed Tom into the kitchen. "I don't think I'll ever be ready for the teen years, Tom. I've been dreading that the very moment I found out we were having a girl."

"I know just what you mean," Tom replied. He opened the fridge and saw that the Seven Up bottle was nearly empty.

"Looks like we're out of pop. I'll go to the store and get some more."

"Want me to join you?" Frank offered.

"Nah, that's okay. You hold down the fort and I'll be back in a bit."

"Okay."

They returned to the family room and Tom gave Peg a peck on the cheek.

"I'm going to run to get more Seven Up—we're fresh out. Anything else anyone needs?"

"Can you get me some cigarettes?" Julie asked.

"Sure. Marlboro Lights, right?"

"Yes, here, I'll go get my purse."

"Forget about it, Julie. As much as I don't want to be a party to your suicide, I will spring for the little killers for you."

"You're a dear, Tom."

"I know it. Back in a flash."

"Be careful, Tom. The roads have surely gotten slick by now," Peg cautioned.

"I will."

Tom went to the closet, took out his coat and gloves then left through the side door. The snow was coming down hard and it looked like Columbus was finally going to get its first blizzard of the season.

Excellent, Tom thought. It was about time.

He got in and started the engine then grabbed the ice scraper lying on the back seat floorboard. He went about the task of clearing the windshield and windows, taking his time as he did so. The frigid air felt good and he was in no particular hurry to get back to the others.

As he backed the Jeep Laredo out of the driveway, Tom found himself pondering his present dilemma. He had in fact been thinking about it the entire day—dismayed to discover that even the euchre game had failed to relieve the incessant nagging thoughts.

Was he doing the right thing? Or should he tell Frank the whole ball of wax and let fate take over from there?

"Yeah, right." he breathed out loud.

Face it, Grayson—this is a no-brainer!

He reached the supermarket and pulled into the parking lot. The Jeep's interior was still uncomfortably frigid so he left the engine running, hopped out and pressed the lock button on the key remote.

Once inside the neighborhood market, Tom began searching for the soft drink section. Although he'd been here countless times, he couldn't recall where it was. He stopped agonizing over his thoughts long enough to walk the entire length of aisles, peering down each one until he finally located the beverage section near the far end of the store.

Tom picked up a liter of Seven Up and headed toward the checkout lanes. He paused at the cigarette counter long enough to pick up Julie's Marlboros then joined the throngs of people waiting in line. It was obvious that New Year's Eve was just around the corner when he observed the enormous amounts of wine, champagne and beer piled up in the carts.

As the thought of New Year's Day entered his mind, Tom considered it's profound symbolism. If he were to do what he should *morally* do, this New Year would mark the beginning of a whole new life for him: the end of his comfortable existence with his wonderful wife and kids in their quaint but beautiful home in suburban Worthington, and the likely termination of his job as art history professor at Capital State College. And to think that he had just received tenure this year . . .

His turn came and Tom paid the cute young cashier with his check card and headed for the exit. He sneezed loudly along the way and cursed his sinuses—how long had it been since he'd been able to smell or taste anything? What he had once thought was a head cold had now become full blown sinusitis. Peg was pushing him to see a doctor about it and he had to admit he was getting tired of not being able to breathe half the time. Maybe he'd go have it checked out after all, he resolved dismally.

The snow was coming down hard now—in fact it was a full-blown blizzard. Tom could barely make out his Jeep parked just twenty yards away.

He got in and stared out at the driving snowstorm. Instead of pulling away, he sat there mesmerized by the wintry scene and resolved that he must come to a definite decision about Tracy Adams. He already knew what the answer would be, but the moral aspect continued tugging at him hard, making it difficult to fully and unequivocally commit to it.

Unfortunately, the fact that Tracy was pregnant with his child wasn't the only issue here—as if that weren't enough.

He had to consider the other person involved in this as well— the poor black girl who had been dumped off in the alley over a month ago. Tom learned from Frank, who was a trial lawyer, that the young woman had in fact been abducted and raped but had no clear memory of what her assailant looked like. The police were looking for anyone who may have possibly seen the woman's attacker or his vehicle on the night of the crime.

This had really thrown Tom for a loop. And as guilty as he felt about not coming forth with any info for the police, he was still too paranoid to even consider getting involved in the investigation.

Once it became public knowledge that the police still had no leads in the case, Tracy started calling Tom on a daily basis to update him on her pregnancy and beg him to go with her to the police station to report what they had witnessed.

But Tom didn't want to hear any of this. He just wanted everything to go away.

A week ago, apparently fed up with his noncommittal attitude toward their unborn child and the rape case, Tracy gave him an ultimatum. If he didn't take responsibility for his actions, she would go to the police by herself and give her account of what they had seen that night. She assured Tom that she would keep him out of the picture, so he needn't worry about being involved. She would have their baby all by herself, without any involvement from him whatsoever, and he would never be allowed to see their child or be a part of its life.

In essence, she was telling him that he would be off the hook.

Tom could hardly believe what he was hearing—he was absolutely elated. For not only would he get out of having to testify in a court case, he wouldn't have to worry about his little secret ever being found out. All would be good again!

Or so he thought.

His conscience was gnawing away at him. The girl obviously loved him and her feelings were hurt. Although that certainly wasn't his fault—he'd made it clear to her all along that he loved his wife and would never leave her—it nevertheless wasn't making him feel any better about this.

But the clincher was that Tracy still hadn't gone to the police in all of this time. Her threat of reporting the incident had just been a bluff—a last ditch effort to heap the maximum amount of guilt on him in hope that he would relent. She wasn't going to go to the police unless he accompanied her—that much he was certain of now.

So in essence, the burden of dealing with this whole mess fell on his shoulders.

Damn! he thought. If only he had never accepted the girl's offer to go out for "an innocent beer" that day. None of this would have ever happened. But he had let her incessant flirting win him over and make him forsake the first cardinal rule of teaching: never get personally involved with a student. And now he was paying the price for allowing the ill-fated May-December romance to go on as long as it had—

Tom's thoughts were suddenly interrupted by the absolute fury of the raging storm that was now obscuring virtually all visibility outside the Jeep. Knowing that Peg and the others would be concerned, he threw the gearshift lever into drive and carefully pulled out of the supermarket parking lot.

He kept his speed at around 20 miles per hour as he deftly navigated the Jeep over the snow-covered roads through the blinding frenzy. Ten minutes later, he pulled into his driveway and parked. Clutching the grocery bag, he got out and headed for the side door.

The first thing he noticed when he entered the house was that the laundry room light was not on. Glancing over at the light switch, he saw that it was in the 'on' position, yet the fluorescent ceiling light was out cold. Odd.

Then he noticed the deadly silence.

The kids had been noisy all afternoon while at play in the living room. Perhaps they were back in the family room with the adults.

He entered the kitchen. The lights were out. The light switch was on.

The storm must have killed the power, he thought. He removed the liter of Seven Up from the bag and took Julie's cigarettes with him into the dark living room. As he neared the family room, he could feel his heart beating faster as the overwhelming silence began to register full tilt.

When he entered the family room, he was utterly shocked at what he discovered—

Not a soul was in sight. The card table was just as it had been before he left—the playing cards strewn around in random stacks, the half empty bowl of chips sitting near the center and everyone's drinks, including Peg's half finished daiquiri, sitting there among the rings on the tablecloth. Three of the chairs were pulled away from the table about the distance they would be if they were occupied. When he noticed this, Tom felt the hair stand up on the back of his neck.

It was as if they had all vaporized.

Then he chuckled to himself nervously. Surely this was some kind of gag. A little pre-New Year's prank dreamed up no doubt by Frank, the perennial jokester. That had to be it!

Tom decided to play along.

"Here are your coffin nails, Julie," he announced to the empty room. "Oh, imagine that! The damn things must have already killed you and your cancer-ravaged body has been carted off to the morgue. Oh well, I guess I better find out where everyone else is and let them know that we need to start making your funeral arrangements."

Half expecting someone to suddenly run out from behind the furniture and reveal their cover, Tom quickly turned around. Nothing. Then he headed through the living room to the stairs leading to the second floor. Most likely they would all be hiding up there somewhere, he thought. He took the stairs at a leisurely pace, giving everyone adequate opportunity to hide themselves. He could almost see the kids, Kelli in the lead, jumping out from behind her parents' king size bed and screaming bloody murder to scare the mortal shit out of him.

He tiptoed to the master bedroom door and opened it slowly.

"Anybody in here?" he said.

He walked past the dresser over to the bed and sat down in it. He fell onto his back and peeked over the edge on the far side. Not a soul.

"Hmm. I wonder if there's anyone in the closet."

He got up, went over to the walk-in closet and opened the door.

"Gotcha!" he cried, his arms outstretched like a ghoul.

But there was nothing but clothes and dark, muffled silence inside.

Tom closed the door and felt his senses sharpen as he left the bedroom and headed down the hall to the kids' rooms. He now realized that his theory was ludicrous — the notion that Peg, Frank, Julie and the three kids had all gotten together while he was gone and decided to play hide and seek just didn't float. It simply didn't seem realistic, especially given the fact that the power was off, which the snowstorm had apparently prompted.

Unless they had decided to trip the circuit breaker themselves, which would be less likely and even more ridiculous. Peg, in her typical level-headed way of running the house, would never have allowed that to happen for such a cheap thrill.

He went to Kelli's bedroom and peeked in. The room was shrouded in semi-darkness but it was clear that nobody was there. He went over to Tyler's bedroom and discovered the same.

The basement was his last shot. Annoyed and put off now by this whole farce, Tom went back downstairs and headed for the basement door located near the entrance to the kitchen. When he opened it, all he saw was absolute darkness. He went to one of the kitchen counter drawers and found a mini Mag-Lite, switched it on and trained the beam on the stairs as he made his descent.

The basement was little more than a large storage room and a place for the rarely used Brunswick pool table. There was also a half-bath and a small area that Tom used as a darkroom for his photography. It took only thirty seconds to determine that the basement was unoccupied.

The silence was intense as Tom went over to the circuit box panel and opened it. He shined the light on the breaker switches and saw that all of them, including the main switch, were on.

So there had indeed been a power failure.

So where the hell is everybody?

Tom closed the panel and went back upstairs, taking two steps at a time. He could now feel his pulse pounding like a drum in his neck as he realized that he was experiencing a keen sense of dread. His wife, kids and close friends were gone—seemingly evaporated from the house!

Coats! He thought. If they had left the house, they surely would have worn their coats.

He ran over to the hallway closet and gazed inside. He saw Frank's gray wool coat and Julie's blue parka along with their kids' winter coats.

Tom's sense of dread now became absolute fear.

In a panic, he ran over to a window and peered out at the street. As expected, he saw Frank and Julie's gray Chevy Tahoe still parked along the curb out front—he recalled seeing it there when he'd returned from the supermarket. He ran over to the front door and stepped out onto the porch. He looked up and down the street as far as could see and noticed that all of the lights in the houses were out, as were the streetlights.

The phone! He thought. He would call the power company and find out what the deal was with this power outage.

But first he would call the police.

He ran back inside and picked up the phone. There was no dial tone. Recalling that the cordless phones didn't work when the power was off, he ran into his study and picked up the old analog office phone on his desk. It was dead as a doornail.

He located his cell phone in his briefcase and booted it up. The sound of the welcoming chime was music to his ears. Now he could finally get to the bottom of all of this.

He stared at the LCD and awaited the welcome screen to come on. When it did, he noted that there were no signal bars showing up as he keyed in 911 and brought the phone to his ear. Nothing but pure silence. He tried again. Nothing.

"Shit!"

Now he was absolutely mystified. There was no power, no phone service and no sign of his family or friends. He stared at the phone a few seconds then flipped it shut and shoved it into his back pocket.

Unsure of what to do next, Tom finally decided to run next door and see if the Chandlers were home. Maybe Bill or Marge would have an idea of what the hell was going on. Maybe they even knew where Peg and everyone had gone.

He fled the house and trudged across the driveway to the Chandlers' front door and rang the doorbell. Realizing that their power was most likely out as well, he knocked on the door and peered through a window to see if he could see anyone. He waited a few seconds then started beating on the door when he noticed their only car parked in the driveway.

"Bill, Marge — are you guys in there?" he shouted.

When nothing happened, he walked around to the rear of the house and peered through the dining room window. There were no signs of life anywhere. Certainly odd, seeing as the elderly couple rarely went out with anyone and their car was here.

Tom decided to try Gary Morris, who lived directly across the street. He knew for a fact that Gary was home because he'd seen him pull into his garage just as he left for the supermarket.

He ran through the driving snow across the street to Gary's and beat on the door.

"Gary, it's Tom!" he cried, wanting nothing more right now than to simply see another human being. He knew that Gary Morris had a penchant for keeping an eye on the neighbors and their goings on. If *anyone* knew what the hell was happening around here it would be good old Gary.

After another minute of pounding and shouting, Tom ran around to the side of the house and peered into the garage window.

Inside he saw Gary's blue '99 Buick. He continued around the side to the backyard gate and lifted the latch. He strode over to the back door that led out from the kitchen and began beating on it. A moment later he went over to a window and peered inside. Tom saw nothing but a darkened room.

Gary lived in a single story ranch that had no basement, only a crawl space. In this tiny house, he most certainly would have heard all of the beating and shouting by now.

Tom went back over to the kitchen door and tried it. It was locked, just as the front door had been. He made a quick decision: he would bust out a window and go inside. Gary was either dead somewhere in there or had vanished mysteriously like the others. He had to find out.

He spotted a snow shovel leaning against the siding and picked it up. He went over to the kitchen window and poked the handle through a single pane of glass near the middle of the frame. The muffled tinkling sound of the shattered glass was all but lost in the raging snowstorm. Tom reached in and turned the latch, hoisted up the window and stuck his head inside.

"Gary—it's me, Tom! You in there?"

When no reply came, Tom slipped fairly easily though the window and onto the linoleum floor. It was dusk now and he could barely see his way around in the kitchen. He rummaged through the drawers until he located a flashlight and switched it on. The first thing he did when he spotted the wall phone was try it. The line was dead. He replaced the phone and went into the dining room.

Tom knew the house well. The living room was straight ahead and the two bedrooms and bath would be to the right. He felt his heart race in his chest as he moved cautiously into the living room.

He flashed the light around the entire perimeter. Gary's easy chair was in its usual position in front of the television. A neatly folded newspaper sat on the coffee table and the remote control rested on a small table beside the chair. Tom went over to the television and touched the screen. It was still warm, just as he had expected it would be.

But where was Gary?

Tom felt like a nervous cat burglar as he crept slowly toward the hallway where the bedrooms were located. He knew that the

first room on his left would be the spare bedroom. He peered inside and saw nothing but a single bed, nightstand and a dresser. He
walked past the bathroom to the only remaining room in the house.
The door to Gary's bedroom was closed. Tom took a deep breath
and turned the doorknob slowly, dreading what he might find on
the other side.

"Gary?" he called softly, startled at the sound of his own voice
in the eerie silence of the house.

He swung the door open gently.

He aimed the flashlight first on the queen sized bed then all
around the room.

Nothing. No body. No Gary.

He was gone, just like the rest.

Tom felt his heart sink like a lead weight.

Where in the holy hell is everybody?

At that moment, something inside Tom snapped.

Like a raging lunatic, he tore out of Gary Morris's house across
the yard to the Williams house and beat on the door furiously with
both fists.

"Mike, Carol—open the door! It's Tom Grayson! Please come
to the door and talk to me!"

He only waited a moment before turning the doorknob to see if
it was locked, which it was. He ran over to their driveway and saw
the Williams' teenage son's Mustang parked behind Carol's So-
nata. Mike's Explorer was parked out front on the street.

Tom sprinted back to the front door.

"I know you guys are in there—answer the damn door!" he
cried.

In a fit, Tom ran around to the side of the house and looked
through a window for any signs of life. Then he ran around to the
backyard and tried the sliding patio door. Miraculously, it slid
open.

Not really expecting to find anyone there, Tom entered the Williams house as though he lived there.

"Just dropping in to see if anyone in this fricking neighborhood
is still around – hope you don't mind!" he hollered as he sashayed
across the family room into the kitchen. He picked up the phone,
which was of course dead, then made his way throughout the
house. There were signs that someone had been home recently—

the television in the den was still warm as was Jason's iMac in his bedroom. But, just like everybody else, the entire Williams family had apparently vanished from the face of the earth.

Tom entered the living room and plopped down on the soft leather sofa. His mind was awhirl, trying to put all of this into some sort of reasonable perspective.

It wasn't possible to do.

He considered the facts thus far. It was a fact that every person he had tried to locate since returning from the supermarket was gone. Where they had gone, he did not know. And, they all appeared to have been in their homes before their sudden disappearance. Everyone involved also shared the following circumstances: the power to their homes was off and their phones didn't work.

Theories, Mr. Grayson?

He had none.

Deductions?

He hadn't an inkling.

What to do now? What would be the most logical thing to do?

Tom pondered this for a moment. He only came up with one obvious answer: he had to find out if anybody, anywhere was still around, period.

And he needed to do it pronto, before it got any later.

Because the last thing he wanted to do tonight was go to bed in utter darkness and total isolation, knowing that when he woke up nothing will have changed.

Tom exited the Williams home and returned to his home. It was pitch dark inside so he gathered up several candles and placed them throughout the house. Afterwards, when he tried the phone again only to find it was still dead, a thought suddenly came to mind: his iBook! It ran on battery power—maybe he could get on the internet!

Smiling to himself at the prospect, he went over to where his laptop computer was plugged into the wall near his fax machine and clicked opened the lid. He recalled that it had been a bit low on power that morning so he had attached it to the charger. It should be fully juiced up by now.

He pressed the power button and held his breath as the computer booted up. Once he saw the desktop, he clicked on Safari in the dock and watched the application appear on the screen. When the window opened, he clicked on the Yahoo bookmark tab and waited.

Two seconds later, a new window appeared.

You are not connected to the internet. Check your . . .

Tom leered at the screen. *Oh, but yes I fricking am connected, you sonofabitch!*

Then Tom laughed out loud lamely as he realized his folly.

But of course you aren't connected to the internet, you idiot! Because although your ethernet cable is connected to your computer, it is connected on the other end to a dsl modem which in order to work requires not only ac power, which you ain't got, but a working telephone line as well, which you also ain't got—

Tom shut down the computer with an agonizing groan. He now realized that in spite of his impending dilemma, he was totally exhausted. He could feel the wind in his sails starting to wane.

He sat the laptop down and went into the kitchen, poured himself a glass of water and chugged it down. He knew what he had to do next. And he was going to have to do it now, in spite of his fatigue and in spite of the fact that the blizzard outside showed no signs of letting up.

He retrieved the flashlight and went around the house blowing out all of the candles. Then he left by the side door and began scraping the freshly fallen snow off of his Jeep. The snowstorm was really raging now.

2

Visibility was very poor as he drove along Hartford toward the police station. Having driven no less than ten blocks, Tom made a frightening discovery: he hadn't seen a single soul nor a single moving vehicle since he'd left his house. Nor had he seen any lights on or any indication that there was power anywhere — not even the traffic lights were working. It was as if he were driving through a ghost town.

The cold kept him alert as he negotiated the hills and dales of Colonial Hills. The sheer darkness and lack of any movement, vehicular or otherwise, was absolutely cryptic. Somewhere in the back of his mind, he was fairly certain that he wasn't going to find anyone no matter where he went tonight. He was and always had been an optimist, but he was also a realist. The fact that he had not seen so much as a single shred of life in Worthington thus far indicated a reality that was, as impossible as it was to conceive, likely.

He nonetheless kept his hopes up as he passed by the supermarket he had been at earlier. There were still several cars parked outside in spite of the pitch-dark. Tom pulled up beside the entrance and threw the Jeep into park. He got out and approached the automatic doors, which failed to open. Inside, he saw nothing but darkness—not even the glow of emergency lighting.

He hopped back in and continued his drive to the Worthington Police department. There was something reassuring about the concept of a police force, he suddenly realized. For if anyone would still be carrying out their duties no matter how horrific or chaotic a situation might be, it would be the local police.

And he hoped and prayed that that would be the case tonight.

There was nearly six inches of fresh snow on the road as Tom swung a right into the police headquarters parking lot. Although he certainly hadn't expected to see the place lit up like a Christmas tree, he was dismayed to find that the station looked as dark and foreboding as all of the other structures he'd passed along the way.

He pulled up beside one of the cruisers and got out. Training his flashlight along the walkway, he reached the door and was surprised to find that he was able to pull it open. But what he discovered inside made his skin crawl.

There was a single red EXIT sign glowing weakly on a far wall beyond the reception area. In the dimly lit foreground, he saw no less than a half dozen desks silhouetted by the eerie red glow, each one equipped with a standard office telephone, a computer tower with an unlit monitor screen, a file cabinet off to the side and an office chair pulled up to it. Complementing the spooky scene was a neat row of walkie-talkies lined up on the desk sergeant's counter beside the police radio array.

There was not a single solitary living soul in sight.

Tom entered the office area. He touched a couple of the computer monitors as he made his way to the rear of the office to see if any of them were warm. When he reached one of the doors, he pushed it open and entered what appeared to be an interrogation room. He went through another door, past the restrooms then saw the entrance to the jail. He checked out the cells, which were uninhabited.

He returned to the reception area and stood for a moment, staring blankly at the deserted Worthington Police station.

So this is it, he thought. He was the only living person in town. Everyone was kaput—not just his family and friends, but his neighbors and even the entire police department!

Jesus, he thought. *This has to be some kind of bad dream! It simply can't be real!*

He could see his breath in the hazy red light and realized that the police station was absolutely frigid. That was no wonder, seeing as there wasn't any power to run the furnace. It was surely going to be a cold night no matter where he went, he thought.

Disgruntled and clueless, Tom made his way back out to the Jeep. He fired up the engine and turned the heat up to the max.

Then he lowered his head and rested it on the steering wheel, closed his eyes and began to pray:

God, please — you got to help me here. I don't know where my family and everyone have gone or what is happening. I need to know what to do. I need to know that wherever they are, they are alive and safe. I don't want to die like this, God, never seeing Peg or my kids ever again. Please God, tell me what to do! Where am I to go?

Where can I find my family?

Tom opened his eyes. He had never been a particularly religious person but he believed that there was a God. And he needed God now more than he ever had before.

Praying helped a little. There was comfort in talking to some-one—even if that someone was only a spirit or whatever God was.

But still, it wasn't quite the same as the real thing.

He had to keep moving. He must not let this thing get the best of him. Somehow he was going to find out where everyone had gone, even if he died in the process.

He shifted into reverse and spun out of the parking lot. He headed west toward High Street and turned left, heading south toward downtown. Within three blocks, he started running through the unlit traffic lights, not even bothering to slow down as he approached them. As he cruised past Morse Road into Beechwald, the next neighborhood south of Worthington, he was not surprised to see that all of the businesses were shrouded in complete darkness. He glanced at the dashboard clock. It was only 7:00 PM. And not a single store was opened to the public.

He approached North Broadway in Clintonville and a thought came to mind. *The hospital!* Riverside Hospital was just a few blocks to the west. Surely there would be some signs of life there!

Elated at the possibility, he fishtailed onto North Broadway and sped as fast as he could toward the hospital, keeping his fingers crossed.

Tom rounded the curve and a smile came to his face—on top of the hospital he saw the brightly lit blue Riverside Methodist Hospital sign.

It was open!

He ran the light at Olentangy River Road and headed toward the main entrance. It was dark in the parking lot but that didn't surprise him. He saw relatively weak lights on in the many of windows, suggesting that the huge complex may be running on emergency power.

He left the engine running and entered the huge glass turnstile. Inside, the lobby was dimly lit and there wasn't anyone at the reception desk. Nor were there any people in the lobby.

Not a good sign.

Perhaps they were operating with a skeleton crew, he thought, due to the power outage.

Tom strode through the lobby until he reached the gift shop, which was also deserted. He went inside and walked over to the counter, aware now that he was totally famished. He grabbed a bag of Fritos off the rack and plunked a dollar bill on the counter. Stuffing a handful into his mouth, he exited the shop and headed down one of the halls toward the emergency room.

He stopped at a bank of elevators and pushed the up button, not expecting the elevator to work. To his surprise, the door whooshed open, startling him. Tom stepped inside and pressed the button for the second floor.

The door shut and the elevator began its ascent. The interior was dimly lit but Tom was just glad it was working. When he reached the second floor, he stepped out into another dim hallway.

He walked toward the nurse's station. It was uninhabited. He entered the area and poked around, noting that neither the computers nor any of the other devices were on. Picking up a phone, he heard a dead line.

Finally, he got his nerve up and walked over to one of the patient's rooms. He knocked on the door, waited a moment, turned the doorknob.

The door was locked.

He went over to the next door and tried it. It too was locked.

Tom tried another half dozen doors only to discover that they were all locked.

Apparently, everyone in this place had either been evacuated or vaporized.

Tom took the elevator to the third floor and checked the rooms. They were all locked as well.

Nothing shakin' but the leaves on the trees.

Heaving a distraught sigh, Tom had to concede that the hospital was a bust. Like the police station, another vital community service center that one would expect to be active in an emergency was DOA.

Screw this.

He wolfed down the rest of his Fritos and washed them down with a slug of the lukewarm bottled water he'd snatched from a fridge in the nurse's supply room. Then he boarded the elevator back down to the main floor.

Tom exited through the turnstile and turned to his right, then did a double take—

The Jeep was gone!

3

Tom quickly glanced around the parking lot and along North Broadway, hoping to catch sight of his Jeep. He saw nothing moving at all. He ran over to where it had been parked and could see the tire tracks clearly in the deep snow where the thief had backed out before moving south toward the exit road from the hospital.

So, he was not alone after all!

His immediate impulse was to find a vehicle he could borrow so he could chase after the driver of his Jeep. There were quite a few cars in the parking lot, every one buried under six or seven inches of snow. He ran over to the first four-wheel drive car he could find, a Subaru Forester, briskly cleared the snow off the door handle and tried it. It was locked. He moved along the row of cars for a few minutes until he finally found a Honda CR-V that was unlocked. He jumped inside and was thrilled to find that the keys were still in the ignition.

The engine was excruciatingly slow in turning over but finally fired up. He jumped out and cleared off the windshield and windows as best as he could then got back in, put it into drive and headed for the exit.

He noticed with relief that the snowstorm had tapered off somewhat as he neared the exit, hoping to ascertain which direction the Jeep tracks led. In the virgin snow, it was clear to see that they headed west toward Upper Arlington. Tom gave the little four cylinder SUV the gas and hung a right in hot pursuit.

As he followed the tracks to Fishinger Road, Tom wondered who had stolen his Jeep and why. The first question was impossible to answer but the second was easy: the guy saw a warm uninhabited vehicle with its engine running in a deserted parking lot so he decided to nab it. Duh . . .

As angry as he was that someone had brazenly ripped him off, Tom nevertheless found solace in knowing that he was not the only human being left on earth. No matter who had stolen his Jeep, that person was apparently alive and well and in the same predicament as he was. That had to be a good thing.

But another mystery was why that person had not tried to contact him. It wouldn't take a genius to figure out that who ever owned the idling Jeep was inside trying to find another living soul in the godforsaken place. Why wouldn't that person attempt to find the Jeep's driver, instead of stealing it and driving off into the sunset?

Unless, Tom thought, that person didn't *want* to be discovered by him. Which would imply that this person could be a potential foe.

Tom raced as fast as he could along Fishinger, continuing west toward Route 33. He barely took his eyes off the road to glance at the houses that were shrouded in darkness. When he reached the intersection at Route 33, the tracks proceeded west over the bridge toward Hilliard.

Although his adrenalin was pumping now, Tom also felt an overwhelming fatigue coursing throughout his body. This whole situation was so bizarre and surreal that he half expected it to end at any moment. He sure *wished* it would end, that was a fact.

The tire tracks continued on the same road for a few more miles until they merged onto the southbound entrance ramp to the I-270 outerbelt. Tom slowed down in order to stay on the curve in the road until he was safely on the interstate.

The highway looked like something out of a science fiction movie as he sped south on it, not a single working streetlight illuminating the way. This source of countless traffic backups, headaches and collisions was now nothing more than a pure white, uninhabited landscape. Sort of like Mars—

Tom suddenly saw a pair of headlights about a mile ahead in the northbound lane, coming toward him fast. He stared over at the car incredulously as it whizzed by in the opposite direction on the other side of the median.

It was his Jeep!

On impulse, he hit the brakes and began fishtailing out of control. He nearly did a three-sixty as the Honda spun around like a top. Tom let off the brake and cut the steering wheel in the same direction as he was spinning until the little SUV was finally under control. He slowed down to a complete stop near the berm heading in the opposite direction.

Tom swore under his breath, turned the car back around and proceeded south—the huge concrete divider preventing him from crossing over to the other side.

He looked out for the next exit and suddenly saw an orange sign that read *Road Closed Ahead*. Tom slowed down a bit until he came upon a huge construction area that encompassed the entire highway in all six lanes. He followed the detour sign to the next exit and quickly got onto the northbound entrance ramp.

As he strained his eyes to spot his Jeep ahead in the distance, Tom thought it odd that the outerbelt was completely shut down southward from this point on. He couldn't recall ever reading anything about it.

Tom was driving as fast as he possibly could and still keep the car under control as he continued in pursuit. He hadn't been able to see the driver when it flew by, but it was clear that whoever it was did not want him to catch up. Which made Tom think that he had best use caution if and when he finally caught up to the thief.

He slowed down at the Hilliard exit where he had first gotten onto the outerbelt and discovered that the Jeep had gone past it. As he sped up again, he noticed that the fuel gauge was near empty. If he didn't have any luck soon, he was going to have to give up the chase before he ran out of gas. The last thing he needed was to be stranded out here on this lonesome interstate.

Tom had driven another four or five miles when he thought he spotted a pair of red taillights up ahead. He began slowing down and when he got closer, discovered that the lights were not moving at all—

The Jeep had run off the road!

He pulled up beside the Laredo, which was still running. It was at that moment that he realized his Jeep had run into a utility pole—just hard enough to dent in his bumper a good half inch or so. He saw no sign of the driver and wondered if he had bailed out.

Then he thought he spotted the top of a head lying against the driver's side window.

The head was motionless—

Tom threw the CR-V into park and jumped out. He ran over and gingerly opened the door, careful not to let the person fall out. He was shocked to discover that the driver was a young woman and apparently unconscious.

He gently lifted the girl upright against the seat. She started to moan softly.

"Hey there, are you all right?" he said.

The girl moaned again and then her eyes fluttered open. When she saw Tom, she let out a scream.

"Don't hurt me, please!" she cried, terrified.

"Don't worry, I won't," Tom said. "Are you hurt? It looks like you may have hit your head on the steering wheel."

"You promise you won't hurt me?"

Tom patted her lightly on the shoulder. "I won't, I promise. I just want to make sure that you're okay. What happened?"

The girl seemed to snap out of it somewhat as she peered into Tom's eyes.

"I thought you were somebody else," she began. "Someone has been chasing me for the last couple of hours. He's very dangerous. I thought I'd lost him a while back and then my car ran out of gas on the north side. I ran on foot until I found this Jeep parked at Riverside Hospital. So I got in and drove out here, trying to find a way out of town.

"Then I ran into the road construction and headed back this way. I saw your car and panicked. I guess I started driving too fast—the next thing I knew I lost control and slid into the berm. I braked until I ran into that pole. Guess I hit my head on the steering wheel and it knocked me out."

Tom wondered why the air bag hadn't deployed as he noticed a lump on the girl's forehead in the dim light. It was bleeding slightly.

"You've got quite a bump there," he said. He leaned over to the dash compartment and pulled out a pack of Kleenex.

"Hold this over it," he said, gently placing the tissue on her forehead.

"Thanks. How did you know there would be Kleenex in the glove box?"

Tom smiled. "Oh, my wife always makes sure that we keep Kleenex aboard."

The girl's eyes widened. "This is *your* Jeep?"

"Yup, sure is. That's why I've been following you."

"God, I'm so sorry! I was just so scared that I didn't give it a second thought when I took it. Of course, I really didn't expect to see anyone else out tonight."

Tom said, "Don't worry about my car—it sounds like you really needed it at the time. Before you tell me who's been chasing you, I'd like to know what you meant by not expecting to see anyone out tonight."

The girl shook her head wearily. "That's going to take some explaining and I am so tired I can hardly keep my eyes open."

"I know what you mean. Let's say we get off of this highway and go somewhere warm. I'll drive."

"You don't know how good that sounds, uh—"

"Tom. Tom Grayson," he said.

The girl smiled. "My name is Erin Myers." She offered him her hand awkwardly. "Nice to meet you."

Tom shook her hand. "The pleasure is mine. How does your head feel?"

"Not too bad, but I wouldn't exactly refuse a couple of Advils, either."

"We'll go to my house and get you some. Maybe we can even find some food to eat."

"Where do you live?"

"Worthington."

"We can't go there!" Erin exclaimed defiantly.

"Why not?"

"That's where he started chasing me—I live in Worthington, too."

"Whereabouts?" Tom asked.

"Near Wilson Bridge Road."

"Don't worry, we're not going that far. Besides, what makes you think he'll find us? And if he does, whoever he is, what could he possibly do?"

Erin shook her head. "Kyle is liable to anything when he's this mad. He would probably kill us both."

Tom was shocked by this response but tried not to show it. "No, he won't. I'll protect you." Spoken like a true superhero.

"No offense, but you don't know just how violent he is. He—"

She stopped herself and closed her eyes. It was clear that she didn't want to go on.

Tom said, "It's okay, Erin. Let's get out of here and we'll make sure that this Kyle character doesn't spot us. I know some pretty obscure routes to my home."

Erin managed a weak smile. "Okay."

Tom helped her out and escorted her over to the passenger side. He checked out the damage to the Jeep, which was minimal, and then parked the CR-V closer to the berm. He debated what to do with the keys and wondered if the owner would ever be reunited with his car again. It was that moment that the full brunt of all that had happened resurfaced in his mind.

He got back into the Jeep and backed away from the pole. "Won't be needing that little Honda anymore—it's about out of gas anyway," he quipped. He glanced at his own fuel gauge, which still had about a quarter of a tank left. Good for about another forty or fifty miles, he estimated.

"Thank you," Erin said.

"For what?"

She looked over at him. "Saving me."

Tom was a little confused by this, but replied, "You're welcome."

They drove a few miles in silence and Tom thought of at least a dozen questions he wanted to ask Erin Myers. He felt it best to wait though—at least until after they reached his house. He caught himself nearly nodding off as he drove through the seemingly endless white vista back to Worthington. He was all but completely spent. The thought of going home, falling asleep, and waking up to find that this had just been an awful nightmare was his greatest wish at the moment.

However, Tom was almost certain that wouldn't be case.

4

Erin Myers was fast asleep by the time they reached Worthington. Tom had caught himself checking the rear view mirror frequently throughout the drive, just in case the mysterious Kyle had picked up their trail along the way.

He felt odd as he pulled into his driveway, aware that his family and friends weren't in the house and that he was about to take a stranger inside. The events leading up to this moment had unfolded so quickly that it nearly overwhelmed him.

Erin stirred when he shut off the engine.

"Is this where you live?" she murmured.

"This is it. Did your little nap help any?"

"No, it just made me feel dumb. And my head really hurts now."

"Let's go inside and get you some pain killers."

The two got out and Tom held Erin's arm as they trudged through the deep snow to the door. Once inside, Tom flipped on the flashlight and lit a candle in the kitchen. As the room filled with flickering yellow light, Tom saw his breath and felt the frigid cold of the house.

On a lark, he went over and turned the knob on the stove. Although it didn't come on, he could smell gas.

"I'll be damned! The gas still works!"

"That's great—it sure is cold in here," Erin shivered.

"We'll take care of that right now," he said. He struck a match and held it near the burner as he turned the knob. A circular blue flame shot out with a whoosh.

"Excellent! We will at least be able to keep warm—we have a natural gas fireplace in the living room."

"Thank God for gas, eh?" Erin said. "My place is total electric. Are your phones dead, too?"

"Oh, yeah. Can't get on the internet either. How long ago did *you* find out that you were the last person on earth?" Tom inquired.

"When I got home from work. It must have been around 5:15."

"Ditto here. I'll go get you some Advil. Would you like something to eat? I'm starving."

"That would be great. You don't have any canned soup do you? I could heat some up," she offered.

"Over there in the pantry—that sounds like a great idea."

Tom went over to look for the soup as Erin stood behind him.

"Chicken and noodle!" she exclaimed.

"Sounds good to me," Tom said and handed her a can. "The pans are hanging over there. I'll be back in a flash."

As he headed for the bathroom, Tom lit candles along the way. He took a bottle of ibuprofen out of the medicine cabinet, stopped in the living room long enough to light the fireplace, then returned to the kitchen.

Erin was warming her hands near the burner while the pan of soup heated up. Tom went over to the sink and filled a glass with water from the tap.

"Here you go," he said handing Erin the tablets and water.

"Thanks."

After they had wolfed down the soup along with some saltines and water, Tom and Erin went into the living room and sat near the fire. For a few moments, they just sat there staring into the flickering gas logs, feeling the warmth seep in.

Moments later, Erin removed her coat and Tom noticed how petite she was. He realized then that she couldn't be much older than eighteen or so. She had long brown hair that fell a few inches below her shoulders, fair skin and very large brown eyes. She was wearing denim jeans, a blouse under a navy blue sweater and loafers. Erin Myers was very pretty but not what one would call beautiful. She possessed a girl-next-door look and an overly serious, cautious demeanor that was somewhat disturbing, considering her young age.

"Is your head getting any better?" Tom asked.

"Yes, it is. I'm finally warming up, too."

"It is getting toasty in here," he said, removing his coat. "Do you feel up to answering a few questions? I know you're tired—I am, too. But I can't let it wait much longer."

Erin gazed at him, her eyes revealing that she too had some questions she wanted answered.

"I'm fine, Tom. I want to know what has happened as much as you do. I hope *you* have some answers for this—because I haven't got a clue."

Tom shook his head. "I wish I had some answers, but I'm afraid I don't. All I know for sure is only what I've seen, and not seen, since I arrived here earlier this afternoon. And none of it is good, to say the least."

Erin nodded. "It's been horrible!"

"Why don't you tell me all what all happened to you today. That is, from the time that things started getting strange."

Erin leaned back in the chair and let out a long sigh.

"Well, let's see. I was driving home from work—I got off at five o'clock—and the snowstorm was getting really bad. I had a hard time seeing and could barely keep my car on the road, it was so slick out. When I finally got to my apartment building, I went inside and noticed that the electric was off.

"I started getting a little nervous because it was getting dark out and I don't do well in the dark. In fact, I can't even sleep without a light on. Anyway, I checked the fuse box and saw that none of the fuses were out so I assumed it was a power failure. I tried to call the power company but the phone wouldn't work. My cell phone wouldn't work either.

"I decided to go to my neighbor's apartment next door and see if she had any idea of what was going on. I mean, it's so weird losing the power *and* the phone at the same time. And I thought it was even weirder that my cell phone wouldn't work—because they work off satellite antennas or whatever, don't they?"

Tom nodded.

"So I went over to Mrs. Kline's apartment and knocked on the door but she never answered. I tried some of the other neighbors as well but no one was answering.

"That's when it dawned on me that something was really wrong. I mean—I've never known *everyone* in that building to be gone all at the same time. It was just too weird. I started freaking out. I ran outside and saw that nobody's lights were on anywhere. I started running up to people's doors and pounding on them, hoping that someone would answer . . . It never happened!"

Tears came to her eyes. Tom went over and kneeled beside her, resting a hand on her arm to comfort her. She was clearly over-wrought. He could understand why.

"It's okay—you're not alone anymore," he said softly.

She smiled faintly, breathed a sigh and continued.

"I didn't know what to do. I wanted to just start running some-where—anywhere—and find somebody to talk too! But the storm was getting worse and worse, and I realized that it probably wouldn't do any good. So I just went back to my apartment and decided to wait it out.

"I lit every candle I had in the house. All of the time, I kept tell-ing myself that the power would surely come back on, or the phone would ring, or something—

"I had some pot so I decided to smoke a joint—you know, to calm down my nerves. I smoked one and had a beer, basically hop-ing that I could get messed up enough to simply pass out. Nothing was really working so I smoked one more joint and had another beer. I finally fell asleep on the sofa.

"The next thing I knew, I heard a horn honking outside. My apartment is on the second floor and faces the street. The horn just kept honking and honking. I got up and went over to the window to look out. I knew right away who it was. It was Kyle! He had driven all the way here to find me. Somehow he had found out where I lived but apparently wasn't sure which apartment I was in. Like I'm sure I was going to just run out there to his car and start chat-ting!"

Erin's wry smile turned into a frown. She suddenly looked dis-traught.

"I couldn't believe it! Kyle had managed to find out that I'd moved to Columbus and I am sure wanted to make me pay for leaving him. He is, so—"

Tom wanted to ask something but Erin continued.

"I saw him glance up at me in the window. He got out of his car and ran toward the building. I totally freaked out! I ran out my door and up to the third floor, hoping that I'd get a chance to es-cape.

"I heard him shout out my name as he ran up the stairs and went into my apartment. 'Where are you, bitch?' he was screaming. I knew I only had a few seconds before he realized I wasn't in there, so I crept back down the stairs and past my door as quietly as I could. When I reached the first floor, I ran out, got into my car and sped off just as he was running out from the building. I saw him get into his car in my rearview mirror as I drove onto High Street and down a side street, hoping to lose him. I eventually got onto Route 315 and headed south until I ran out of gas near the North Broadway exit. That's when I ran on foot to Riverside Hospital and stole your Jeep."

Tom was taken aback by her story. He wanted to know more about Kyle and why he was pursuing her so ferociously.

"Why was this Kyle fellow chasing you down? You said something about leaving him—is he an old boyfriend?"

Erin's expression changed dramatically. She paused for a moment and replied, "It's a long story, and I'm way too tired to get into it right now. Let's just leave it at that, okay?"

Tom decided not to push her. It was more than obvious that Erin didn't want to divulge much more than she already had about this particular topic.

"Okay. I certainly don't want to be prying into your personal life, Erin. I guess what is eating at me is why this Kyle acquaintance of yours is apparently the only other person left in this town besides you and myself. Is there a reason, or is it just coincidence?"

Erin shook her head. "I don't know. All I can say is that Kyle is the last person on earth I ever wanted to see and this is just my luck! I'm sure glad you're here, though. I'm more grateful to you than you can even imagine."

"I feel the same way about you, Erin. I would not want to be alone right now with all of this weirdness, and just having you here has given me hope that we can somehow beat this thing, what ever it is."

"What about you, Tom? Is that your family in that picture?" she asked, pointing to the eight by ten family portrait on the mantel.

Tom went over, picked up the photo and showed it to Erin.

"This is my wife Peg and our two kids: Kelli and Tyler."

Just saying their names made his voice waver noticeably. "I'm sorry. I just can't believe they're not here—"

Erin gently placed her hand on Tom's and squeezed it. "It must be horrible for you—I'm sorry, Tom."

Tom stared into Erin's eyes. Her compassion seemed genuine and he felt the overwhelming urge to hug her, which he did. A moment later, a thought suddenly came him. "How old are you, Erin?"

She pulled slowly away from him. "Why do you ask?"

"Just curious. You had mentioned drinking beer a bit ago but I have a funny feeling you're not old enough to legally purchase it. Am I right?"

Erin looked somewhat indignant. "Well, I'm only eighteen—but I'll be nineteen in a couple of months."

"That's old enough for 3.2 beer when I was your age. So how about a beer now that I know I'm not serving a minor?"

She laughed heartily. "I'd love one!"

Tom stood up and headed for the kitchen. He took a pair of Michelobs from the fridge and returned to the living room. Erin was sprawled out on the floor in front of the fireplace as he removed the caps and handed her one of the beers.

"Cheers," he said.

"Cheers," the girl replied.

Erin took a swig and looked at Tom, who had sat down beside her on the hearth. "So now it's time for you to tell me about *your* day, Tom. When did you realize that everyone was gone?"

Tom chugged his beer and savored it as it went down. "Well, we were playing euchre in the family room . . ."

Tom proceeded to tell his side of the story. When he finished, he sensed that the extent of their dire situation hadn't really sunk in with Erin until now since she had spent most of her time running from her raging mad ex-boyfriend.

"I can't say this enough, Tom. I am so glad you found me. I don't think I could've made it without you."

Tom took her hand and held it tight. "I'm glad I found you, as well. Somehow, we are going to get through this. Together."

She looked sad and a little skeptical. "I know we will."

Erin killed her beer and yawned.

"Let's turn in," Tom said. "Tomorrow is another day. Why don't you sleep on the sofa and I'll take the chair."

"Okay."

"I'll find some blankets."

He went up to the bedroom and picked up a couple of blankets and a pillow then went through the rooms, dousing all of the candles. He stopped by the phone long enough to pick it up and hear the dead line.

Erin was fast asleep on the sofa when he returned to the living room. He tucked the pillow under her head and spread a blanket over her. She looked like an angel lying there and Tom bent down to kiss her on the cheek.

He didn't know why he did that. It just felt right.

Then he put out the rest of the candles, sat down in the chair and closed his eyes. He was fast asleep within seconds.

5

Tom's first conscious thought when he awoke was to be sure to tell Peg the bizarre dream he'd just had while it was still fresh in his mind. When he started to turn onto his side to face her, he realized that he was not in their king size bed.

He was on a chair in the living room.

It had not been a dream!

The events of the following day cascaded into his head in no particular order: the stark reality that his entire family was gone. The huge snowstorm and discovering that there wasn't a single soul in Riverside Hospital—and how the doors to all of the patient's rooms had been locked. When he recalled Erin Myers, he bolted upright and turned to look at the sofa.

She wasn't there!

Tom bounded out of the chair just as the aroma of freshly brewed coffee hit his nose. He had a smile on his face as he headed for the kitchen.

He saw Erin at the stove just getting ready to crack an egg on the edge of the skillet.

"Good morning," he greeted.

"Good morning. I thought I'd fix us some breakfast. I sort of improvised with the coffee maker," she added, glancing toward the counter.

Tom looked over to where she had poured boiling water through the coffee maker basket into the Mr. Coffee carafe.

"Excellent! I'll pour us a cup. Cream and sugar?"

"Lots of both," she replied.

Tom prepared their coffees and handed a cup to Erin.

"How did you sleep?" he said.

"Like a log. I don't think I've been that exhausted in my life!"

"Me neither."

Tom went over to the window and peered out. There were shafts of brilliant morning sunshine slicing through the trees in the back yard. The sky was clear blue.

A perfect day to go out and find out what happened to the rest of the world, he thought to himself with a wry smile. He still couldn't believe that this was really happening. He glanced over at the young stranger cooking at his stove. The scene was so incredibly surreal and bizarre that he almost felt like laughing out loud. But he didn't.

Because this, amigo, is no laughing matter.

Where in the holy hell had his family gone? And everybody else? When were things going to get back to normal? Were they *ever* going to get back to normal? What in the hell should he do now?

He had no answers to any of these questions. All he knew was that he couldn't just sit around this house and hope for some kind of miracle to come along and make it all go away. He was going to have to get into his car and go somewhere. Somewhere where the electric was still on, the phones still worked and people still existed.

So where should he begin?

Downtown would be a start.

And if he had no luck there, then where should he go?

He would just have to cross that bridge when he got to it.

"Here we go," Erin said, carrying a pair of plates over to the table. On each was a huge pile of scrambled eggs. Forks, knives, napkins and glasses of water were already neatly set up on the table.

Tom went over and sat down. "It looks like you have some experience at this."

"I've waited tables at a few places over the years."

Tom thought it odd when she said this—it suggested that she'd had several different waitressing jobs in her young life. And she was only eighteen?

"That's interesting. Any restaurants that I know of?" Tom asked.

She shook her head. "I don't think so."

Tom had the feeling she didn't want to go any further with this—just like the old boyfriend topic. He felt it best not to pry, at least not at the moment.

"These are really good. It's refreshing to see a youngster who knows how to cook nowadays. Cooking seems to be going out the door in today's society—especially with your generation."

"I wish you wouldn't lump me into some statistical bullshit, Tom! I mean—you make me feel like I'm five years old. I'm a *woman*, not some little kid!"

Her outburst left Tom dumbfounded. Her age seemed to be a particularly sensitive issue with Erin Myers.

As did her past.

Tom began to wonder what the real story was with this peculiar young lady. As much as he was dying to find out, he knew it would simply have to wait. The most pressing issue now was to try to get out of the predicament they were in and find out where everybody had gone.

"I'm sorry, Erin. I didn't mean to offend you. But when you get to be my age, you look at the world differently with regard to some things. I guess that I was stereotyping and I apologize for that. It's a bad habit of mine, I'm afraid."

"That's okay. I'm sorry I lashed out at you. I'm just a little too freaked out by all of this. What are we going to do?"

"I guess we'll just get into the Jeep and drive around. Look for signs of life somewhere. I figure we can start out downtown and take it from there. There's the police station, the city building, and so on. Surely, there has to be *something*."

Erin nodded. "I guess you're right."

Tom took a gulp of coffee and stood up. "I'll go start the Jeep so it can be warming up. Thanks for the breakfast."

She smiled at him. "You're welcome. I'll clean up the dishes."

Tom was intrigued by this young lady's resourcefulness. She would make somebody a great wife some day.

He went outside and got into the Jeep. After he started it up, he noted the fuel gauge and realized that they would have to get gas soon. He wondered if the gas pumps would work without power, then answered his own question. Of course not—virtually everything needed electricity to work nowadays. He'd have to either si-phon out some gas from another car or—

"Hold it right there!" a voice commanded.

Tom turned to see a gun staring him in the face. A man in his late twenties or early thirties was standing outside the Jeep poking a gun through the open door, glaring at him with malice.

"Who are you?" Tom said, his heart racing.

"Don't you worry about who I am, motherfucker. You just need to worry about how you're going to do as I say so I don't pop you with this piece. Got it?"

Tom had never had a gun in his face before in his life. Nor had he ever been as scared as he was that moment.

"I got it."

"Now, get out of the car, slowly. Don't make one false move or I'll blow you away. I may just blow you away for the fun of it if it moves me. Hell, who knows?"

"I'll move slowly. Please, don't shoot me!" Tom cried.

The man roared with laughter. "What a pussy! You sound like an old lady, you know it?"

Tom was not concerned with what this guy thought about him. All he wanted to do was stay alive.

"Turn it off. You're not going anywhere," he said as Tom started to get out.

Tom turned off the ignition and stepped out slowly from behind the wheel. The man backed away, keeping the gun pointed at his chest as Tom stood up.

"Now, let's go see where my Erin girl is. I believe you shacked up with her last night in there, didn't you? Did she give you a good blowjob? Or maybe she let you bang her from the rear—she really likes that."

Tom, despite his fear, wanted to punch the bastard's smug face. What in god's name was this guy's *problem?*

"She didn't do anything but sleep here."

"Right! And I'm the president of the United States!" the stranger laughed.

It was then that Tom realized this must be the infamous Kyle.

And he was even worse than Erin had described him.

Much worse.

"Come on, shithead, lead the way. Slowly. And don't make a sound or I'll waste you."

Tom led the way to the door. He considered spinning around and trying to knock the gun out of Kyle's hand, but knew that only worked in the movies. This was no movie and he was no James Bond.

Tom reached the door.

"Open it—slow and easy. Don't try to be a hero."

Tom opened the door and entered, Kyle following closely behind.

They went through the laundry room and into the kitchen. Erin was washing the dishes.

"Well looky there! It's my little girl-whore playing housewife! How goddamn *cozy!*"

Erin dropped the plate and spun around, the look of shock, dread and terror on her face.

"*Kyle!* What are you doing here?" she cried.

"Why, I'm coming to take what is mine, honey. And you know you're mine, now don't you?"

"God, Kyle—let Tom go! He doesn't have anything to do with this!" Erin pleaded, staring past Tom toward his captor.

"What do you mean, 'he doesn't have anything to do with this?' He has a *lot* to do with this! He took you in and banged you last night! Now that wasn't a nice thing to do at all, taking another man's woman and dissing me like that. No, I'm afraid that Mr. Tom here is gonna have to pay for that."

"I told you—" Tom said.

"Shut your goddamn mouth! Or I'm gonna make it so you can't ever talk again!"

"Kyle, please don't hurt him! I'll go with you—I'll do anything you say! Just don't hurt him!"

"Why, it sounds like you've really taken a liking to Tom here. You must have had a real good time screwing him last night. Jesus, girl—don't you think he's a little *old* for you? Not that that has ever stopped you before. But then, that's a different situation altogether, now isn't it?"

"Kyle, please don't—"

Kyle laughed hideously. "I think I got a pretty good idea what's going on here. I have a feeling that you haven't quite told this guy everything about our special relationship, have you? I can tell by the look in your eyes."

Erin started weeping. She convulsed so violently that Tom ran over to her side, forgetting the gun pointed at him.

Suddenly, the gun fired. The sound was so loud that Tom's ears rang. He saw a hole in the shattered ceramic tile to the right of his sink.

"The next one is for you, asshole. Now go over and sit down at that table before I get tempted to quit wasting any more time on you."

"Are you all right?" he said to Erin.

"Now, motherfucker!" Kyle roared.

"Go Tom!" Erin pleaded.

Tom went over to one of the chairs at the kitchen table and sat down. He realized that he could be dead now and knew that he was going to have to cool it if he was going to have any chance of getting out of this alive.

"Now, Erin girl, I want you to sit down next to your friend. And if you cry like that one more time, I'm going to kill him. You know what I think about those crocodile tears, don't you? And I'm not gonna put up with any of that bullshit, I can tell you that right now!"

"I won't cry, Kyle. I promise." Erin declared warily as she sat down beside Tom at the table.

"I know you won't, you ho! Now, you two sit there while I figure out what I'm going to do. I'm so goddamn tired I can hardly think straight. And that's your fault, you cheating slut! Keeping me out all night trying to find you after you sneaked out on me. I liked to never caught up to you, but luckily there weren't exactly a helluva lot of tire tracks in the snow out on the roads."

Kyle kept his gun trained on Tom as he walked over to the refrigerator and opened the door. He pulled out a bottle of Chardonnay, popped off the cork and took a long swig.

"Jesus, I needed that! I don't suppose you have any decent road food around here, do you old man? Some chips or peanuts—something like that?"

"There are some chips in the pantry."

"That's real hospitable of you," he said. He went over to the pantry and rifled through the shelves, keeping a close eye on Tom.

He took out a bag of potato chips, a box of Ritz crackers and a jar of salsa dip.

"This is a start. Well, I think we should be shoving off now, dear. We've got a long way to go. Kiss your old buddy here good-bye, but only on the cheek, now! I wouldn't want you to get all excited and want to screw him again!"

"What are you going to do to him, Kyle?" Erin asked suspiciously.

"Not sure yet. Probably shoot him."

"Kyle, you *can't!* He hasn't done anything wrong! Just take me and leave him here—"

"Quiet, bitch! We've already been through this. He has done plenty wrong and I am going to make him pay for it. Just not sure how much he owes me, but I'm thinking his miserable yuppie life ought to make us about even."

"Kyle, if you kill him, you might as well kill me, too."

Kyle feigned a chuckle. "What a laugh! That's just about the funniest thing I've heard all day! But your supreme sacrifice isn't going to do me any damn good at all, so you might as well forget *that* offer. I'm going to give you a break though, darling, just because I'm such a sweet guy and all. I'll let your buddy live if he really means that much to you."

"Thank-you Kyle! You won't regret this!"

"You're gonna owe me *big time!* You hear me?"

"Yes, I know. I will make it worth your while."

"You bet your sweet ass, you will! Now, Mr. Yup-shit, maybe you can tell me where you keep your duct tape. And if you tell me you don't have any, the deal's off. I'll just blow your head off."

Tom thought for a moment. "I think there's a roll in one of the cabinets in the laundry room."

"You better pray it's there or you're out of luck. I want to get the hell out of this place and I don't have time to be looking around for a roll of goddamn duct tape. Go get the tape, Erin. And hurry before I change my mind."

Erin nodded and ran to the laundry room. Tom heard some shuffling around and a moment later, she returned with a roll of duct tape.

"What took you so long? Now, you're going to have to pull out that chair a little, old man, so I can get this tape around you."

Tom scooted out a foot or so from the table. Kyle pulled out a length of tape and starting at Tom's elbow, began wrapping it around his chest and the back of the chair. He wrapped it around no less than a dozen times. Tom could hardly breathe it was so tight.

"Now, your feet."

He bound Tom's feet together several times then continued wrapping the tape around the front legs of the chair.

"And now, just in case you get a notion to try chewing . . ."

Kyle proceeded to slap a four-inch strip over his mouth.

"There, now. Sorry you can't say goodbye, old man, but that's just the way it goes. Come on, wench. Lead the way out of this place."

Erin stood up and faced Tom. "Thanks for your help, Tom. I hope you find your family. And don't worry about me. I'll be okay."

"Let's fucking *go!*" Kyle shouted.

"My coat, I left it—"

"I'm losing patience here. You have thirty seconds to get it or I blow him away!"

Erin ran into the living room and returned a few seconds later with her coat.

"Grab that stuff and let's blow this Popsicle stand."

Erin gathered up the food, glanced at Tom with a look of sadness and regret, and then ran out the door.

The moment she was out of sight, Kyle stared directly into Tom's eyes.

"And this is for humping my girl!"

He brought the handle of the gun down cleanly into Tom's skull.

6

When Tom came to, he started to bring his hand to the aching lump on his head and realized that he couldn't move either of his arms. In his dazed state, he couldn't immediately recall why he suddenly found himself bound and gagged in his kitchen or what had led up to it.

Then the events began to unfold.

Erin! She had been taken away by her old boyfriend, Kyle!

He wondered how long ago they had left. He glanced down at his wristwatch and realized that it must have been an hour or so ago. Too much time for him to catch up with them—

Even if he knew where they were headed . . .

He had to get out of this chair. He tried to force his arms out of the duct tape but it was hopeless—he could hardly move them even the slightest bit. He looked around the kitchen and wondered if he could somehow scoot himself over to the drawer where the kitchen knives were stored. He decided to give it a try.

He started rocking back and forth in an effort to get the chair to move forward. It took all he had to get it to budge. But at least it was possible. He continued rocking until he had moved a few inches, then stopped to rest. At this rate, he estimated it would take him three hours to get to the other side of the kitchen. If he didn't have a coronary first.

Got to be a better way—

There was a possibility that he could get his hand into his pants pocket if he was able to get into the right position. He recalled that he still had the keys from the CRV he had borrowed the night before. With some luck, he might be able to use them to cut off the duct tape.

He squirmed to his right in the chair and at the same time dug his right shoulder into the back of the chair in an effort to guide his hand into his pants pocket. After several attempts, he managed to get his index finger inside. He squirmed and groped around until he finally had his finger inside the key ring.

Withdrawing his finger from the pocket along with the key ring was a grueling process. But finally, after a lot of squirming, stretching and grunting, he managed to get the keys out.

The car key was a computer type with several vertical grooves cut into it and lacked any sharp edges. The other key, which looked like it might be the owner's house key, was a standard brass variety with several sharply cut ridges running the length of it.

Tom managed to position the key between his thumb and index finger with the ridges facing upward. He brought the key against the outermost wrapping of duct tape and began cutting into it with a back and forth sawing motion. It was like trying to cut a thick steak with a butter knife, but at least it was working.

Fifteen minutes later, Tom had managed to cut most of the duct tape away from his chest and arms. When he was down to the last wrapping, he brought his arms out from his sides with all his strength and tore through the remaining strip.

He tore off the strip from his mouth in a swift single motion, grimacing at the pain. A moment or two later he had removed all of the tape from around his ankles.

He was free at last!

With his head throbbing, Tom stood up too quickly and nearly passed out. Moving slowly, he made his way to the bathroom and looked at himself in the mirror. There was a thick matting of blood in his hair where Kyle's gun handle had slammed into his skull and a golf ball sized lump beneath it. The bleeding had already stopped, he was pleased to discover, and with a little luck he just might survive his first ever brush with a gun-wielding lunatic.

And he hoped that it would be his last.

He took out three ibuprofens from the medicine cabinet, returned to the kitchen and chased them down with a slug of cold coffee. Recalling the deplorable way Kyle had treated Erin—as though she were no more than a common possession expected to be at his beck and call—left Tom outraged. The man's total lack of respect for her and his humiliating accusations made Tom livid and wanting nothing more than to get Erin away from the miserable prick before he hurt her any more.

His anger and hatred toward Kyle notwithstanding, Tom also found himself curious about some of things the man had said and what had prompted him to say them. Things like immediately assuming that he and Erin had slept together—mentioning blowjobs and doing it from the rear. Why such damning, graphic accusations, given the unusual circumstances by which they had gotten together?

And what about his comment that Tom was too old for Erin, but that that had "never stopped her before?" What had he meant by that?

But the real stopper was what Kyle had said next—that he had a feeling Erin hadn't explained their "special relationship" to Tom.

What special relationship would that be?

And why had he incessantly referred to her as a whore?

These questions left Tom uneasy about Erin and wondering what had gone on prior to her coming to Columbus. Why had she ever had a relationship with such a lowlife scumbag like this Kyle character in the first place? It just didn't make any sense.

He had to find Erin and get her away from the violent, unstable asshole before it was too late.

Tom suddenly laughed out loud. He had to laugh to keep from crying. In less than twenty-four hours he had lost his wife, his children, his best friends and their kids. And, as it turns out, everyone else in this town had suddenly mysteriously disappeared. Now, after finding the one person he thought was the only other living soul in town, she gets taken away by the *other* only living soul in town.

Leaving him right smack dab where he had begun: alone, clueless and utterly directionless.

When will this nightmare end?

He could only do what he had to do. He had to track down Erin—that was a given. If he could find her, he would somehow get her away from Kyle the madman.

Then, hopefully, they could move on from there. Find out what in the hell was happening in this ghost town.

He went into the living room to get his coat, still draped over the chair. He was putting it on when he noticed a small piece of paper on top of the sofa. He walked over and picked it up. Hastily scrawled on the paper were three letters: *nyc*.

New York City. That must be where Erin and Kyle were heading—Erin had somehow managed to jot this down while getting her coat!

But why New York? She had mentioned that Kyle had driven 'all the way here' to find her. Is that where he had come from?

He had no idea. But it was clear that she wanted him to know where they were going. And that she wanted him to follow.

So follow he would.

Tom spent the next few minutes hastily packing a few clothes, some food and a few other items into a duffel bag. He took a moment to wash up in the bathroom, grabbed his laptop and headed back downstairs.

Two minutes later, he was backing the Jeep out of his driveway.

Erin and Kyle's footprints headed south toward Meadow Street, which meant that Kyle had most likely parked around the corner from Tom's house to avoid detection. Coasting near the curb, Tom kept his eyes peeled on the couple's tracks until they suddenly disappeared near the corner of Kenton and Meadow—where they had apparently boarded Kyle's car.

Tom could clearly see where Kyle had backed into a driveway to turn around before heading east toward the freeway.

As Tom sped up and began following the tire tracks, it dawned on him that he had no idea what kind of car Erin and Kyle were traveling in. All he knew for sure was they were heading in the direction of I-71, which meant they would head north on the interstate toward Cleveland and probably pick up either I-80 East or the turnpike through Pennsylvania en route to New York City.

And unless he saw other cars along the way, it wouldn't really make any difference what kind of car Kyle was driving—

It would be the only one on the road.

Tom drove to where Morse Road and the access road to I-71 intersected then pulled over to the curb. It was time to do some serious thinking. New York City was a ten-hour drive in good weather. Should he risk spending that kind of time on what may well be a wild goose chase?

Two thoughts nagged at him in equal measures. On one hand, he knew that Erin was in serious trouble and that he needed to try to find her before it was too late. Not only was it more than obvious that Kyle was a maniacal control freak but he also had a gun and had already proven that he wasn't afraid to use it when things don't go his way.

On the other hand, he had to continue trying to locate his family and find out what in the holy hell had happened to everyone else in this town. He was so overwhelmed by the absurdity of all of this that he had to keep pinching himself to make sure it wasn't all just a horrible nightmare.

He finally decided that he would drive downtown to make absolutely sure there weren't any signs of life there. If it was as desolate and lifeless as everything else he'd seen thus far, he would turn back around and head for New York City.

But first he was going to have to gas up. The thirsty Jeep's fuel gauge was resting precariously on "E."

He already assumed that the fuel pumps weren't going to work without any electricity so he would have to come up with an alternative method to get fuel into his tank. He pulled back onto Morse Road and headed for the Sunoco station a block away. He pulled up beside a pump, got out and gazed expectantly at the instrumentation. Not a single lit up numeral.

Tom strode over to the mini mart and entered, not surprised at the frigid air inside. He poked around the aisles in search of a hose of some kind but had no luck. He then located a maintenance closet across from the restrooms and spotted a length of garden hose hanging from a hook. Removing the hose, he headed outside and walked over to a massive Ford pickup parked off to the side. He was elated to find a gas can in the bed of the truck, suggesting that the driver had run out during the storm. He lifted out the can, which was empty, and placed it on the ground beside the truck.

Luckily, the truck's fuel cap was not locked. He unscrewed the cap and stuck the garden hose in as far as it would go.

Tom brought the open end of the hose to his mouth. Taking a deep breath, he placed his lips around the hose and started sucking. It had been decades since he'd siphoned anything and the first time he'd ever siphoned gasoline. The smell nearly knocked him out by the time he got his first mouthful of the burning wet fuel. Nearly gagging, he quickly plunged the hose into the gas can, spilling several ounces along the way.

Tom siphoned enough gas to fill the two-gallon can a half dozen times. When he'd emptied the last of the gas into the Jeep, he tossed the can along with the hose into the cargo section and got back behind the wheel.

Tom backtracked to the I-71 south access road. Radiant sun was coming from the southeast as he drove along at a brisk speed. In another ten minutes, he pulled off onto the Broad Street exit and began his search for signs of life in downtown Columbus.

As expected, there were cars parked along the streets, no working traffic lights and not a glimmer of life. He swung by the Columbus Police Department, double-parked and ran up to the door. He went inside and glanced around the darkened reception area. Not a single soul. It looked just like the Worthington P.D. but a lot bigger.

Columbus, Ohio was absolutely shut down and totally evacuated—save for one solitary soul. And it looked like that soul would be abandoning the city as well.

With a shrug, Tom hopped back into the Jeep, drove east to the I-71 entrance ramp and headed north to New York City.

7

By the time he reached Akron, Tom was totally lost in thought. He thought back to the last time he'd been in New York, which was nearly twenty years ago. He had lived in The Big Apple for over five years in search of his idea of the American Dream: becoming a self employed, successful artist.

After graduating cum laude from Ohio University with a B.F.A. to his credit, Tom had returned to his hometown of Smithtown long enough to realize that he was going to have to get out of there pronto if he had any aspirations of making a living at his chosen career. Not only was the tiny town economically challenged, as was the case of virtually every other Appalachian town in southern Ohio, it was absolutely depressing. He had enjoyed his childhood there but it was time to spread his wings and go somewhere that had a future.

After several weeks of serious deliberation, he opted for New York. After all, he figured, if you're going to be serious about a career in art, you may as well go to the art capital of the country. And besides that, he knew of a friend living there who had offered to put him up until he was able to get on his feet.

So it was off to a new city and a new life. After several agonizing weeks of pounding the streets, he had finally found a job with a salary decent enough to allow him his own loft space in Soho. Although the nine-to-five gig as an archive photo intern at the Museum of Modern Art was interesting and fairly prestigious, Tom would much rather have been creating his own art instead of preserving others.'

But it was a job nonetheless. And in addition to a generous salary, it offered him a great opportunity for establishing connections in the art community. Tom had dove into his new job with a positive attitude and worked on his art in his spare time. Photography was his discipline of choice but he also spent time drawing and painting.

Between his full time job at the museum and spending the rest of his time in his loft studio, Tom had enjoyed his life in New York for the most part. His social life, however, was nearly non-existent. He preferred to pursue his art with as little distraction from outside influences as was humanly possible. That isn't to say he was a self-ordained monk by any means, but the sum total of his socializing was limited mostly to the occasional night out bar hopping with a small circle of coworkers from the museum and the even rarer one night stand with some girl he'd meet at a bar. Tom adamantly refused to get involved in any serious relationships. He had a career to think of first.

But his life seemed lackluster and he still wasn't making a living at what he wanted to do. He had amassed a considerable body of work after living five years in the city but had found very few galleries interested in displaying any of it. In fact, he had only sold one piece of art in all the time he'd been there—a black and white portrait of one of his coworkers from the museum.

The job at the museum became less and less challenging and more of a grind than anything else as time passed by. But at least one good thing came out of his employment there: he had made up his mind to become an art teacher – perhaps to specialize in art history. He decided to move back to Smithtown and eventually enrolled at Ohio State University to pursue his MFA. OSU had an excellent art program and was located only a couple of hours away in Ohio's capital and largest city—

A deer suddenly darted out into the road and Tom swerved hard to the right to avoid plowing into it. The sudden move caused the Jeep to spin a full 360 degrees. He watched the white tail bound into the woods and felt his heart race wildly as he finally managed to bring the car under control.

This abrupt reality check made Tom snap out of his reverie. He had driven over three hours and still hadn't seen a single vehicle or a single soul. It had started snowing again and was becoming more and more difficult to see the road. He decided he would stop off in

Youngstown long enough to eat and wait to see if the snow was going to let up any.

Tom pulled off onto the first exit for downtown Youngstown. Five minutes later, he was driving down one of the main streets in search of a place with something substantial to eat. He finally opted for a gas station with a mini mart. He pulled up beside the entrance, got out and went inside.

It was at that moment that Tom nearly lost it completely. He took one look at the deserted store and realized that it looked just like the one he had been at in Columbus. In a single sickening moment, he considered the notion of being the last man on earth. The proverbial Omega Man. Feeling weak in the knees and beaten down, he leaned over and rested his head on the counter, feeling tears come to his eyes.

His family had vanished into thin air along with the rest of mankind and now here he was in this goddamn deserted mini mart in Youngstown searching for a decent meal.

It was as daunting as it was absurd.

Why had this happened? he thought. And when was it going to end? Would he ever see Peg and the kids again? As he thought back to the whole unreal scenario he had left behind in Columbus, he now found it difficult to believe it had ever happened.

But the ten thousand dollar question came down to this: had he made the right decision traveling to NYC while his family could at this moment be in harm's way somewhere back in Columbus?

Tom shivered and dashed the impending urge to break down totally. What sobered him up was the innate desire to live and a compulsion to find out what was happening. He was only human— what other options did he have? He could either continue standing there bawling like a baby until he froze to death or be grateful that he was still alive and go where his heart told him to go.

Smiling faintly, looked around and snagged a candy bar off the shelf. He unwrapped it, took a bite of the frozen rock hard Milky Way and nearly chipped a tooth in the process. Perhaps something a bit more palatable? he thought.

He browsed the aisles and picked out a large bag of potato chips, some Planters whole cashews and a semi-hard giant Slim Jim. Tom wondered why the latter wasn't frozen solid then considered the salt and preservatives that prevented the leathery junk from crystallizing totally. And to think of what it would be doing to his body . . .

Tom returned to the warm Jeep and settled down to eat his lunch. He reached over for one of the three bottled waters he'd packed and began munching on his junk food as the snow continued falling hard against the windshield. It didn't look like the storm was going to let up anytime soon so he took his time eating. When he was finished, he had the overpowering urge for a cup of hot coffee. He recalled seeing canned fuel in the mini mart and made the easiest decision he'd made all day: to brew a cup of hot coffee.

Then he would gas up and continue his journey after the storm broke.

8

Tom's anxiety grew more the closer he got to Manhattan. Night had fallen about halfway through Pennsylvania and that was intimidating enough. But as he approached the Lincoln Tunnel and got his first glimpse of the Manhattan skyline in over twenty years, he nearly came undone—

The famous skyline he had known so well was all but invisible in the misty darkness. Missing were the countless rectangles of light in the towering skyscrapers, the lights tracing the spans of the Hudson and East River bridges, the familiar gleaming stainless steel apex of the Chrysler Building, the illuminated tiers of the Empire State building and most apparent of all—the World Trade Center altogether. He hadn't been back since the 9/11 tragedy.

In fact, had the skies not just cleared up enough to reveal an amber quarter moon hanging low in the southwest sky, Tom would be unable to make out anything distinguishable from his present perspective. But the weak light afforded by the moon revealed the eerie silhouetted forms of the towering buildings on Manhattan Island.

"Christ," he breathed aloud into the silent interior of the Jeep. "It's even worse than I imagined."

The skyline disappeared abruptly as Tom made a wide turn and drove past the deserted tollbooths. He entered the Lincoln Tunnel and slowed down to a near crawl, still overwhelmed by the scene he'd just seen a moment ago.

This was simply too much for him to grasp right now.

Tom continued letting up on the accelerator until he had almost coasted to a dead stop, trying to ascertain what he might find on the other side of this tunnel. He had just driven ten hours alone on an abandoned highway in search of the only two living souls he'd seen since arriving home from the supermarket the day before. And now that he had finally arrived at his questionable destination he found himself clueless as to what he should do next.

He was absolutely terrified.

He stared out at the headlights as they sliced through the blackness of the tunnel and took a deep breath. What difference did it make? He was here, what had happened had happened and now he had to do what he had to do to survive. It was as simple as that.

This simple rationale rekindled his spirits a bit as he inched his speed up to forty-five and focused on the road ahead. Maybe, he thought, he would see the usual throngs of people on the streets. After all, with a population of over eight million, the odds were certainly greater than anywhere else he'd been thus far. Surely there would at least be some signs of life—the odds had it if nothing else.

Surely.

He spotted the exit looming in the near distance. Impulsively, he let off the gas and slowed down to a glorified crawl. By the time he actually emerged from the tunnel, he felt as though he were driving in wet cement.

His first observation when he suddenly thrust into the manmade canyons of midtown Manhattan was the near total darkness and mind-boggling silence. He had never known the city to be dead silent. This, along with the absence of any working lights whatsoever, made it all the more foreboding. Columbus, Ohio was one thing. The desolate mountain highways of Pennsylvania were another thing.

But to be in the city that never sleeps and experiencing *this* was absolutely paralyzing.

Tom puttered east along Thirty-fourth Street with no destination in mind, numbed by the silent darkness. He spotted the occasional abandoned taxi or truck parked along the curb but didn't see nearly as many vehicles as he had expected to see. This made the enormous cityscape seem all the more desolate.

Nervously, he turned up the volume on his CD player and continued driving east. Ironically, the song playing was *Omega Man* by the Police. When he reached Herald Square, he slowed down to a complete stop directly across from Macy's.

It just wasn't possible, he thought. To be sitting there in one of the most congested pedestrian venues in the country and not seeing a single soul. He turned down the volume, tentatively rolled down his window a few inches and listened intently. Not a sound. He turned off the engine. Nothing but dead silence, except for the clicking of the Jeep's hot engine manifold.

Tom sighed and turned the key. The engine turned for a moment but didn't catch. He switched off the headlights and tried again. The starter whined a couple of times and stopped dead.

"Shit!" he spat.

He tried a few more times to start the Jeep but without success. The battery finally became so weak that and all he got was the clicking of the solenoid.

The Jeep was dead.

Excellent.

In a semi-panic, he looked around for another mode of transportation. He spotted a couple of cabs parked up ahead near the corner of Sixth Avenue. He could only pray that the keys were still in one of them.

Tom cursed to himself once more as he fumbled for the flashlight in his duffel bag. He switched it on and stepped out onto the street, thankful it had stopped snowing by the time he'd entered New Jersey a few hours ago.

Training the flashlight's pinpoint beam along the sidewalk, Tom walked briskly toward the first cab. He heard the sound of his footsteps echo crisply as he glanced at the storefronts along the way. He suddenly stopped dead in his tracks when he noticed the smashed window of an upscale clothing store. Looters? he wondered. If that were the case, it was the first sign of looting he'd seen since this nightmare had begun—which seemed a little odd, he now realized. But at the same time, it was an encouraging sign. It meant that perhaps someone other than himself was alive and kicking in Gotham City.

Tom walked up to the shattered glass window and shone his flashlight into the store. Nothing seemed to be out of place as far as he could see in the weak light. He wasn't about to go inside to look any further.

He continued walking until he came upon the first cab. He tried the door but it was locked. He shone the light into the front compartment. No keys.

Frowning, he ran up to the next cab and discovered that it too was locked and keyless. He trained the light up the street and spotted a panel truck parked on the corner of Broadway. He ran over and peered expectantly through the passenger window as he tried the door handle. It worked. He opened the door just as he noticed that the driver side window was bashed in, shards of safety glass lying all over the front seat.

Another looting?

Tom stepped back to read the sign on the side of the white panel truck: *Tri-State Heating and Air Conditioning*. The address showed a Union City, New Jersey address. Tom hopped into the truck.

He shone the flashlight into the glove compartment, which was wide open. Nothing much there but it was clear that someone had rifled through it. He moved in between the seats and shone the light into the rear compartment. He saw a few Freon gas cylinders, an empty tool belt, what looked like a couple of small air compressors and a few odds and ends. All of the items had been cased out and shuffled around hastily, or so it appeared. Whatever the thieves had chosen to take was anyone's guess. If they had taken anything at all.

But the significant thing was what the broken store window and truck break-in implied: someone was stalking the streets of New York and had most likely done so since all of this lunacy had begun. Which to Tom was a good thing.

Could this have been the work of Kyle and Erin? he thought. Or someone else? Tom had a feeling the answer was the latter. It just didn't seem likely that Kyle and Erin would blow into town only hours ago and randomly elect to break into a store and a truck right from the get-go. This had to be the work of someone else. And whoever that was, he hoped to discover.

Or did he?

Tom realized that the mere presence of other life forms here might not be a good thing after all. In fact, it could make his finding Kyle and Erin that much more difficult. Maybe even dangerous—especially if the unknown city stalkers weren't particularly in a hospitable mindset.

What he didn't need now was someone standing in the way of his finding Erin and Kyle. His plan was to save the girl and get the holy hell out of here pronto. His desire to stick around in this skeleton of a city had evaporated a long time ago . . .

Tom hopped out of the truck and pointed his light down Broadway in either direction. He couldn't see any more vehicles within the limited range of the tiny flashlight. He retraced his steps to Sixth Avenue and looked north and south, but it was the same story there.

Decision time again.

He walked back to the Jeep, got in and stared out at the darkness. Should he continue looking for a vehicle or stay here and wait until daylight? The prospect of wandering too far from his only sense of security—his faithful but flawed Jeep—wasn't particularly inviting. In fact, it would be foolish to even attempt it. He was dead tired from the drive in spite of the inert adrenalin coursing through his veins, it was dark as pitch, and his only source of light was a piddling two-AA cell mini Mag-Lite that was about as effective as a fart in a windstorm.

All of this and the fact that he was scared shitless.

The rational thing to do was stay here in the Jeep for the night, try to catch a few winks and resume tomorrow morning in the daylight. At least then he could see what the hell he was doing.

His mind made up, Tom cracked his last bottle of spring water, took a slug and downed a handful of cashews. Feeling his eyelids droop for what had to be the hundredth time since this grueling trip through hell began, he rummaged through the duffel bag for the blanket he'd packed and spread it out over himself. He locked the doors, pulled the recliner lever up, leaned back in the seat and stretched his legs out until his feet were rested up against the carpeted firewall. Within a minute he was fast asleep.

9

Tom awoke with a start. An instant later, he heard a crash and felt shards of glass fall into his lap. Before he could react, he heard the click of a door lock and saw the Jeep's interior bathed in light as the driver's side door suddenly swung open.

In an instant, huge hands clawed at his chest, pulling him up and out of the Jeep. His heart beating like a jackhammer, Tom could see the face of his captor in the dim light of the Jeep. The face was young, about eighteen or so, and a grimy gray. The boy pulled Tom onto his feet while another youth came out of nowhere and punched him in the gut.

"Look what we have here, mates! Another intruder to our domain!"

Tom crouched forward from the blow long enough for a knee to uppercut his jaw. His head whipped backward as he reeled in pain.

"Jesus Christ!" he wailed. "What the hell—"

His first captor held him in a full nelson from behind and spat into his ear, "Now matey, there'll be no more words from you now!"

Tom got a good look at the other adversary as he stood there leering at Tom, brandishing what looked to be a three-foot long iron bar. This boy was also young, maybe sixteen or so, tall, lanky and black.

"That is unless you want to feel some more pain from this," the black youth cried, drawing the bar back menacingly.

Tom instinctively tried to raise his arms to protect himself but the grip on them was too great.

"Nice wheels ya got here," another voice said. Tom spotted a third youth who had been standing in the shadows. He was white, stocky and not quite as tall as the other boys.

"This is the first Jeep we've seen," he added.

"Say, you're right, Bummer!" the boy with the English accent replied. "We can go anywhere in this thing!"

"Four wheel drive—motherfucker!" Bummer exclaimed.

'Let's just see what he has inside for us. Hoops, you check it out. And why don't you cuff our guest so he doesn't get any wise ideas, Bum," the young Brit said.

"Got it, Chappy," the stocky boy replied.

As the black youth boarded the Jeep and poked around, Bummer came over to Tom, pulled a pair of handcuffs from his back pocket and cuffed Tom while the other boy held him. The stench emanating from Bummer was unbearable—a disgusting mix of sweat, alcohol and human excrement. Tom nearly gagged.

"There, now. That should keep ya under control. So tell us your name, bloke. No sense in being a stranger!" Chappy chirped.

"Tom. Tom Grayson."

"Well, Tommy-Boy, it's a pleasure to meet you. Allow me to introduce you to the troops here. This is Bummer and that's Hoops in there casing out your ride."

Tom's jaw was pounding as he stood there before his captors.

"What do you plan on doing?" he managed to say.

Chappy laughed heartily, a sort of girlish giggle. "Did ya hear that, blokes? Tommy-Boy here wants to know our plans!"

Bummer snickered moronically. "That's a laugh and a half!"

Chappy stood directly in front of Tom, smiled and pulled out a long barreled pistol – the kind that Dirty Harry used. He pointed the gun directly at Tom's forehead and pulled back the hammer. Tom froze, his heart in his throat.

This is it, he thought.

"I'm afraid our plan is to kill you and take your wheels, Tommy-Boy. So why don't you make your final request before I blow your brains out. But make it quick—we've got other things to do."

"Why? Why are going to shoot me? I haven't done anything to you," he pleaded.

Chappy giggled again. "Oh, but you *have,* Tommy-boy! You've done something very bad. You have busted into our fair town without an invitation. And that just isn't a happening thing, is it, Hoops?"

Hoops had joined them, holding Tom's iBook and cell phone up for everyone to see.

"Definitely not happening, dude. Check it out, men! An iBook and a phone. Pretty good shit, eh?"

"Not bad—any juice in that computer, Tommy?"

Tom replied weakly, his voice cracking. "I think so."

"Excellent! I'll say one last thing before we say our goodbyes, Matey. You've brought us some damn good shit here. I mean, a fucking Jeep, a phone and a Mac—absolutely awesome!"

Tom wished he could share in the joy of their spoils but couldn't. All he could do was stare at the .44 Magnum pointing at him and wait to make Chappy's day—

Hoops said, "The Jeep won't turn over, Chappy. Something's screwed up."

"Screw it. We'll come back later when it's light and see if we can get it running. At least we got the 'puter and a phone, and for that we thank you very kindly, Tommy. In fact, I think we'll grant you one final request for all of these wonderful contributions. What would you fancy, Tommy-Boy? Pizza? A beer? Or maybe you'd like to give us all a blowjob! Hey, hey, whatayasay, Tommy-Boy?" Chappy taunted.

"Yeah, a blowjob! C'mon Tommy, let's make that your final request!" Bummer shrieked as all three boys laughed in unison.

Tom's head was spinning wildly as he tried to figure a way out of this situation. He could make a run for it, but he knew he wouldn't get far with that loaded .44 in Chappy's hand.

But what if he could he kick it out of his hand? Was it possible?

Got to stall them longer—got to think this through.

"Uh, hate to disappoint you boys, but a beer is actually sounding like a better choice," Tom finally said, forcing a smile.

Hoops got right up into Tom's face. "What the hell makes you think you *got* a choice, Tommy-Boy? You didn't think we was gonna *really* let you choose your own final request did you?"

Chappy shook his head slowly and said: "I'm afraid Hoops is right, Tommy. In case you haven't already guessed, *we* are calling the shots here. And you are just gonna have to go with whatever we decide on. So what's it gonna be, mates? Shall we give this man a beer or let him suck our weenies?"

The other two looked at one another, snickered and shouted in unison, "Weenies!"

Tom felt his heart sink and his blood boil. He would rather be shot—

In a flash, he kicked the Magnum out of Chappy's hand. The gun went flying into the air. Before it touched the ground, Tom was twenty yards away running for his life.

"Catch him, lads!" Tom heard Chappy holler from behind. He never looked back as he sprinted east down Thirty-Fourth Street.

He heard a deafening shot ring out and a bullet ricochet off a nearby wall as he ran with all his might toward the store with the broken window. Although it was pitch dark, he knew to stay on the right side of the sidewalk and that it wasn't much further ahead. His plan was to duck into the building before the others caught up to him.

In another forty yards, he reached the store and glanced back toward his pursuers. He could see a long shaft of light aimed in his direction from about thirty yards back.

Tom groped around until he felt where the break in the window was, sliced two fingers in the process and hopped through the window into the store. The broken glass made a loud crunching sound beneath his feet as he scurried toward the rear of the store. A beam of light danced around on the east wall just as he bumped into a large object. Tom groped around and realized that it was a sales counter, ran his hands along the top until he reached a corner, rounded the corner and crouched down behind the counter.

At that moment, he clearly heard the boys' voices and saw the beam shine on the ceiling directly above him.

"I'll bet he ran in here!" he heard Hoops say.

The light shone randomly all over the place as Chappy chanted, "Tommy, Tommy, come out and play! We know you're in there!"

Tom felt his heart nearly beat out of his ribcage and held his breath. Cold sweat poured down his face and stung his eyes as he struggled to remain still in his awkward position.

"Let's go in and get him," Bummer said. "Apparently he doesn't want to play with us," he added with a guffaw.

A shot rang out and the slug tore through the counter Tom was hiding behind. Tom could actually smell the singed hole in the wood as he nervously felt around for the point of entry. He discovered a three-inch hole near his head—the bullet had missed him by only a couple of inches.

"The next one is for you, Tommy-Boy! Don't make us come in there and track you down—it's just gonna make you suffer that much more when we find ya!" Chappy warned.

Giving himself up was not an option. He would stay where he was and wait it out. And pray for a miracle.

"Okay, Matey—we're coming in!"

There was a shuffling of feet as the boys climbed through the broken window and entered the store. Tom felt around behind his back for a weapon of some kind but got only floor, counter and air.

His ass was cooked.

The boys spread out and came toward him, Chappy in the center of the charge with the flashlight in one hand and the .44 in the other. Tom watched helplessly as the beam shone on the floor just to his right. He suddenly saw a foot appear and knew that Chappy was one step away from killing him.

Tom did the only thing left to do. He stuck his leg out into the aisle in a desperate attempt to trip Chappy up.

The ploy didn't work. All he managed to do was ram his shin into the edge of the counter, causing him to howl in pain.

"Well, well—what have we here! By god it looks like 'ol Tommy-Boy!" Chappy exclaimed in delight, training first his flashlight then the gun directly into Tom's eyes.

Tom braced himself and awaited the gunshot. He wanted to say a silent prayer but didn't have time—

"Bang!" Chappy cried. "You're dead!"

All three broke out laughing.

Tom stared up at Chappy warily, trying to get a read on the demented sadist. What makes this scary son of a bitch tick? he wondered.

"Not quite yet, Tommy-Boy. We aren't gonna let ya off that easy, are we blokes?"

"Not even," Bummer said.

"Nope, Tommy. I'm afraid that you've just earned yourself some real pain. Now, get the hell up and I mean *now*, not tomorrow!"

Tom managed to get up onto his feet, his shin writhing in pain as he did so.

"Let's get the hell out of this morbid place. Lead the way toward the street, Tommy-Boy. And don't try anything funny or believe me, I'll shoot your balls off one by one before I totally waste you."

Tom stumbled toward the window and climbed out onto the sidewalk. He was so whipped now that he could only pray for salvation when they finally killed him.

"Let's take him back to camp, boys. I've just got an idea and it is freaking *brilliant!*"

"What is it, Chappy?" Bummer asked excitedly.

"Oh, I'm afraid it's just too good to give up right now, lads. But I can tell ya this—Tommy is gonna be in a for a howling good time when we get back!"

"Shit, Chappy—give us a hint, anyway," Hoops pleaded.

"Hmm. Well, let's just say that we may have our *other* guest put on a real nice show for Tommy-Boy here. A show that I think he'll enjoy beaucoup!"

The three had drawn up alongside and Tom glanced over at Chappy. A sinister smile came to his face as Bummer exclaimed excitedly, "Oh shit, man—I think I got a pretty good idea what you're talking about. Too freaking awesome, dude!"

The mention of this "other guest" made Tom wonder whom they might be referring to. Could it be Erin? Was it possible? If so, then what had happened to Kyle? Or maybe the guest was Kyle and Erin hadn't been caught yet.

He needed to find out.

"Who is your other guest?"

The moment he spoke the last word, Tom felt something crash into his ribcage.

"Silence, Tommy-Boy! It is none of your goddamn business and you had best keep your trap shut if you know what's good for you. You don't have any idea how close I am to maiming you with this piece. Are you getting the picture, mate? Or do I need to prove that I mean business here?"

Tom glanced over at Chappy, not sure if he should answer or not. He nodded instead.

"There you go, man. And let's just keep it shut until I say so."

They had returned to where the Jeep was parked; but instead of stopping they moved past it. A moment later, Tom saw the vehicle they had apparently arrived in and did a double take.

Parked in the middle of the street was a shiny black Cadillac hearse, complete with curtained windows.

"What do ya think of our wheels, Tommy? Not many miles to a tank of petrol but nice and roomy!"

Tom gasped, but remained silent.

"Let's put Tommy in the back, Hoops. Along with the stiff."

Tom glanced in horror at Chappy. The boy suddenly broke into laughter. "Just kidding, Tommy-Boy! No coffin back there, I promise!"

Hoops took Tom around to the rear of the hearse and opened the tailgate. He gestured for him to climb in, no small task while wearing handcuffs. He managed to wrestle himself in and lie down on his side in the rear compartment, his head resting forward. Hoops slammed the tailgate door shut and came around to the side. All three of them got in with Bummer driving, Chappy in the front passenger seat and Hoops in the backseat.

"We forgot the iBook," Hoops said after Bummer fired up the V8.

"Go get it—and the cell phone," Chappy ordered.

Bummer pulled up beside the Jeep, Hoops hopped out, gathered up the items and got back in.

"To camp, James," Chappy ordered.

Bummer floored it, laid a patch and sped east on Thirty-Fourth. Tom's vision was partially obstructed by the hearse's curtained windows but he caught a quick glance of the Empire State Building as Bummer zoomed past it.

A few minutes later, the hearse swung a left onto what looked to be Park Avenue. Bummer slowed down a little as Tom peeled his eyes through the curtain in an effort to get a fix on where they were going.

"What we gonna do about that heap, Chappy?" he heard Hoops say.

"Oh hell, I don't know. It's in really bad shape—about all it's good for is petrol. That poor bloke was about as worthless as they come, eh?"

Bummer replied, "No shit. Crap car, no good stuff except that cheap .22 and nothing but attitude. Sweet hot lady, though."

"*Sweet* is an absolute understatement, Bum! That hottie is gonna provide us with many a premium ride—makes me willy stiff just thinking about her!"

All three chortled.

"Jesus, damn—our own white slave anytime we want her! But just wait'll she gets a shot at my throbbin' johnson! She won't want shit to do with you lily-white punks after that!" Hoops exclaimed.

"Hate to break it to you, mate, but size isn't everything. English charm and incredible longevity will have her crawlin' back for more from yours truly," Chappy said.

Then Bummer chimed in, "Screw both of you! Did you see the way she was looking at me after I made mincemeat of her boyfriend? That was the look of *respect!* She wanted to give it to me that very minute! Well, maybe once she got over the fact that I'd just split her loverboy's skull in two, that is. But I swear that whole goddamn whupping turned her sweet ass on!"

"Bummer, you are one sick dude," Hoops declared.

"Screw you, Hoops!"

Tom's mind was reeling as he felt the hearse begin to slow down again. *Erin!* he thought. *And Kyle! They had to be talking about Erin and Kyle! Who else could it be?*

"Well here we are—home sweet home," Chappy announced. "Let's get Tommy-Boy out of this crypt and show him our humble abode."

Tom squinted his eyes to see where they were. It looked like they were still on Park Avenue.

Hoops came around to open the tailgate.

"Out, Tommy."

Tom scooted on his ass toward the rear of the hearse and sat on the bumper long enough take in the surroundings—

The hearse was pulled up in front of 301 Park Avenue—*The Waldorf-Astoria!*

As Tom let out a gasp, Chappy came around and pulled him on to his feet.

"So what do ya think, Tommy-Boy?"

"I'm speechless," was all Tom could say. The mere thought of these skuzzy delinquents inhabiting one of the world's most elegant hotels was inconceivable.

"You freaking should be," Chappy replied. "And let's keep it that way."

Chappy shoved Tom forward as they headed for the entrance of the famous Waldorf. Bummer held the door open and Tom was unable to remain silent after seeing the inside. "Where is all of the light coming from?"

Chappy glared at him and Tom saw murder in his eyes for speaking out of turn. The English boy's misguided pride, however, prevailed.

"Backup generators, Tommy. Practically everything in this place is fully functional. And quite comfortable, I might add."

Tom squinted as he took in the elegant beauty of the Waldorf's lobby, bathed in light. A huge crystal chandelier cast delicate jewels of reflected light onto the marble floor. The stunning effect of the lush lobby lighting was a study in contrasts from the dark foreboding world he'd just left outside.

"Hungry, Tommy?" Chappy asked offhandedly.

Tom could eat a horse. "Starving."

"Too freaking bad!" he quipped and giggled his girlish giggle. "Can't feed ya, I'm afraid. But I'll tell ya what I *can* do for you while my mates and I enjoy a little snack."

Tom saw Bummer grin a moronic grin out of the corner of his eye. Tom simply stood there and braced himself for whatever came next.

"This way, please," Chappy said, taking Tom by the arm and leading him across the lobby. "I have a special place for you to gather your thoughts and ponder the meaning of life."

He led Tom over to a pair of doors located at the far side of the lobby as Bummer and Hoops followed behind.

"You're roommate awaits you." Chappy announced as he swung open the doors.

What Tom saw nearly made him vomit.

Suspended by a wire cable attached to a chandelier on one end and wrapped around the wrists of his outstretched arms on the other was, or what used to be, Erin's boyfriend Kyle. He was totally nude and covered from head to toe in crimson trails of blood. His skull was shattered in several places, swollen to twice its original size and horribly disfigured—presumably Bummer's handiwork.

Kyle had been used as a human piñata and now resembled a slaughtered animal hanging in a butcher shop.

Tom stared for a moment in horror then turned away. Chappy immediately pushed him into the room so hard that he fell to the floor.

"Take a good look at this luckless wretch, Tommy-Boy! Now you see what happens to intruders to our domain! And this piece of crap actually had the nerve to call me a 'limey asshole'—imagine that! Before I could recover from this untimely insult Bummer was on the bloke quicker than flies on shit, worked him over real good with his crowbar. Couldn't bring myself to stop him, actually. I'd be lying if I told you I didn't enjoy watching this worthless shit being turned into hamburger by my loyal mate. Loved every minute of it, in fact!"

Tom's shoulder winced in pain from the fall. He sat for a moment and stared up at the three misfits standing before him, wondering where Erin was at this moment. The last thing he wanted to do was let on to them that he knew Kyle and Erin; that much he was sure of.

"Why is he—" Tom began to ask.

"Strung up?" Chappy finished the question for him. "Let's just say that we had a little fun with the bastard before Bummer finished him off and leave it at that. You'll know the rest soon enough."

Tom gulped. He had nearly forgotten that he was a condemned man—or maybe he didn't want to remember after seeing Kyle hanging from the ceiling like a sacrificed animal.

Have to find Erin and get the holy hell out of here! he thought. He did not want to stick around long enough to find out 'the rest.'

"Well Tommy-Boy, I'm getting pretty hungry so we'll leave you here so you can and your new friend can 'hang out' together until we finish eating. When we come back, you are in for one big surprise!"

I can hardly wait, Tom thought. Chappy led the other two out of the room and the doors swung shut behind them. He heard the click of a deadbolt and the muffled sound of their chuckles as they left him there in this death chamber.

Tom tried not to look up at Kyle as he got to his feet and began casing out the room for some way out.

10

The room was cavernous and may have been used for banquets or as a meeting room—he'd never been in the Waldorf and could only guess the room's purpose. He was aware that the historic site had a rich past and had played host to a number of balls and similar get-togethers for socialites and countless big names throughout history.

Tom knew he didn't have much time—Chappy and the boys could be back any minute—so he sprinted along the perimeter of the room, checking every door for a possible escape route. He was forced to turn with his back toward each door in order to turn the doorknobs since his hands were still cuffed behind him. It didn't take long for to discover that every door in the huge room was locked securely.

Since he was trapped inside, his only chance for survival would be to make a break for it through the main doors when the lynch mob returned. He may need a weapon, though—

If he could just get these fricking handcuffs off . . .

He stored this fantasy away on his wish list and looked around for a weapon, well aware that there was little he could do without the full use of his hands and arms. Noticing how the silverware was wrapped inside the neatly folded linen napkins, he went over to one of the tables and turned his back against it, managed to grasp an enveloped silverware packet in his left hand and pulled out a serrated dinner knife with his right. Pretty weak defense against a .44 magnum or a crowbar but better than nothing.

Next, he looked around for a suitable table to hide under. Fortunately, they were all large with white tablecloths draped over them that fell nearly all the way to the floor. This would enable him to conceal himself fairly easily under any one of them. He moved toward the entrance and searched for the best vantage point. If he were to hide under a table perhaps fifteen feet away and to either side of the door, he just might be able to sneak out past the punks before they had a chance to realize what was happening.

Which he realized was a long shot at best.

Suddenly, he heard voices outside that were getting louder. He scurried over to one of the tables, crouched down onto his knees, fell onto his right side, then scooted in under the table. He noticed in despair that the tablecloth was still flapping in the breeze when he heard the sound of the doors fly open.

"We're back, Tommy!" Chappy shouted in his signature cockney accent. "I certainly hope that you and our— What's *this?* I don't see you Tommy-Boy! Oh, Tommy, Tommy, Tommy—it's really not a good idea for you to try to hide from us. It is definitely going to make your demise all the more painful!"

Tom could see two pairs of feet from his vantage point under the table. Where was the third set? he wondered. Please don't tell me that one of these cutthroats is still outside in the lobby! If that were the case, he didn't have an ice cube's chance in Hades of—

A shot suddenly fired out. It sounded like a cannon going off.

"Frick an *a*, Tommy! You'd best be giving yourself up this very moment or you are going to regret it! I'm going to make it a point to yank off each and every one of these bloody tablecloths until I find you. Then, I shall proceed to make you a very, very sorry bloke!"

There was a short pause.

"Okay, mates, let's do it!" Chappy cried, followed by cheers and the shuffling of feet.

Mates, he had said, as in *plural!*

Tom peeled his eyes to locate all three pairs of feet. A second later, he saw the third set walk directly past him toward the far side of the room. He held his breath and paused a moment, then quietly backed his way out from under the table.

After he had cleared the tablecloth and found himself out in the open, Tom glanced around and saw Chappy working the tables to-

ward the far end, Bummer to his left and Hoops immediately behind him. All three were yanking the tablecloths off the tables with
a flourish, like aspiring magicians. Miraculously, none of them had
yet spotted him nor were any of them facing his way at that particular moment.

Tom hunched forward as far as he could and hurried toward the
doors on his knees.

"I'm gonna get you, Tom-Boy!" he heard Hoops cry from behind. With his heart in his throat, Tom stood up and ran toward the
doors as quickly as his legs would carry him. He reached the entrance, shoved one of the doors open with his shoulder, slipped
through and turned his back against the doors. He heard Hoops
holler "he's escaped!" as he fumbled anxiously with the dead bolt,
trying desperately to slide it home. Finally, he heard a metallic
clack as he managed to lock the door.

One to go—

He fumbled with the other bolt as he heard the boys running
toward the entrance. He was able to slide the bolt home an instant
before he felt the weight of the door smash against his back.

"Open this door, motherfucker!" Chappy snarled from the other
side. A shot rang out and Tom saw the hole where the slug had
torn through about an inch from the handle.

Tom sidestepped the doors and ran across the lobby toward the
Park Avenue entrance, spotted a ring of keys lying on a table between a Heinekin and a plate of French fries, managed to snatch
them up just as he heard two more shots ring out.

*They were going to shoot their way through that door any sec-
ond—*

He needed to make a quick decision: either bolt out onto the
street and run as far away from these crazy shits as earthly possible
or stay in the hotel and likely become a piece of dead meat. The
decision was a no-brainer. Erin was somewhere in here and he had
to find her.

He wondered if the elevators were working. Then he recalled
Chappy's words: "practically everything in this place is fully functional." He could only hope that included the elevators.

Tom sprinted across the lobby to the bank of elevators, pressed
the "up" button with his elbow and held his breath. The door slid
open with a quiet whoosh.

Awesome! he thought.

He hopped in, pushed the button for the fifteenth floor for no particular reason except that it seemed far away from where he stood now, located the 'close door' button and pressed it repeatedly. He heard another gunshot come from the lobby and the muffled sound of running madmen through the door as it closed.

Tom nervously watched the floor indicator panel as the car ascended. The elevator slowed down and stopped at the fifteenth floor, the doors slid open and he bolted out into total darkness.

Perhaps not such a good choice, he thought to himself. Were the lights off on *all* of the upper floors or had he just happened to choose the only one that was?

No time to ponder—he caught the door before it closed and re-entered the elevator.

The odds of the power being on were probably greater near the lobby, he theorized. Although he didn't really want to go back toward the pursuing posse, he knew he was going to have to chance it. Besides, he wasn't even sure if these bad boys were still in the hotel at the moment. They may have thought he fled outside instead—in fact, that was most likely the case. After all, they didn't know that he knew Kyle and Erin—so there was no reason for him to stay in the hotel as far as they were concerned. They would assume that he had fled the same way he had come in: via Park Avenue.

Of course! he thought. Right now was his best shot at finding Erin while they were out looking for his ass.

He pressed the button for the fifth floor. He would try it and then work his way down. Erin would most likely be on one of the lower floors.

The doors closed and the elevator plummeted at a fairly good clip. When it reached the fifth floor, Tom crossed his fingers as the door opened.

The floor was lit up like a Christmas tree!

He stepped out and looked in either direction, noting that the floor consisted of numbered guest rooms as far as he could see. He went to the nearest room and turned the knob. Locked. He glanced at the ring of keys in his hand, wondering if there was a master key to the rooms or a key to the handcuffs.

He stepped over to one of the chairs sitting near the elevator, turned around and dropped the keys onto it. He searched for a small key that might be the one for the cuffs. Most of the dozen or so keys were of average size and appeared to be door keys. There was also a GM car key—perhaps the one for the hearse.

Tom spotted a tiny brass key that looked like it could be the one he sought. Excitedly, he picked up the key ring, went over to a mirror and began the arduous task of trying to slip the key into the tiny hole of the cuff. Sweating profusely, he eventually managed to get the key into the hole and nearly snapped his wrist fumbling around trying to get the key to rotate inside the hole. Five minutes later, he heard a crisp click as the manacle sprang away from his left wrist, freeing his hand.

A victorious smile came to Tom's face as he brought his hands around and unlocked the other cuff.

He'd done it, by god!

Tom picked up the keys, chose one randomly and tried it in one of the guest room doors. The key went in but wouldn't turn. What he needed to do now was find the room holding Erin captive and worry about the keys later.

The problem was that she could be anywhere in this huge hotel and there was really no way to know where to start. He would just have to give it his best shot and pray for a miracle before Chappy and his entourage returned to the Waldorf.

He quickly worked his way down the corridor, knocking on each door and listening for a sound. Then he advanced to the adjacent hallway and repeated the process until he'd covered nearly the entire fifth floor. When he suddenly heard a sound coming from the direction of the elevators, he froze where he stood and then quietly backtracked toward the direction of the sound. He arrived at the end of the hallway and cautiously peeked around the corner.

At first, he didn't see anything. Then suddenly, he saw the door to the stairway open and someone stepped out into the hallway.

It was Bummer!

Tom thought Bummer had spotted him so he ran down the corridor, thankful that it was carpeted. He could only pray that Bummer wasn't headed toward him because if that were the case, he was a goner. The corridor dead-ended and he would have no time to get inside any of the rooms.

He heard Bummer running down the hall toward him and started looking around for a possible escape route. There was nothing. Bummer would be rounding the corner any second.

Tom tried the handle of the nearest guest room door and couldn't believe it—the door was unlocked! Quickly, he opened it, ran inside and closed the door behind him. He slid the deadbolt as quietly as he could, praying that Bummer wouldn't hear—

"Room service," he heard just outside the door.

Bummer had found him.

Tom glanced around the room then heard a huge crash at the door. He turned around and saw the sharp edge of an ax sticking out where it had sliced through the door.

Feeling like he was in a scene from *The Shining*, Tom watched in horror as the ax blade withdraw then sliced into the door again about a half-inch to the right of the first hole. He ran over to the bed, grabbed a lamp and stood off to the side. It was at that moment that he spotted another door in the room with a deadbolt on it.

A door that led to the adjoining room!

Tom ran over to the door, slid open the dead bolt and tried the doorknob. It turned. He opened the door, ran into the adjoining room and locked the door behind him. He was safe for the moment.

But how long would it take for Bummer to break into the other room then proceed to this room?

He needed to get away quickly or he would be a dead man.

Tom heard the ax continuously crashing into the wood as he stepped over to the room entrance. Quietly, with his heart beating hard in his chest, he cracked the door an inch and looked out into the corridor. Fortunately, the door swung in the direction that allowed him to see Bummer next door hacking the hell out of the door with his ax. Unfortunately, there would be nothing standing between him and Bummer once he ran out into the hall.

So he would have to wait until Bummer axed his way through the door then take off like a bat out of hell.

"You just wait till I get in there, asshole!" Bummer grunted, short of breath from his labors. "I'm gonna make you look like a pile of raw ground beef!"

Tom watched as Bummer swung his ax one more time then poked his hand through the gaping hole in the door. He heard the deadbolt slide and watched as Bummer swung open the door. The moment he went inside, Tom bolted out of the room.

"Gotcha!" Tom heard the stocky slob shout the moment he hit the hallway. He sped after Tom and was directly behind him in an instant. Tom suddenly turned around and saw Bummer holding the ax high over his head, poised to strike.

That's when Tom swung the lamp as hard as he could into Bummer's fat face.

The boy was so shocked that he dropped the ax and simply stood there dumbfounded for a second, a look of hideous stupidity on his face. Tom swung again, this time landing the brass base of the lamp squarely into Bummer's jaw.

Blood literally squirted out as Bummer howled like an animal. Tom hesitated a moment, then gathered up all his strength and let him have it one more time, this time from overhead into his huge hairless skull.

Bummer slumped and fell like a limp dishcloth onto the floor, out like a light.

Or dead as a doornail—Tom wasn't really sure.

He dropped the lamp and sprinted down the hall toward the elevator, wondering if any of the other boys were in the hotel. Just in case, he opted for the same stairway Bummer had taken instead of risking the elevator.

Tom made his way quietly down the stairs to the fourth floor, listening carefully for any sounds. All he could hear was his own footsteps echoing off the walls.

He went through the stairway door. He saw more guest rooms in either direction. He started down the hallway and resumed methodically knocking softly on each door. About halfway down the corridor, he thought he heard a sound come from inside one of the rooms. He knocked again. This time he was sure he heard a sound—a sort of weak, muffled whimper.

He turned the doorknob, which was locked.

"Erin, is that you?" he whispered through the door.

Nothing.

"Erin, it's me—Tom. Can you hear me?"

He heard more muffled sounds, more staccato than before.

It had to be her.

"I'm gonna get you out of there, Erin. I just need to find a way inside. Hang in there!" he whispered excitedly.

Tom frantically pulled the key ring out of his back pocket and tried each key, praying that one of them would unlock the door. He was hoping that the keys were masters for each floor of the hotel, or something like that.

The next to the last key turned smoothly in the keyhole.

He unlocked the door and entered the room.

11

The room was pitch dark. The muffled whimpers sounded louder now and were coming from halfway across the room. Tom fumbled around for a light switch along the wall, located it and flipped it up. The room remained dark. Frustrated, he swung the door open all the way to let more light in.

Once his eyes adjusted, he could make out two queen-sized beds and what looked like a body lying on the furthest one. He made his way across the room, went in between the two beds, located the lamp on the nightstand, found a switch and clicked it on.

There lying face down on the bed was Erin Myers, her hands tied behind her back with thick rope. Her head was turned so that she was facing him, her mouth bound by duct tape, her eyes swollen red.

"Erin!" Tom cried.

He leaned down and removed the duct tape from her mouth as delicately as he could.

"Jesus, am I ever glad to see you!" Erin cried when the tape was off. "How did you ever find me here?"

"I was confronted by your captors at Macy's. They brought me here to join their little party but I haven't been feeling particularly welcome, to say the least. Here, let's get you onto your feet."

Tom rolled Erin onto her side and pulled her over toward the edge of the bed. The moment she was on her feet, he encircled her thin waist and hugged her tightly. Tears of relief and joy came to his eyes as he embraced the girl.

"I'm so happy to see you! I wasn't sure I'd ever see you again after you left my place."

Erin laid her head on his shoulder and heaved emotionally. "God, Tom, I can't believe you found me! I've been so scared!"

Tom pulled away and faced her. Erin planted a big kiss on his cheek and stared directly into his eyes.

"You've been my savior twice now. Thank you so much," she said softly.

"It's the least I could do," Tom replied, wishing he could have done more.

He went over and rummaged through the nightstand drawers in hope of finding something to cut the rope binding Erin's hands. All he found was a small notepad, a TV remote and a Gideon's Bible.

Then he remembered the serrated bread knife he'd stuffed into his back pocket. He pulled it out, stood behind Erin and began working on the rope.

"Kyle's dead, Tom. You wouldn't believe what they did to him—it was horrifying!"

Tom tried to imagine what it had been like for this young girl to be forced to stand by and watch while these misfits mutilated her ex-boyfriend. No matter what her feelings may have been for Kyle, it had to have been absolutely terrifying.

"I saw him, Erin, down in that room. I'm really sorry. No one deserves to be subjected to that kind of inhumane torture and violence," was all he could say.

"Those boys are *animals!* I couldn't believe how they strung up Kyle like that and did all of those awful things to him. And then they made me—oh shit, Tom! It was so sick and insane!"

Tom wondered what the demented bastards had forced Erin to do but he didn't ask, not sure he really wanted to know. He continued sawing back and forth on the rope with the knife, becoming more and more nervous and frustrated at how long it was taking. He knew they needed to move, quickly, before the two boys found them.

Tom said, "They are certainly a screwed-up crew, that's for sure. And we are going to be their next victims if we don't start moving soon. Jesus, this knife is about as useless as tits on a boar hog—pardon the expression!"

Erin managed a weak smile. "Now that's one I've never heard before."

"Showing my roots and old age, I reckon. Listen, we need to go somewhere to find something better to cut this rope off with. They could bust in here any second."

"Where should we go?"

"Hell if I know—just out of this room would be a start. Let's work our way down to the lobby. I'm not sure, but two of them may still be out on the street looking for me now. There's really no way of knowing for sure. If we make it to the lobby and see that the coast is clear, we'll book out of here before they get back."

"You said two of them. Where's the third one?"

Tom paused a moment then said, "I think I killed him. He's up on the fifth floor."

"Good—it serves him right! Which one was it?" Erin said, clearly feeling no remorse.

"The short stinky one—Bummer."

Erin grinned triumphantly. "That's the one that beat Kyle to a pulp— I hope he burns in hell!"

"I'm thinking that they will all end up there eventually. Let's get going now."

Tom held Erin by the arm and led her out of the room to the corridor. They stood there for a moment, looking both ways and listening quietly.

"Let's take the stairs down," Tom whispered.

He led the way down the hallway and held the door open for Erin. They descended briskly until they reached the third floor. Tom slipped through the door first, took a peek in either direction then motioned for Erin to join him.

"This way."

Erin followed him down the corridor until they reached what appeared to be a huge deserted banquet room. They proceeded further through the corridors until they reached The Grand Ballroom. Erin let out a gasp.

"Look how big it is!"

"Yeah, and unless my eyes are deceiving me, I see *food!*" Tom exclaimed when he spotted a crate of apples, several boxes of Carr's stoned wheat crackers and a wheel of cheese stored on one of the serving tables.

"God, I am so hungry! Let's eat!"

"We have to be careful, though—this could be a trap," Tom cautioned. "Stay here until I case it out first. I also want to get something to cut that rope off. If the coast is clear, we'll snag some food then go somewhere to hide out while we eat."

"Okay."

Tom walked cautiously across the ballroom toward the table that was located along the wall near the east entrance. As he drew closer, he saw a double-handled cheese knife lying beside a ten-inch wheel of smoked cheddar. When the aroma of cheese greeted him, his pace quickened appreciably. He reached the table, looked either way, snatched a firm ripened gala with one hand and the knife with the other.

There wasn't a soul around, thank god.

He returned to where Erin was standing at a brisk pace.

"Try this," he said, offering her the apple.

"Thanks!" Erin said. She took an enormous bite of the fruit and gobbled it down ravenously.

Tom began sawing at the rope binding her hands with the cheese knife. In twenty seconds, the rope was off.

Erin rubbed the welts where the rope had rubbed her raw. "What a relief that is!"

"Now, let's go get some more of that food."

They ran over to the table and Erin sliced off several wedges of cheddar while Tom picked out a half dozen apples. Grabbing an unopened box of wheat thins, Tom said, "Let's go back toward that meeting room. We'll find a place to hide out and chow down."

Erin nodded and followed Tom out of the ballroom. They discovered a cluttered storage room and meandered their way through the stacks of tables, chairs and serving carts to the rear of the room and sat down. Nearby was a second door that opened up to a small closet that could be used for a quick hideaway if need be. Erin winked at Tom as she pointed her finger at a six pack of bottled Evian water stored on the shelf.

"That should complete our meal quite nicely," she said before reaching up for the water.

Tom sat across from Erin on the floor with their bounty lying between them. Like a couple of hungry wolves, they proceeded to stuff their mouths as if they hadn't eaten in weeks.

"That sure hit the spot!" Tom finally said, chasing his last bite of cheese down with a slug of water.

"For sure," Erin replied. "Now I'm so full I can hardly move!"

"I hear you. Unfortunately, we don't have time for a siesta. We need to see if we can get out of this place before our luck starts running out."

"Do you think either of them is in the hotel right now? I mean, we're just above the lobby and haven't heard or seen anything at all."

"I'm beginning to think they're still outside looking for me. When I escaped, I'm pretty sure they didn't see which way I went. They probably assumed that I'd bale out of this place rather than stick around."

"So why *did* you stick around?"

"I wasn't going to leave without you," Tom replied simply.

Erin reached over and gave him a huge bear hug. "I still can't believe you drove all the way here to look for me. I wrote that little note out of sheer desperation, not really sure if you'd even see it and definitely not thinking you would actually act on it!"

Tom held her tightly. "I'll admit I was a little confused at first. I mean—I was faced with the dilemma of either continuing to look for my family or go chasing after you. It didn't take me long to realize that it was useless to search Columbus for Peg and the kids any longer."

"I feel really guilty, you know."

"Don't, Erin. I will find my family eventually if they are anywhere to be found. But we need to get moving now—we can talk later. All I want to do is get the hell out of this hotel, out of New York and back to Columbus!"

"Me, too!" Erin said.

They both stood up and Erin hastily gathered up the plates. Tom was reminded of her experience as a waitress and smiled to himself.

"Let's go check the lobby and if the coast is clear, get out of this godforsaken place," Tom said.

12

Tom's heart was pounding hard as he and Erin slipped through the stairway door and into the lobby. He brought his finger to his lips and motioned for Erin to wait while he went ahead to scout the area. Then he tiptoed along the wall toward the lobby's main corridor.

When he reached the end of the corridor, he peeked around the corner past the registration desks toward the Park Avenue entrance. He spotted the table where he'd snatched up the keys and saw the plates of food and beer bottles, still in the same positions they'd been before. Encouraged by this, he walked quietly along the registration area toward the entrance several yards further, stopped, looked around and listened.

Not a sign of anybody.

He walked back until he saw Erin then motioned for her to come over to him. She moved toward Tom stealthily until she drew up beside him.

"Looks good," Tom whispered. "If we can get as far as the entrance, we should be home free."

"Great, let's do it!" Erin whispered excitedly.

"Stay right behind me and don't make a sound. They could still be around the corner for all we know. We're just going to have to creep along until we can case the scene better."

Tom started moving with Erin close behind. He stayed glued to the wall, keeping his eyes trained on the entrance and to his right, just in case he spotted someone around the corner. In another few steps he could see the doors to the death chamber where Kyle no doubt was still hanging from the ceiling. The thought made Tom feel nauseous and he inadvertently turned and glanced at Erin. Her face was white as a sheet as she stared in the same direction. God only knew what she had been forced to endure in there, Tom thought.

He squeezed her hand in encouragement. They were about twenty yards from the foyer leading to the Park Avenue entrance. It was obvious now that no one was in the immediate area.

They were almost home free.

Tom took Erin by the hand and quickened the pace when they reached the foyer. He could now see the doors clearly and the waning darkness outside.

"Let's run for it!" he whispered to Erin.

"Okay!"

The two sprinted toward the doors. Tom flung open one of them and ran out onto the street, Erin right on his heels. He immediately noticed that the hearse was gone, prompting Tom to think that they just might make it after all. They headed south on Park Avenue.

"We'll head back to my Jeep and see if we can get it started—maybe the battery has recharged itself after some rest. If we see any kind of vehicle on the way, we'll check it for keys just in case," Tom told Erin between breaths.

"Sounds good—where is it parked?"

"On Thirty-Fourth Street."

They ran all the way to Forty-Sixth Street then stopped long enough to peek inside a parked taxicab: unlocked but no keys. They continued their run and paced themselves, slowing down to a moderate gait to conserve energy. Tom was already winded and marveled at Erin, who was barely breathing hard. Of course she was still a kid and had youth on her side. He was not, did not and felt like an old man.

They ran a few more blocks, checked another cab for keys and discovered that it was unlocked but had been vandalized. The windows were all busted out, the seat covers sliced and indecipherable graffiti was scrawled all over the hood and side panels. Apparently Chappy and the boys had been particularly bored one night.

By the time they approached Forty-Second Street and spotted Grand Central Station, Tom knew he was going to have to rest before his lungs totally collapsed.

"Gotta stop and catch my breath," he told Erin breathlessly. "Used to smoke and it's catching up with me."

"Me, too," Erin replied, probably just to make him feel better.

"Let's duck in there for minute," Tom said, pointing toward an electronics store with a busted out door window on the north side of Forty-Second Street.

The two headed toward the store and stepped inside. Tom stood for a moment to catch his breath then started searching the trashed display cases for anything they might be of value in them. He found a decent flashlight/radio combination then looked around for batteries that would fit the thing. When he found a pack of double A's, he popped them in, turned on the flashlight and the radio.

Nothing but static on the radio. He twirled the tuning knob and continued getting static across the band.

"Oh well, at least we have a decent flashlight now. Speaking of light, it's getting lighter every minute. We'd better get going before day breaks."

"What are we going to do if the Jeep won't start?" Erin asked.

"Hell if I know. I guess we'll have to take a battery out of one the cabs parked nearby. That could be a real problem, though. I don't know if we can afford that kind of time."

"I can't believe we haven't seen them yet! I wonder where they are."

Tom led the way out of the store. "I have no idea. All I know is that the odds are running against us every second we stay in this place. Manhattan may be huge, but they know we can only get so far without any wheels."

Tom looked both ways on Forty-Second Street and recalled how lively and bustling the popular venue had always been when he'd lived here. Now it looked like the set of a Hollywood ghost town.

The two broke into a run down Park Avenue.

The eastern sky was now becoming a dark blue over the tops of the buildings on Park. It was light enough now for Tom to recognize some of the places now—the posh apartment buildings with their awning adorned entrances, the delis and pizza shops, a Duane Reade drugstore.

When they approached Thirty-Eighth Street, Erin let out a gasp. "Kyle's car!"

Up ahead, Tom saw a beat up Toyota Tercel parked near the corner of the street. When they reached the car, Erin opened the door and began rummaging through the back seat. She found her coat, got out and put it on.

"I love this coat!" she said. "It was expensive, too."

"Any chance this thing still runs?" Tom asked.

"No way. It totally broke down. Kyle said something about dropping the transmission. That's how we got caught in the first place."

"Oh. Hell, it's damn near daylight out—we have got to get moving!"

"I'm with you!" Erin cried.

They sprinted the remaining four blocks to Thirty-fourth Street fueled by sheer anxiety and adrenalin—they knew they would be sitting ducks if the boys found them now. They rounded Thirty-fourth and made it as far as the Empire State building before Tom finally admitted to himself he simply had to stop to rest—even though they had only one more block to go.

He pushed one of the doors open and the two ducked into the lobby of the historic skyscraper. As he stood there catching his breath, Tom looked around and recalled the many times he'd been in this lobby, for he had made frequent trips up to the observatory to view this wonderful city whenever he needed encouragement or reassurance. It had always worked miracles.

The memory made Tom recall how many questions he had for Erin once they got out the city and back on the road. He especially wanted to know about her connection with New York and what part Kyle had played in her life.

"Let's do it," he panted, making a silent vow to start working out again if and when things got back to normal.

They exited the lobby and broke into a full run west on Thirty-fourth. In another forty seconds, Tom saw his Jeep parked ahead in the growing light, looking like an oasis in the middle of the Sahara.

"God, I hope the damn thing starts!" he exclaimed, casting a final look behind for any sign of the hearse, elated that they had made it this far. Now, if only their luck would hold out and the engine would turn over—

The loud blare of a car horn suddenly broke the silence. Tom whipped around and to his horror, saw the hearse flying directly toward them—

"Jesus, there they are!" he cried.

"Screw it—we're dead!" Erin exclaimed.

"Not yet, kiddo. Step on it and see if we can make it to the Jeep!"

Tom glanced back quickly again and saw that the hearse was only a couple of blocks away. It was going to be awfully close—and a fricking miracle if the Jeep started.

They stumbled up to the Laredo, flung open the doors and hopped inside in unison. Tom reached for the keys in the ignition only to discover that they were gone. Chappy and the boys had taken them. The hearse was now less than a block away—it almost seemed to be moving in slow motion now—which meant that this nightmare was almost over and he would suddenly wake up the moment he died.

They were screwed . . .

Then Tom remembered his spare key—the one he had ditched in the console after misplacing his keys one too many times.

"Frick an *a!*" Tom shouted. He reached over between the seats, snatched the key out of the compartment and fumbled around trying to guide it into the ignition. Tom looked in horror at the hearse heading straight for them at full speed—

They were going to ram them head-on!

Tom turned the key. The engine cranked once and died. He turned it again. The engine cranked twice, faltered for a split second then fired up.

But it was too late—the hearse was only yards away now. Tom could see Hoops and Chappy grinning from ear to ear in the front seat of the Caddie as they prepared for impact.

Tom threw the gearshift into reverse and floored it. The Jeep lurched backward so fast that Tom's head hit the steering wheel almost hard enough to knock him out.

The Jeep fishtailed wildly to the left and swayed like it was going to fall onto its side as it plowed toward the entrance of Macy's. The hearse continued speeding toward them, nearly sideswiping them as Tom saw Hoops whiz past the Jeep—

They'd missed them by a coat of paint!

Tom slammed on the brakes just as the Jeep jumped the sidewalk and plowed directly toward Macy's main entrance. It skidded backward into the door and smashed the plate glass with a huge jolt. Tom threw the gearshift into drive and floored it, flying back out over the curve and east on Thirty-fourth.

"Christ, that was close!" he gasped.

"No shit!" Erin said. "I can't believe they just missed us!"

Tom looked in his rear view mirror and saw the hearse pull a U-turn and head toward them again.

"We're not out of the woods, yet. Here they come!"

Tom tried to get his bearings as he flew down Thirty-fourth. What was the best way to lose these bastards? he thought, struggling to recall the streets of Manhattan. Heading back to the Lincoln Tunnel was out of the question—he needed more time to put some distance between themselves and the ghouls. Should he keep heading east and see if he could shake them before he got to the FDR, then head back toward the Tunnel? Or should he cross over to Queens or Brooklyn and take a totally different route out of here?

"They're gaining on us!" Erin shouted.

"I know—that hearse must have a goddamn 427 in it!"

"How can we lose them?"

"I'm thinking—I wish we had a gun so we could blow out one of their tires!" Tom blurted, feeling like an extra in a "B" movie.

"Maybe you should turn onto one of these streets," Erin suggested.

"Nope, I don't want to do that. We need to keep going as fast as we can; turning will just slow us down."

Tom's heart was in his mouth as he glanced in the mirror and saw that the hearse was no more than three or four car lengths behind them. The accelerator was all the way to the floor and he now regretted not getting a V-8 Cherokee instead of this doggy six-banger.

He had flown by Lexington Avenue and crossed Third Avenue when Tom realized that they were running out of road. There was Second then First Avenue before they dead-ended into the FDR. He wasn't going to be able to lose these guys by any stretch of the imagination before then—he had to think of something else.

Suddenly he had an idea: The Queens Midtown Tunnel! It was coming up any time now and maybe, just maybe he could throw them off by taking the tunnel at the very last second . . .

Tom knew it was a gamble because he would lose precious seconds turning off for the Midtown Tunnel instead of continuing on to the FDR. But there was a good chance that these demented shits were assuming he would be taking the FDR—heading for Queens wouldn't make any sense.

And that was exactly what he was banking on.

Tom flew through the intersection of Second Avenue and saw the sign for the Midtown Tunnel up ahead. Instead of applying his brakes to slow down for the access road and thereby give his pursuers a cue, he waited until he had almost past it, slammed the gearshift into second, turned the wheel hard to the left, jumped the curb and headed north on the access road.

Tom looked in the rearview mirror. The hearse had missed the turn! He heard the sound of the hearse's tires squealing as he floored it and headed toward the ramp to the tunnel. Another turn and they were inside the pitch-dark underground passage.

"We lost them!" Erin exclaimed as she looked back.

"Yeah, but just for a moment. I'm sure they'll be back on our tail in a flash. But at least we managed to put some distance between us."

Tom glanced at the fuel gauge just as he saw the headlights coming at him in his rear view mirror. He was on empty!

"Shit, here they come again!" Erin cried.

"Yeah, and that's just part of the bad news. I'm running on fumes."

"Oh, no! When do think we'll run out?"

"It won't be long, trust me. We're never going to outrun them now—we'll be at a dead stop any minute!"

"Oh, Tom, what are we going to do?"

"If we just had a weapon of some kind."

Erin shouted, "They're almost on us already! What are those sparks coming out of the side of their car?"

Tom looked in the mirror and saw intermittent sparks flying from the hearse. Apparently, they must have hit something when they turned around after he had eluded them. As the hearse drew closer, he saw that the chrome bumper of the old Caddy had somehow gotten smashed in and caused something, maybe the license plate, to drag along the pavement and create the sparks.

"Man, I'll bet they're pissed now! Hoops must not be too swift of a driver. Chappy will— Whoa, wait a second! I think I've got an idea!"

"What?"

"We have to hurry, though—they're only a couple hundred feet away! Quick, Erin, climb back to the cargo compartment!"

"Why?"

"I'll tell you in a second—just go!"

"Okay!"

Erin whipped off her seat belt, turned around and bolted in between the seats to the back. She climbed over the backseat and into the cargo area.

"Good girl. Now, I'm going to release the rear window lock and you push it open. See that gas can sitting back there? Once you get the window open, unscrew the cap and chuck that gas can outside. Hurry!"

Tom pressed the rear window release button and heard a click.

"It's unlocked!" Erin shouted.

"Push it open! Christ, hurry before they get any closer!" Tom cried.

Tom watched Erin in the rear view mirror as she pushed the window open, his ears popping from the sudden vacuum it created. He saw her hoist the gas can up and rest it on the edge of the tailgate, unscrew the cap then push the can out the window.

"Geronimo!"

"Hit the deck, Erin!" Tom shouted.

That second, there was a huge orange/red blast of light that completely illuminated the tunnel, followed by an ear-deafening explosion. Tom saw the hearse explode into flames and continue speeding toward the Jeep like a meteor gone wild.

"You all right?" he hollered back.

Erin's head popped up over the back seat. "Wow, that was *crazy!* Shit, they're still coming at us!"

Tom realized just then that he had lightened up his foot on the accelerator after the explosion so he floored it again. The ball of fire that was once a Cadillac hearse appeared to slow down as the Jeep sped quickly away from it.

"We did it!" Erin yelled.

"It sure looks that way," Tom said. "Now I just hope we get to the end of this tunnel before we run out of gas."

Erin began making her way up toward the front seat. The fireball was smaller now but still lit up the tunnel like a Christmas tree.

"Great job, kiddo!" Tom said, giving Erin a high-five as she sat back down in the passenger seat.

"Thanks—god, that was so *exciting!*"

"Yeah, a little *too* exciting for this guy! I think I left my heart about a mile back or so!" Tom declared.

"This was just like out of an action flick! What made you think of the gas can idea?"

Tom smiled dryly. "Seeing the fuel gauge on "E." Then remembering that I had a couple of gallons back there in the can."

"Cool—just like James Bond!"

"Well, I don't' know if I'd go *that* far," Tom chuckled, impressed that Erin had apparently checked out a Bond movie or two.

"I see light up ahead!" the girl cried.

"Thank God—if we can just get out of this tunnel before we run out of gas, I'll be forever grateful."

In another moment they emerged into Queens and headed directly into a beautiful sunrise. Now on the Long Island Expressway, Tom sped past the tollbooths and got off on the first exit they came to.

"Got to find a gas station pronto—keep your eyes peeled," he said to Erin.

As luck would have it, the engine suddenly sputtered a couple of times then died altogether. Tom coasted to a stop.

"Screw it. Well, at least it's a beautiful morning—perfect for a stroll in Bumfuck, Queens," Tom groaned.

"At least we're *alive,*" Erin reminded him.

He glanced over at his young passenger and smiled. "Point taken. Let's be sure to keep it that way."

They got out and started walking north on Twenty-First Street. It was surreal, walking along on such a bright, crisp morning and hearing nothing but their footsteps echoing dully off the concrete. As had been the case in Manhattan, vehicles were scarce and there wasn't a soul in sight, not even a bird singing a song.

"Do you think things will ever be the same?" Erin asked solemnly.

Tom looked around at the deserted streets and empty sidewalks. In all of the time since being captured by Chappy and his sidekicks, he hadn't given this ongoing dilemma much thought. He'd thought of his family of course, but only in fleeting moments. He'd thought of the fact that virtually everyone in the world had vanished, but had not dwelled much upon it. When your life was on the line and you were fighting to survive, all else seemed to fade into the background.

Now, at least at that particular moment, he and Erin seemed out of danger. And now, like a bad penny, the bitter reality of their bizarre situation suddenly appeared again.

"I just don't know, Erin. I mean, here we are in the most populated city in the country and all we've seen are three other people—and I'm using that word loosely. Not only are there no other human beings—there isn't even a single animal or insect! It's so hard to conceive that what might seem like an impossible scenario has become real and that there is no rational answer to where we will go from here. I'm sorry to say this, but I don't feel too good about any of this. I mean, to be perfectly honest, I really can't see things just suddenly going back to the way it used to be."

"I know what you're saying—I feel the same way. All I can say for sure is that I'm glad I have you. If it weren't for you, I would not be able to handle this."

Tom put his arm around her. "Believe me, kiddo, I feel the exact same way."

Within another few blocks, they came upon an Exxon station. Tom felt the same feeling of déjà vu as he went inside and began poking around for another fuel can. Erin shopped around for snacks in the meantime. Amazingly, the shop was very well stocked and actually had a two-gallon size gas can for sale. Tom picked one up and headed outside.

There wasn't a single vehicle on the lot but Tom spotted an old Buick further up the street. Erin stepped outside with her groceries in a plastic bag and joined him as he walked toward the car.

"I hope this old clunker has a lot of gas—I just want to get on the road and out of this godforsaken place ASAP," Tom said as he unscrewed the fuel cap and inserted the hose.

"Want Coke or a water?" Erin asked. "Got Sprite, too."

"Coke, please. It'll be a perfect chaser for the gas."

Erin giggled and watched Tom as he began sucking on the hose. In a moment, he pulled his mouth away just before gas began flowing out of it. Quickly, he jammed the hose into the gas can.

"Well, whatdya know—I'm getting better at this!"

When the gas can was full, Tom pulled the hose out of the Buick's fuel tank.

"Let's go back to the Jeep," he said to Erin. "I'd let you wait here but I'm not taking any chances on losing you again."

She handed him an open bottle of Coke. "I'm not going anywhere without you, ever again!"

Tom considered what she had just said and a funny thought came to mind. What would happen between he and Erin in the event that he was actually reunited with his family? Would the two of them simply part company and go their separate ways? Or would they try to continue their relationship in some capacity? A strange thought, indeed.

He knew one thing for certain: he was oddly attracted to the girl in a way that he couldn't really put a finger on. It wasn't sexual or anything like that—it was more like an invisible bond he felt between himself and her. An indefinable attachment.

Not surprising, really. After all, they had already gone through a lot of intense situations together. Erin had been his only ally in this whole absurd thing—his cohort and in fact his only tangible hope for survival. Had he not discovered her, he would probably still be back in Columbus right this moment combing the streets relentlessly for signs of life that may never again exist.

Whatever the case, he felt certain that he could never simply forget about the girl and deny himself any contact with her in the future. He felt a certain responsibility for her now—to be there to protect her and guide her if need be . . .

"Tom?" she suddenly said. "What are you thinking about?"

He realized that his mind had drifted off.

"Oh, nothing in particular. Just daydreaming, I guess."

"About finding your family?"

"Yeah, you could say that. And about you, too."

"What do you mean?"

"I mean that I'm very glad I met you, in spite of the horrible circumstances under which we have met."

"That's funny. I feel the exact same way but couldn't find the right way to put it. You just did it for me!" she smiled brightly.

Tom put his arm around her waist and pulled her close to his side. Erin followed suit.

He said, "Let's get gassed up and head back to Ohio, what say?"

"Sounds like a plan," Erin replied, holding him tighter.

13

As they drove through Easton, Pennsylvania, Tom felt bold enough to ask Erin a few questions about her past. She had slept most of the hour and a half drive and awoken moments ago. The girl was still a little groggy but in good spirits.

"You warm enough?" he asked.

"Yeah, like toast. It sure is a lot warmer today than it was yesterday."

"I hope this weather holds out. The turnpike can be rough when it's snowing."

Erin chuckled. "Kyle almost totally wiped out at least twice. His car was lousy in the snow—not to mention that he is, or was, a pretty bad driver."

"How long had you known Kyle," Tom asked, trying to sound as nonchalant as possible.

She thought for a moment then replied, "About two years."

"Where was he from—Ohio?"

"No, he was from Long Island. I met him in Ohio, though."

Tom could already sense the hesitation in her voice. Time to back off? He'd play it by ear.

"When I lived in the city, I used to go out on Long Island quite a bit. Some really nice beaches out there."

"I know—we went to Montauk one day, out on the very end of the island. It was so pretty! So much nicer than the city."

"So you lived in New York, too?" Tom asked, surprised she had never mentioned it before.

Again, the slightest hesitation in her voice. "Yeah, for a while."

"With your family?"

Silence.

Tom looked over at Erin. Her head was turned and she was staring out the window. He waited a moment and said, "Erin—you okay?"

"I'm fine," she replied, continuing to stare.

"I hope I didn't say something wrong."

Erin turned and faced him, a tear in her eye. "No, you didn't. I just don't really know how to answer you."

"What do you mean?"

"I haven't really ever had a family, Tom. I was adopted."

Tom realized he had hit on a very delicate subject. He also wanted to know more about it.

"I'm sorry, Erin. If you'd rather not talk about it, I'll understand."

She smiled wanly. "No, it's fine. There's really not a whole lot to say other than I was adopted as a baby and that I've been in several foster homes throughout my life. That's about all there is to it."

"How long have you been on your own?" he asked, recalling that she lived alone in her own apartment.

"Oh, about six months."

"Do your foster parents live nearby—I mean in Ohio?"

"If you're referring to my last ones, yes. In Cleveland."

"You keep in touch with them?"

"Not really. Listen, Tom. I appreciate your interest in my past but I'd prefer not to say anymore about it. No offense, but I really don't think I can do it. Not now, anyway. Maybe later, I don't know. Do you understand?"

Tom was angry with himself—he realized that he'd pushed her too hard much too soon. He should have taken more time with her.

"Sure, I understand. I'm sorry, Erin. I won't pry anymore."

She held his eyes for a moment and said, "I didn't think you were prying, Tom. It's just that, I don't know, my past has not been the kind that anyone would be proud of. In fact, it has been horrible and disgusting. I don't want you to think badly of me. I'm afraid that if you knew about my life, you . . . you wouldn't like me anymore!"

Tom's was stunned. She couldn't be any further from the truth.

"That's ridiculous, Erin! I don't care what you've done or not done before—it won't change how I feel about you now. I really like you. A lot. And I care about you a lot. Nothing you could do or say would ever make me think any differently of you."

She smiled sweetly. "You really mean that?"

"Of course I do."

"I think that's the nicest thing anyone has ever said to me," she said, her eyes welling up again.

"Well, I just want you to know that it's true," Tom said, offering his hand to her.

She took his hand in hers and squeezed. She breathed a long sigh of resignation, as if she were about to shed a great weight off her shoulders. "My life has been so, so *pathetic!* You are not going to like what I'm about to tell you."

"Try me," he said encouragingly.

Erin sighed deeply. "Well, I guess I'll start at the beginning. My first memories of growing up were in Youngstown. My first foster parents were very nice to me and it wasn't until I was older, seven years old to be exact, that they let me know that they weren't my natural parents. That crushed me."

"Why would they tell you that in the first place, especially at that young age?"

"Because they could no longer afford to raise me, that's why. My foster dad had lost his job and my mother had just been a part time waitress. They tried to make ends meet but simply couldn't— Youngstown had fallen on some hard economic times. So they had to send me back to the adoption agency."

Tom was speechless. Surely her foster parents could have tried harder to make it work instead of taking that route. He bit his tongue, though.

"So what happened then?"

"I was adopted by another family. They had a couple of other kids, too, so it was sort of neat. At first, anyway."

"What do you mean, 'at first?'"

"Let's just say that my new father was—well, he molested me."

Jesus! Tom thought. How much worse could this get?

"Oh Erin, I'm so sorry to hear that," was all he could say.

"It went on for three years. Finally, he got caught. By my foster mother. I was out of that place in a flash."

"You had never told anyone before?" Tom asked, bewildered.

"No, are you kidding? He told me he would kill me if I told anyone, and I believed him!"

Tom was speechless. All he could think of was this poor orphaned girl who had first been rejected by one family only to be relocated to another one with a parent that was supposed to be raising her molesting her. How in Christ's name could anyone be that cruel?

Erin said, "I know what you're probably thinking now: *oh poor little Erin.* But don't think that way, Tom. It wasn't the end of the world and I don't need your sympathy. I probably deserved what I got . . ."

"That is an absurd thing to say, Erin! No child deserves to be abused, period. I can't believe you would even think like that."

"You could never understand, Tom. No one can. I felt lucky just having a roof over my head and living a fairly normal life instead of being forced to live in some awful orphanage. I can't begin to describe what goes on in orphanages but trust me, it's worse than you could ever imagine."

"All I know is that I hope they punished the bastard who did that to you. What ever became of him?"

"I don't know—I never heard any more about it. I had to go back to the orphanage after that, which was in Cleveland, until someone else adopted me again."

"And how long was that?"

"Too long. I started picking up some pretty bad habits at the orphanage."

"Like?"

"Stealing. Smoking cigarettes. Lying. Drinking. Should I go on?"

"I've got the idea. Go on," Tom said, feeling sick in the pit of his stomach. He had a feeling of what was coming next.

"By the time my most recent foster parents adopted me, I was a teenager. And they were very good people. The only problem was, I didn't realize that at the time."

"How's that?"

"Oh, I put them through so much hell! I was a horrible kid—I hated school, got into fights, drank and smoked much of the time. I even got into shoplifting just for the thrill of it! And my parents tried so hard to get me under control. But it was useless. *I* was use-less . . .

"I eventually fell in with a pretty bad bunch of kids, to say the least. We skipped school all the time, went out to the lake and got high instead of going to classes. Basically, I was an incorrigible delinquent. By the time I was a sophomore, my high school career was all but over before it had really begun."

"What do you mean?"

"Well, I got suspended twice and almost got expelled alto-gether. Yeah, I was that bad! But before I could totally screw up at school, Kyle came along to save me."

Tom noted the sarcasm in her voice. She continued.

"I was partying with some friends one night when I met Kyle. He seemed like this really cool dude because he dressed so weird and was from New York, which we all thought was about as awe-some as you could get! We got high together and talked about all kinds of stuff and I just went crazy over him. He really seemed to like me, too.

"He told me all about New York, and how he had his own movie production company in Manhattan. I was impressed and asked him how old he was. He told me he was twenty-three and had graduated from N.Y.U. with a degree in film the year before. Then he told me that I should go back to New York with him—that I could be a model or an actress if I was willing to work hard enough. He said I had a great look and that he had all kinds of con-nections. He told me that the industry was always looking for cute young girls like me.

"I was of course floored by all of this! I mean, New York City—a model or an actress—*me?* I basically asked him when we could leave and if now was too soon!"

Tom imagined the scenario Erin had just described: wayward teenage girl, potential school dropout at age fifteen or sixteen and seasoned partier who had zero self esteem being confronted by Mr. Big City Shit, dressed hip and years older, with his own "movie production company" in Manhattan at age twenty-three, ready to make a star out a vulnerable young girl whose life already seemed like a dead-end street . . .

Could Erin have fallen for a character like Kyle any easier?

"So that night, literally, I went home, told my folks I was going to bed, then packed up and snuck out my window without them even hearing me. Then I left with Kyle to the city."

Tom was floored. At the drop of a hat, this young impressionable girl had run away with a virtual stranger who was eight years her senior to New York to pursue an acting or modeling career. The rest of this story could only get worse.

"So how did that go?" he asked.

"Well, at first it was exciting. I mean, it was pretty obvious that Kyle had exaggerated somewhat—his movie production company wasn't much more than an extra room in his apartment. But I really didn't care, I was just so thrilled to actually be living in New York City! The people, the buildings, the lights, Broadway, everything!"

"So his apartment was in Manhattan?"

"Well, no. It was actually in Brooklyn. But we were only twenty minutes from midtown," she added. "Anyway, I decided to call my foster parents to let them know I was okay. They of course wanted to know where I was and begged me to come back. I just told them that I would keep in touch and not to worry about me. I felt bad for them, but I really thought I was doing the right thing at the time."

"So how did you make ends meet? Did Kyle have a regular job to pay the rent?"

"Not exactly."

"What do you mean?"

"He, uh, sort of had his own side business," she replied slowly.

"You mean making movies?"

"Well, he did that, too. But he got most of his money from dealing."

"Great," Tom muttered.

"I'm not going to make any excuses for him. He was a drug dealer and it got scary at times. I mean, strange people bopping in at all hours wanting to score some weed or coke. I once begged him to give it up because it was only a matter of time before we got in trouble and he, uh, wasn't very happy with me."

"Meaning?"

"He beat the crap out of me—I sure learned not to do anything like that again!"

"Jesus, Erin. Why did you stay with him?"

"I don't know—I was just young and ignorant. I really believed that I could go somewhere there, model or something. And besides that, I didn't have anywhere else to go. I was stubborn and did not want to go back to boring Cleveland. So I figured I was better off where I was.

"It wasn't always as bad as it sounds—at least not for awhile, anyway. Kyle was a really good photographer and shot a modeling portfolio for me. It was really good. I showed my book around and went to a few go-sees. I almost got a couple of jobs, too, but it is really competitive in the modeling industry.

"Kyle started getting pissed off that I wasn't getting hired any- where so he thought of another way to bring some money in." She said this under her breath so softly that Tom could barely hear her.

"What was that?"

"Porn. He started taking shots of me for the internet."

She saw the expression on Tom's face and quickly added, "I *told* you I wasn't proud of my past! Now you hate me, don't you?"

"Erin, I do not hate you. And I wish I could say that I'm sur- prised to be hearing all of this but I'm not. Kyle reminded me of a very shady character who was quite capable of taking advantage of a young impressionable fifteen year old if given half the chance."

Erin sighed. "Well, it gets worse," she declared dismally. "At first he shot stills of me and uploaded them to kiddy porn sites. He had me, uh, get naked and pose in all kinds of positions. Then he decided that that wasn't enough, that he needed to 'spice things up a bit,' as he put it."

Tom braced himself. "How was that?"

"He had a friend, Gino, who started posing with me. He had me—do stuff to him. It was disgusting! I told Kyle I didn't want to do those things!" she cried.

Tom reached over and placed his hand on her shoulder comfort- ingly. "Erin, you don't have to go on with this. It's only getting you upset."

She gazed at him in earnest. "No, Tom, I *want* to tell you this. I need to get this off of my chest and be up front with you about me."

"Okay, kiddo, it's your call."

"Kyle basically didn't give a damn *what* I didn't want to do. You see, by this time he had gotten more and more into drugs—not just selling them but taking them, too. He started doing a lot of crack and his personality changed a lot for the worse. He didn't really care about me anymore, he just wanted to use me. I realize that now, of course, but I was clueless back then. You see, I was starting to do drugs, too. I was messed up half the time."

Tom thought: surprise, surprise. As much as he felt bad about Kyle's violent demise, right now he was glad the son of a bitch was dead.

Erin went on. "Anyway, Kyle made me keep doing the porn shots and apparently made good money off of them on the web-sites. He was thrilled at how much money was rolling in 'for such little work,' as he put it. But it wasn't enough—he always wanted more and to expand his horizons. So, he started shooting porn movies."

"Don't tell me—"

"Yes, I was the star of them, too. There were a few other guys he knew that joined in as time went by. Kyle would create these retarded 'screenplays' where I would like, come home from school, wearing my plaid skirt with my hair in pigtails, and start watching television in my bedroom. I'd hear a knock at my win-dow and it would be some older guy staring in at me. I'd let him inside and start undressing while he played with himself. It was so stupid and disgusting!

"There were a couple of other girls he would occasionally use in the videos, too. One of them was only ten or eleven. That was when I finally drew the line. I told him flatly that I was not going to be a part of this sick shit anymore!"

"What did you do?"

"Well, he of course beat the shit out of me. He said that I would do what he wanted me to do or he would throw me out on the street. I told him that was fine, that I was going to leave him any-way. That made him even madder and he beat me some more. He beat me so bad that I was knocked unconscious for hours. When I came to, it was morning and Kyle wasn't in the apartment. But he had tied me to the bed and locked me in the bedroom."

"What happened when he returned?" Tom asked.

She smiled. "I don't know—I wasn't there when he got back!"

"You managed to escape?"

"Yeah! What Kyle didn't know was that there was a pair of scissors in the nightstand. I managed to get close enough to work them out of the drawer and cut off the rope. Then, I figured a way out of the bedroom. There was a fire escape outside the window but Kyle either forgot about it or figured that even if I did manage to untie myself, I would never have the nerve to climb out onto the rickety thing. That's where he misjudged me," she added.

"So I packed up a few things, took some money I had stashed under the rug and left by way of the window. When I stepped out onto the fire escape, it shook and squeaked like it was going to collapse with me on it. But I was determined to get out of that place one way or another, so I walked over to the edge, tossed my bag onto the sidewalk and hang-dropped twelve feet onto the concrete. I sprained my ankle, but at least I made it!"

"Good for you. Where did you go?"

"I didn't waste any time—I took the subway to the Greyhound station on Eighth Avenue and bought a one-way ticket to Cleveland. It took every cent I had."

"So you went back to your parents?"

"No. I knew that Kyle would come looking for me so I stayed with my best friend, Courtney for awhile to figure out what I was going to do next."

"But what about your foster parents? Why didn't you simply go back to them and let them take care of Kyle in case he ever tried to track you down?"

"You know what he's capable of! The man was a raging druggie by then and would have done anything to force me to go back to New York with him. The last thing I wanted to do was put my parents in the same dangerous position you had been in."

Tom realized that she had indeed been very wise keeping her parents out of the picture. "So what did you do?"

"I needed money so I called my foster parents just to see if they would loan me some. That was the stupidest thing I could've done, obviously. They begged me to come home, but I told them I couldn't, that I needed to live my own life. After I realized that they weren't going to give me any money, I told mom goodbye and that I loved her. That's when she broke down and cried, then told me that someone had been looking for me earlier that day."

"Kyle," Tom said.

"Yeah. He'd actually had the nerve to call the house and ask for me! I couldn't believe it!"

"So what happened next?"

"Courtney had a friend she knew who offered to drive me to Columbus if I wanted to go. I didn't have much choice since Kyle was in town and hot on my tracks so I said yes. Courtney gave me all the money she had—seventy-five dollars—and Matt picked me up later that afternoon. And that's how I ended up in Columbus. I stayed with a friend of Matt's who went to Ohio State until I could find a job and get on my feet. I eventually earned enough to get my own apartment in Worthington and the rest as they say is history."

"So why did Kyle try to find you again after all of this time, you suppose?" Tom asked.

Erin shook her head. "The guy was sick, that's all I can tell you. He got so strung out on drugs that he just suddenly lost it and decided that he had to get me back—apparently to start exploiting me again, judging by our conversation on the way to New York. All I know for sure is that there was no way he was ever going to let me leave him again. He would've definitely killed me first."

Well, at least you don't have to worry about that now, Tom thought with more than a little satisfaction.

They lapsed into silence. Tom thought about Erin and wondered how she had managed to remain so together after all of the baggage she had been carrying most of her young life. He thought back to the way Kyle had spoken to her—his condescending and demeaning attitude toward her and total lack of respect. How could someone put up with someone like him as long as she had? And how could someone have the gall to imply that she was a slut when in fact Erin had done nothing but what she been forced to do at his hand?

But perhaps the most troubling aspect about Erin Myers was that she literally had no family now, and never really had. Her foster families had been either unwilling to make any sacrifices to keep her or dysfunctional and abusive. What would it be like to never know who your biological parents were? Or if you had any siblings, aunts, uncles, grandparents somewhere out there?

It all seemed inconceivable to Tom. He tried to imagine going through life being tossed into random homes with random people who were expected to pretend to love and care about you as if you were their own but in reality lacked the real, rock-solid commit-ment that true blood parents possessed. Granted, it was better than nothing he supposed, but there were no guarantees and plenty of risks, considering what Erin's second adoptive "father" had done to her.

Tom's thoughts shifted to his own family and he wondered where they were now. He stared out at the dark highway, void of any traffic just as it had been the entire return trip, and realized that most likely nothing had changed since leaving Columbus the day before. Peg and the kids would still be gone. The rest of the world would still be gone . . .

And all that would be left in the world would be he and Erin.

14

It was 8:20 PM when Tom pulled off the I-71 exit at Morse Road. They hadn't seen a single vehicle the entire trip and Columbus looked the same as the day before except for the snow that had begun melting away in the warmer temperature.

Tom was exhausted and wanted nothing more than to go home and sleep. He would of course gladly trade that in to see his family again. Erin had mentioned that she would like to go to her apartment to get some clothes, so Tom drove past Indianola toward High Street.

"It looks as dead as ever, Tom," she said quietly.

"Yeah, I know. But I don't think either of us is too surprised."

"Nope, I'm not. After all, when you drive thirteen hours and don't see a single car on the road, you don't expect to arrive here and see all kinds of people milling around."

"I wish I could say that I'm getting use to any of this, but that would be a lie," Tom declared.

"God, do I need a shower! I'll even take a cold one—I have never felt so funky in my entire life!" Erin exclaimed.

"The good news is that we have a gas hot water heater at the house, so we can at least enjoy a hot shower."

"Awesome—I can't wait!"

Erin told Tom how to get to her apartment, which wasn't far from downtown Worthington. He parked in front of the four-story brick structure and kept the car running.

"You want to come in? It will just take me a minute or two," Erin said.

"Yes, I do. It's going to be dark as pitch inside."

"Forgot about that."

Tom grabbed the flashlight and followed Erin up the walk. Erin led the way inside and up to the second floor. Her apartment door was still wide open—the way Kyle had apparently left it.

"Can I borrow the flashlight? I need to find my clothes," she said.

"Sure," Tom replied, handing it to her.

Tom stood near the door and watched Erin as she made her way across the small living room to her bedroom. He heard her rummaging around for several moments before she came out carrying a backpack. She went into the bathroom, stuffed some items into the backpack then rejoined Tom.

"Now take me to where that hot shower awaits!" she smiled.

Back in the Jeep, Tom yawned for what had to be the twentieth time since leaving New York. He tried to recall the last time he'd slept and realized it had been the night before while parked in front of Macy's—about forty-five minutes worth in all before being rudely awakened by Chappy and his cronies.

He needed about eight uninterrupted hours of shuteye and a square meal.

After a shower.

He turned onto his street, pulled up in front of his house and did a double take—

There was a car parked in the driveway!

Although he didn't recognize the car, its presence could only be good news: maybe someone had brought his family back home!

"Whose car is that?" Erin said.

"I don't know but I'm hoping that Peg and the kids are in there right now. Maybe somebody found them!"

"That would be great!"

Tom pulled up behind the car and shut of the engine. He glanced at the license plate and recognized the name of the auto dealership advertised on the frame, which was located in Smithtown.

That was odd, to say the least.

"Maybe you'd better stay here while I check this out, come to think of it," he told Erin.

"But you said—"

"I know what I said, but I want to be sure it's safe before you come in. Once I'm sure that it is, I'll come back and get you."

Erin was visibly miffed. "I want to go, too! It's not fair!"

Tom looked directly into her eyes. "Listen, Erin. We have no idea who is in my house right now. It could be a good thing or it could be trouble. I just don't want to take any chances."

"Okay. I'll wait here. But come back as fast as you can, you promise?"

"I promise."

Tom grabbed the flashlight and opened the car door. He shut it gently and made his way to the side door. It was dark as pitch inside, which was not a good sign. If Peg and the kids were in there, they certainly would have at least lit some candles or fired up the fireplace.

He paused before opening the door and glanced back at the mysterious car parked in the driveway. It was an older model Pontiac, green, and looked to be around a mid-nineties model. Who in god's green earth would be visiting from Smithtown? he wondered. Peg's family hailed from Columbus, so it almost had to be either a friend or a relative of his—someone with an awfully good reason to warrant the two-hour drive.

Tom crept over to the garage. He was not going to go into the house without some kind of weapon. He found a crowbar, recalled Bummer for a second, then carried it with him over to the side door. Opening the door as quietly as he could, he stepped inside.

From the laundry room, Tom could just make out a tiny orange glow coming from inside the kitchen. It looked like the end of a lit cigarette. He took a whiff and recognized the pungent smell of burning tobacco. At that same moment, the glow intensified as the person at the other end of the cigarette took a long drag.

"Come on in, Tom," a voice suddenly rang from the darkness.

Tom flinched.

A flashlight flicked on and its beam shone directly into his eyes.

"And ya can put down that goddamn crowbar."

The man's voice was gruff sounding with a heavy southern Ohio drawl. It wasn't the least bit familiar.

"Who are you?" Tom asked, feeling his heart rate go up a notch or two.

"Right now, that's for me to know and you to find out. I want you to drop that piece of iron (pronounced *"arn"*) and walk toward me real slow-like," the voice commanded.

"No way—this is my house and I'm not going to drop any-thing!"

Click.

Tom knew that was the sound of a gun cocking in the darkness.

"Ya sure about that, Tom? I'm bettin' ya might wanna recon-sider if ya don't want a slug in yer haid"

"Okay, I'm dropping it!"

He let the crowbar fall to his feet; the dull clanging nearly deafening.

"There ya go. Now come toward me real slow. Or as God is my witness, I'll waste yer sorry ass."

Tom moved tentatively toward the man holding the flashlight. He couldn't make out any of his features except that he was thin.

"That's far enough, right there," the man said. "Now, I'm gonna light a candle so we can see each another. I want you to just stand there nice and still for a second."

Tom watched anxiously as the stranger grabbed a butane lighter off the kitchen table, flicked it and lit a candle. As amber light filled the kitchen, Tom gazed at the man's face, trying to determine if he'd ever seen him before. He was heavily bearded, had a broken nose and wore his long, greasy hair in a ponytail. Tom was fairly certain he had never laid eyes on him before.

"There. Now have a seat and we can begin our little chit-chat," the intruder said, gaping at him with bug eyes that looked like he was on crystal meth.

Tom sat down across the table from him and said, "What do you want with me?"

"Hold on and I'll tell ya in a minute. First I want to get some-thing to drink."

The man got up, went over to the refrigerator and took out two warm Michelob Ultras. "Here," he said, offering one to Tom.

"No thanks, too early for me," Tom said, trying to appear under control while in fact he was terrified of this scary-looking redneck.

"Suit yerself," the stranger said, screwing off the bottle cap. He kept the gun trained on Tom as he sucked down several huge gulps of beer.

"Ahhh, that's better. Now down to the business. I don't reckon you remember me, Tom, but I lived on the west side of Smithtown back in the eighties around the same time you shuffled off to New York. I'd seen you around in the bars from time to time but we never talked none because you were one of them city fellahs and I was just what you thought of as a hillbilly or whatever. Which I didn't really give a big shit about because I figgered as long as you never messed with me or any of my buddies, I wasn't gonna start no trouble with you."

Tom thought back to those cobweb-shrouded days twenty years ago, trying to place this guy's face in a bar. He looked just like the other typical hicks from the sticks: ultra-long dirty hair, full beard and that same sort of startled, demented look as the good ol' boys in *Deliverance*—

But the guy didn't ring any bells.

"Anyway, my name is Donnie—Donnie Shortridge. Now, does that name sound familiar to you?"

In fact, it did, but only faintly. Tom recalled the name Donnie Shortridge but couldn't place exactly where he'd heard it before.

"Not really," he said. "Should it?"

"Aww, it sure as hell *should!* But like I said before, your type of folk didn't give a shit about my type so you probably don't *want* to remember. Don't really make any big shit to me, anyway."

Tom noticed that the longer this Donnie character talked, the more anger showed in his face. He was scowling at him now, looking like a time bomb ready to blow any second.

Tom needed to keep this in mind, whatever the guy wanted from him.

"My memory is pretty fried, Donnie. Too much booze over the years, I guess," Tom quipped, attempting to add a little humor to the conversation.

Donnie's expression didn't change one iota.

"You're a goddamn pussy, Tom. You don't know what drunk *is*."

Hmmm, Tom thought. He's getting downright nasty now.

"Let me throw another name at ya, Tom, and I'm betting that you're gonna remember *it!* How about the name Mindy Conkel?"

Mindy Conkel. Tom did recall her name. She was the girl he'd picked up at a bar one night. Really good looking but a little on the sleazy side. He'd taken her to her place and had a pretty good time. And that was about it—he'd never seen her again.

"Yeah, I do remember Mindy. Why do you ask?"

Donnie's expression went from angry to furious. *"Because, motherfucker, she was my wife and you fucked her!"*

Tom's heart skipped two beats and his head felt like a lead weight all of a sudden.

Shit! So that's what this is all about . . .

He decided to play it cool. "I *what?* No way, Donnie! What makes you think I did that?"

Donnie drained the bottle, opened the other one with his yellow buckteeth and spit the cap out onto the table. "Because I just know, fucker! She told me!"

Tom thought back, trying to recall exactly what had happened the night he had picked up Mindy Conkle—

He'd been at the Short Stop Pub with Mike and Jeff that night. They had all been fairly smashed when all of a sudden these two chicks came over and sat down at their table. One was Mindy and the other was—hell he couldn't remember what her name was. She was pretty ugly though, which made Mindy look all that much better.

One thing led to another and Mindy began flirting with him big time, rubbing his leg and pressing her tits against him every time she said something into his ear. Before long, she asked him if he wanted to go to her place and he had happily agreed.

They had gone to her downtown apartment, which was a little rough and seemed to fit her personality to a tee. They drank some more and eventually went to bed together. About all he could recall from that point on was that she was a good lay but he couldn't wait to get the hell out of there the next morning. Mindy Conkel was not exactly the stuff that dreams were made of. But he'd had a very good time, and that was a fact.

Mindy had never said anything about being married or mentioned any boyfriend. And she definitely had not been wearing a wedding band—he would have been keeping an eye out for that no matter how drunk he'd been. In fact, he could recall her mentioning a roommate named Sarah—

So she had definitely not been married to Donnie Shortridge at the time—

"Donnie, I swear to you that Mindy was single when I went out with her. And I only went out with her one night. I think you have the facts wrong—"

Crash!

Donnie's fist came down so hard on the table that the beer bottle jumped an inch or two into the air.

"Don't tell *me* I ain't got my story straight, you fuckin' shit! Whether or not we was married at that exact time don't make no difference—you banged her when she was my woman!"

"Donnie, listen. If you were dating Mindy at the time, she never told me, and that's the truth! Had I known she had a boyfriend, I would never have uh, been with her. I swear!"

"You mean you would have never fucked her, that's what you mean."

"Donnie, I did not do that. We just played around a little."

"Played around a little, my ass! That's the same goddamn thing she tried to tell me at first. Then she couldn't deny it anymore because she was knocked up!"

Tom suddenly felt lightheaded—like something buried deep in the muck and the mire for years had risen to the surface. This story was beginning to have a very unpleasant ring to it.

He had in fact gotten a call from Mindy Conkel one day. Not long after he'd moved to New York. And he had put that call so far out of his mind, it wasn't until now that it came back to him.

Mindy Conkel had called to tell him that she was pregnant with his child.

He had blown her off, telling her that it was next to impossible that he had gotten her pregnant, given the circumstances. They had only slept together once, he had argued. The odds were totally against it.

Besides, he had thought, there was no way he was going to let this chick screw up his new life in the Big Apple!

Mindy continued to insist that the child was his and Tom had finally gotten so angry that he simply hung up on her. As it turned out, he'd never heard from her again.

So he had promptly forgotten all about it—

Until now.

Tom knew he had to find a way out of this situation. If he didn't, there was little doubt that Donnie Shortridge was going to kill him.

"Are you trying to say that I got her pregnant?" he said.

"That's right, I know ya did!"

"How could you know that, Donnie? What makes you think it wasn't you?"

"Because, asshole, I took a paternity test. I started having my doubts about her when she got knocked up once I found out that she had fucked you, too. And even though the bitch swore up and down that you weren't the father, I didn't believe her.

"But the clincher was that the kid had dark brown hair and brown eyes. Mindy and I both have blue eyes and blond hair. This kid didn't look one goddamn bit like me! So I got tested one day. And sure enough, the kid wasn't mine.

"I got real mad and real drunk after I found out the results of that test. When Mindy got back from work that night, I beat the crap out of her. Broke her arm, a couple of ribs and smashed her face in pretty good. The cops came and I ended up getting a prison term. All because of *you*, motherfucker! You messed up my whole goddamn life!"

The man was so roaring angry now that the veins were popping out of his neck. Tom almost shot up and ran but the gun pointed at him made him reconsider.

"Donnie, I'm sorry. But that still doesn't prove I was the father—it could just as easily have been someone else—"

"You stinkin' sonofabitch—now you're makin' Mindy out for an even bigger whore than she is! No, she may be a bitch but I'm sure you were the only other bastard she'd screwed. So that makes you the daddy and the one that not only screwed up my family but got me sent to the southern Ohio pen for *five fucking years!*"

"Even if I were the father, which I really doubt, that wouldn't make it *my* fault you got sent to prison, Donnie. I mean, it sounds like you could've used a few anger management sessions or something—"

Tom knew as soon as it came out that this had not been a wise thing to say.

Whack!

Donnie backhanded him with a beer bottle. It hurt like bloody hell.

"Fuck you, man! Don't be telling me about needing anger management!"

Tom almost laughed out loud at the irony, but his jaw hurt too much.

It was at that moment that he spotted Erin in the living room—creeping toward the kitchen with the fire poker in her hand. Donnie's back was toward her so he was unaware of her presence.

Ignoring Erin, Tom touched his aching jaw gingerly and said, "Look Donnie, I'm sorry about all of this—I truly am. But surely you could have just forgiven Mindy's infidelity and raised the child as your own, right?"

Donnie guffawed heartily. "You gotta be shittin'me! First of all there was no way I'd do that. I wasn't gonna live with no whore and rear some other dude's kid. Wouldn't have made no difference any way, even if I had been foolish enough to do that. She had a restraining order on me when I got out of the joint and she'd given the little shit up for adoption. Seems she couldn't afford to raise the kid on her own. Serves her right for pressing charges against me. Nope, screw it all. The only thing that's gonna make me feel better is to take this out on your ass since it was your goddamn fault."

"What do you mean by that?" Tom asked, trying not to stare at Erin who was now only a few feet from Donnie, the poker held high over her head.

"I'm gonna kill you and clean out yer beautiful home, that's what I'm gonna do."

A sickening thought suddenly came to mind. "Do you know where my family is right now, Donnie?"

The man smiled malevolently. "Wish I could say I do, but no—the place was empty when I got here. You expecting them anytime soon?"

Erin was directly behind him now. Tom watched in awe and relief as she came down hard with the poker and hit Donnie square in the head with the iron handle. His expression switched from rage to total shock just before he slumped over the table, out like a light.

"A direct hit!" Tom shouted, "Great going, kiddo!"

Erin dropped the poker and ran over to Tom. She stared at the unconscious man.

"Did I kill him?"

Tom arose, gave her a warm hug and walked over to Donnie to feel his pulse. "No, he's still alive, unfortunately. But he's going to be out of it for quite some time. How in the hell were you able to sneak into the house so quietly?"

Erin grinned. "I learned how to sneak around a long time ago, remember? Who is this man, anyway?"

"Someone from my hometown. He apparently has it out for me and came all the way up here to rob me blind and murder me."

"What did he mean when he said it was your fault that he was sent to prison? I didn't catch all of the story."

Tom hesitated a moment before answering. He didn't really want to tell Erin the details of that matter so he was careful to choose his words carefully. Like she and her own past, this wasn't something he was particularly proud of about his.

"It's sort of hard to explain, really. Basically, this guy is a lunatic and was accusing me of something I didn't do. He got into some trouble and was sent to prison and decided to blame me since he couldn't blame anybody else, I guess. Anyway, I am eternally grateful that you did what you just did. You have in fact just saved my life!"

"I almost blew it when I saw him whack you with the beer bottle! I nearly ran into the kitchen at that instant but realized that I had no weapon. That's when I picked up the poker from the fireplace and plotted my move."

Tom gestured toward the poker lying on the floor. "Good thing you didn't hit him with the business end of that—he'd be dead as a doornail now."

"I must confess that I was wanting to hit him with the poker end, but I changed my mind."

"It wouldn't have been any great loss but I'm glad you didn't. That would have been hard to explain to the cops."

Erin outstretched her hands and chuckled. "What cops? Haven't exactly seen too many of them around lately."

Tom laughed. "Good point."

"So what are we going to do with him?" the girl asked.

Tom stared at the unconscious man and said, "Tie him up, I guess. I wonder if Kyle left me any duct tape."

"Looks like there's still some left," Erin said, pointing at the roll still lying on the kitchen counter.

"Why don't you go ahead and take that hot shower while I tie him up?" Tom suggested.

"Yes!" Erin smiled broadly. "I'll go out and get my things."

Erin left and Tom lit up a couple more candles, grabbed the duct tape and bound Donnie Shortridge securely to the chair. He heard Erin come back in the front door and make her way upstairs to the bathroom. When he was finished with Donnie, he went to the living room fireplace, lit a match, valved in the gas and watched as the gas logs came to life. With a long yawn, he sat down on the sofa and leaned his head back.

He heard the faucet squeak and the water running upstairs as Erin started her shower. He thought of how grateful he was that the girl had the courage and moxie to do what she had just done. Most girls her age probably would never have taken the risk to come to his aid as she had. The more he got to know Erin Myers, the more he realized what a truly unique individual she was.

His thoughts shifted to Donnie Shortridge and what had just occurred. A number of questions came to mind as he fought the fatigue gnawing away at him.

For starters, why had Donnie shown up in the first place—and why *now* of all times, when there were only a few people still existing on earth as far as he knew? Why someone from his hometown—someone he had never known before yet someone who apparently knew plenty about him?

And how much of this man's insane story should he believe? Yes, he had had a one-night stand with Mindy Conkel twenty years ago. And yes, it was possible but unlikely that he had gotten her pregnant. But why had Donnie been so *adamant* that Tom had been the father of her child?

And what about Mindy Conkel, who had at first insisted that Donnie was the father then recanted once it was discovered that Donnie's DNA didn't match the child's? Why would she all of a sudden insist it was Tom instead? How could she be so certain?

Unless, Tom thought, he had actually been the only one who had slept with Mindy that particular month. There was an outside possibility, and if it were the case, then she would have been correct in assuming that Tom was the father.

Tom swallowed hard and stared intently into the fire. What if he really *had* been the father of Mindy Conkel's child? What if the call she had made to him in New York had been a legitimate cry for him to take some kind of responsibility for her desperate situation?

His thoughts flew into a tailspin. He had been so much in denial of the situation at the time that he had totally dismissed its seriousness. And this denial was ultimately what had kept him from accepting responsibility when he should have.

How convenient, he thought.

And the fact that Mindy had called him once and only once had made it even easier for him to forsake his responsibility.

Tom leaned back on the sofa. He was so exhausted now that he could barely keep his eyes open. He yawned and promptly drifted off to sleep . . .

*   *   *

"Tom?" he heard Erin say softly.

He opened his eyes and saw her sitting beside him on the sofa, her expression apologetic.

"I hate to wake you up but I wasn't sure if you wanted me to or not. You had mentioned wanting to take a shower."

Tom sat up straight. "Oh, yeah, I'm glad you woke me up. I guess I just dozed off for a moment there."

He rubbed his eyes and noticed that Erin was wearing nothing but a white oversized tee shirt that went down to just above her knees and that she smelled as sweet as a rose after her shower. Her hair was still damp, combed out poker straight, falling onto her shoulders in shiny strands. For the first time, Tom realized that Erin Myers was attractive in an oddly compelling way that made her unique—as unique on the outside as she was on the inside.

"How long have you been sitting here?" he asked.

She giggled. "Would you believe about five minutes? You were really dead to the world—and you were snoring, too!"

Tom smiled. "Yeah, that doesn't surprise me. I feel like I could sleep for a week."

"You'll feel much better after a shower—I sure did. But I wouldn't have any trouble falling asleep now, either."

"Why don't you go to sleep, then—I'll take my shower and do the same."

"Okay."

Tom stood up. "Are there enough blankets for you?"

"Yes, I'll be fine," Erin replied.

Tom decided to go into the kitchen long enough to check on Donnie Shortridge, who was still out cold, then returned to the living room and headed for the staircase.

"Tom? Who is Mindy?" Erin asked suddenly.

Tom halted in his tracks. He turned toward her and replied, "You mean the Mindy we were discussing in the kitchen? She was Donnie's wife. Why do you ask?"

"Oh, I don't know, I just love that name—Mindy. It was my biological mother's name, too."

"Oh, really?" Tom said, intrigued at this revelation. "You mean you actually know who your real mom is?"

"Not exactly. All I know is that her name was Mindy. I've got a picture of her holding me when I was a baby. I've had it for as long as I can remember. You want to see it?"

"Of course I would."

Erin opened her backpack. Tom sat down beside her and waited as she located her billfold and began thumbing through it.

"Here it is," she said, taking one of the photos out of a transparent sleeve. She flipped it over and showed Tom the back, which had writing in blue ballpoint pen. It read, *"To my lovely daughter. Please know that I will always love you."* At the bottom it was signed, *"Mindy, your mommy."*

"See, she even signed it," Erin said proudly.

She flipped the photo over. "There we are—my mommy and me." Tom stared at the photo. It was in color and showed a young woman about twenty or so holding a tiny baby in her arms—

The woman was Mindy Conkel!

Tom looked closer. No doubt about it, the woman in the picture was Mindy.

He was dumbfounded. Not sure what to do or say, Tom struggled for the best way to deal with this.

"She's very pretty. How in the world did you get this picture, anyway?"

Erin continued holding on to the picture lovingly. "I think my first foster parents gave it to children's services who in turn gave it to me after I'd been adopted by my second foster family. Since I had already been told that I was an orphan I guess they figured I may as well have it."

"Did you ever want to find her—your biological mother?" Tom asked curiously.

"Of course! But I haven't known where to begin. I heard that you could trace your family tree online so I tried that once, but had no luck. It really helps when you have a last name to start with," she added dismally.

"I wonder if you could post that picture on the internet. There's a chance that someone might know who she is," Tom suggested, feeling more and more guilty the further he went with this charade.

"I tried that, too. In fact, Kyle put it online for me, which is about the only nice thing he'd ever done for me. We never heard back from anyone. It's useless. I'll probably never know who she is—or was."

Tom wanted nothing more than tell her who her mother was. And that he knew who her father was, too. That it just so happened that her dad was the same man sitting there with her right now.

But he couldn't do that. Not yet, anyway. He had to be certain that he was truly the girl's father before running the risk of leading her on with something that might not be true. And the only way to be absolutely certain would be for them to have their DNA tested.

Furthermore, he wanted to be sure of Mindy Conkel's feelings on this. After all, she had given Erin up for adoption in the first place. It was really her place to decide if Erin should know who her biological mother was. Somehow, he was going to have to track her down and find out what her thoughts would be on seeing her daughter again after all these years. Perhaps he could find out Mindy's whereabouts from Donnie when he came to.

Tom stared thoughtfully at Erin for a moment as she continued studying the wallet print in her hand. Did she look anything like him? She did have brown eyes and hair, just as he did. And her face was rather long and thin like his. And didn't the shape of her nose resemble his, or was it just his imagination?

Suddenly, the bizarre nature of this entire situation hit him straight on. What in the hell were the astronomical odds of he and Erin and Donnie Shortridge all being together in this house right now at this very moment? The world was virtually deserted right now for all he knew, yet here he was with a daughter he never knew he had and the man who had once been married to her mother—

There had to be a reason for all of this.

But what was it?

He had no idea.

He would have to think about this.

But first, he was going to have to get some sleep. His thoughts were so jumbled up now that it was useless to try to make any sense of anything.

He observed how Erin was looking longingly at the photo in her hand. His heart bled for her. The girl had had a miserable life through no fault of her own. Yet she still yearned to know who her mother was. And no doubt, her father, too.

It was enough to make him want to break down and cry.

He gently placed his hand on her arm. "Well, you never know, kiddo. You may still find her some day. I wouldn't give up if I were you."

She smiled as she continued staring at the photo. "I know I'll never give up. Even if she doesn't want me in her life, I want to know what has happened to her. And why she had to give me away. This photo proves she loves me. I think she had to do it for a good reason. And whatever the reason was, I know that I'll forgive her. I just want to *know her!*"

Tom put his arm around Erin and pulled her against him. "If you want, I'd be more than happy to help you find her in any way I can."

"Oh Tom, that would be so nice! And I'll help you find your wife and kids."

Tom had almost forgotten his own family for a moment. Almost. This was all just too much to bear. All he could hope for was that things would be better in the morning.

"Well, I'm ready to take that shower and turn in."

Erin slipped the photo back into her wallet. "Me too."

Tom got up. "I'll see you in the morning."

"Okay. Night."

"Night, Erin."

Tom went upstairs, undressed and took a long, hot shower.

After changing into a pair of sweatpants and sweatshirt, he quietly descended the stairs to the living room. By the light of the fire, he saw Erin snuggled up on the sofa under the blankets. He went over to where she lay, leaned down and kissed her gently on her forehead.

He went into the kitchen to check on Donnie. The hillbilly was still out like a light and breathing regularly. With luck, the bastard would be out for another eight hours so he and Erin could get some much needed sleep.

Tom returned to the living room, picked up one of the blankets, sat down on the recliner and covered himself up. He felt a bit more focused after his shower and had come up with a plan for tomorrow morning. He would take Donnie aside, safely out of earshot of Erin, and ask him where he might find Mindy. If he refused to comply or claimed not to know, he would be out of luck. If he flatly refused to talk, Tom would use some kind of tactic to get him to speak. What that would be, he had no idea and in fact hoped it wouldn't come to that.

Then after making certain that Donnie was securely bound, he and Erin would take a drive down to Smithtown. Tom would make up an excuse for going there—maybe tell her that his family could possibly be there with relatives or something.

The truth of it was, Tom now found himself obsessed with the idea that Erin might be his daughter. He had to find out if it was true. And locating her mother would be a start.

Tom pondered why he had become obsessed with the truth about Erin and came up with a very good one . . .

She could very well be the only family he had left on earth.

Tom glanced over at the sleeping girl, wondering if she would ever be able to forgive him if she were indeed his child. Would she be as forgiving of him as she was of her mother?

Only time would tell.

Tom felt his eyes get heavy. He finally gave in to the absolute need for sleep, closed his eyes and fell into a dead slumber.

15

"Tom? Can you hear me?"

The voice seemed far away. Miles and miles away.

"Tom, please wake up!"

He wondered how long the voice had persisted. It seemed like he'd heard it for the last hour or so. He wished it would go away. He was so damned tired—

"Please, Tom! Open your eyes!"

He realized now that the voice was not going to go away. He was going to have to get up, damn it!

Tom opened his eyes. His vision was so blurry that all he could see were blobs of random shapes. And it was bright—he had to shut his eyes immediately to avoid being blinded.

"He's awake!" the voice cried. "Tom, honey, can you hear me? It's Peg!"

Peg? he thought. Figures. He had probably overslept again and she would have none of that!

He opened his eyes again, blinked a couple of times and shut them promptly. "It's so bright!" he said.

His throat felt raw. Great, he was getting a cold.

"My throat. Dry. Sore."

"Have some water, honey. Pour your father some water, Kelli."

"Okay, mommy."

"And can we turn down those lights down some?" Peg said.

Another voice replied, "Surely, Mrs. Grayson, I'll get them. I'll page the doctor, too."

"Thanks, Nancy. Here, drink some of this, dear."

Tom felt something touch his lips and opened his eyes. It was not as bright now and he could see the Styrofoam cup that his wife was holding to his mouth. He parted his parched lips and sipped the water. It felt like heaven going down.

As his senses sharpened, he realized that he was lying in bed in a hospital room, causing him to suddenly panic—

"Jesus, what happened?"

Peg took his hand and squeezed it. "You passed out, honey. In your car."

"Passed out! What do you mean?"

"At the supermarket. You were overcome by what the doctor said was a mixture of raw gasoline fumes and carbon monoxide."

Tom tried to get a grip of this. The supermarket? When had he been at the supermarket? His eyes were wide open now and everything was in focus. He saw Kelli and Tyler standing near the foot of his bed and suddenly all he wanted to do was hug them.

"Come here, you two!" he called, reaching out his arms toward his children.

Kelli got there first and he gave her dad a big bear hug. Then came Tyler, who seemed a little embarrassed as Tom held him tight.

"I can see where *I* stand now," Peg mumbled from the bedside.

"Aw, let me hug you too, sweetie," Tom said emotionally. He wasn't sure why he felt so sensitive toward his family now but for some reason he was extraordinarily grateful for their company.

"You could have *died*, Tom!" Peg cried passionately after they kissed. "I am so glad they found you in time!"

Just then, the doctor came into the room and went over to Tom. Peg arose and stood off to the side as he examined him.

"I'm Doctor Wheeler, chief resident on call. And you are one lucky man, Mr. Grayson," he said as he shone a penlight into his eyes.

"That's what I hear. So what happened? I don't really remember."

"Well, apparently you drove to the store in the snowstorm and left your motor running while you were inside. By the time you returned to your car, fumes had built up inside to a fairly dangerous level. I was surprised you didn't smell the raw fuel until your wife informed me that you had sinusitis and couldn't smell much of anything. Carbon monoxide of course is odorless."

Tom struggled to remember. He could vaguely recall being at the supermarket but couldn't remember why he would have gone there without Peg.

He looked over at Peg. "What was I getting at the store?"

"Pop and cigarettes, remember? We were playing euchre with Frank and Jules." Peg was visibly alarmed that he couldn't remember.

Tom thought back for a moment and it came to him in bits and pieces. The Warrens had been over to play cards, euchre of course, in the family room. The kids had been playing in the living room. It had been snowing hard. He'd gone to the supermarket to pick up more Seven Up and smokes for Julie.

"I remember now. So where are Frank and Julie now?"

"They went home about an hour ago. They've been here all evening but finally decided to take Brittany home and put her to bed."

"So exactly how long have I been in the hospital?" Tom inquired.

Peg glanced at her wristwatch. "About six hours."

"Jesus! And I've been passed out all this time?"

Doctor Wheeler replied, "You've been totally unconscious from the effects of the poisoning. Fortunately, you were not exposed to enough CO to do any permanent damage. We've given you oxygen to raise your O2 level. Basically, you have been in a very deep sleep all this time."

"So I can go home now?"

Peg and Tom both stared at the doctor expectantly.

"Actually, I don't see any reason why not. Let us get a few more readings and if everything looks okay, we'll turn you loose."

"Great, doctor!" Tom said, elated. "Thanks for everything."

"My pleasure."

Dr. Wheeler did a check of Tom's vitals, spoke briefly to the nurse then left the room.

"I can't believe this!" Tom declared. "I wonder how long my Jeep has been trying to kill me."

Peg glared at him accusingly. "I don't know, but I hope this has taught you a lesson, Tom. How many times have I told you that I smelled gas when we were out in that thing? And every time you said I was just imagining it."

"Hell, I was telling you the truth—I really haven't ever smelled gas in it."

"Which is exactly why you need to do something about your sinuses! This just shows how important it is to be able to smell properly. It almost cost you your life!"

Christ, Tom thought, does she ever let up on the I-told-you-so's? "Okay, dear, you've made your point. I'll go see an ENT specialist next week. So where is the Jeep now?"

"At the dealership. I told them to tow it there so it could be getting repaired."

"Thanks. Will they give me a loaner, you think? I need a car."

"I'm sure they will."

The nurse returned with the discharge papers and went over them with Peg and Tom. He was to get plenty of rest and call 911 immediately if he felt any shortness of breath, heart palpitations, became nauseous, got a headache that wouldn't go away or if he started hallucinating. Twenty minutes later, the Grayson family left the hospital with Peg driving her Accord.

Tom was surprised at how exhausted he felt by the time they pulled into their driveway. He could barely keep his eyes open but insisted on helping Peg put the kids to bed. After kissing them both goodnight, he undressed to his shorts and undershirt, climbed into their king size bed and promptly fell into a deep, fitful sleep.

16

Tom slept in until 10:30 the next morning. Although he had been asleep for nearly eleven hours, he still felt weak and somewhat out of it. He could hear the kids playing downstairs as he lay in bed, mulling over what had happened the day before.

He was in utter awe of the fact that he had actually passed out in his Jeep while parked in the supermarket parking lot. How in the hell could he have missed smelling raw gasoline fumes for chrissakes? Granted, his nose was on the fritz with sinus issues, but to miss smelling *raw gasoline?* It was hard to fathom.

But evidently, he had done just that. And he had been told that inhaling the potentially lethal cocktail of gas fumes and carbon monoxide (Jesus, were the gas line and exhaust system *both* leaking?) would have *killed* him if it hadn't been for someone coming to his rescue. Tom now wondered who had discovered him and made a mental note to ask Peg so he could properly thank him or her for saving his life.

He also wondered why the fumes had overtaken him so quickly—almost immediately after he'd gotten back into his Jeep, evidently. That didn't make any sense at all. The doctor hadn't elaborated on this phenomenon and had probably been wondering the same thing himself. It seemed as though he would have had to be inside the Jeep several minutes before the fumes would have enough time to knock him out like that. He made another note to ask Peg if she had an explanation.

He thought back to his grocery run and recalled that he had been thinking about Tracy Adams and the rape incident the entire time, just as he had been for weeks now. In fact, he had been so engrossed in the matter that he was still racking his brains over it when he'd left the supermarket and got back into the Jeep—

That was it! He had decided to sit there in the Jeep and deliberate until he came to a decision once and for all on what to do!

And in the process, he had breathed in enough noxious fumes to render him totally unconscious for six hours . . .

Scary stuff, he thought.

And now, as he lay there, Tom realized that he wasn't any further along on that matter than he'd been before.

But he had a very good idea of what his decision was going to be: let the whole thing slide and don't rock the boat. He would be a complete fool to get involved and jeopardize his marriage and his career.

Case closed.

Tom stretched, yawned and got out of bed. After splashing cold water in his face, he went downstairs and made a beeline for the coffee maker.

"Morning, sweetie," he said when he entered the kitchen. Kelli was sitting at the kitchen table eating cookies and milk.

"Hi, Daddy," Kelli said. "You slept really late!"

"Yeah, I was pretty tired, I guess. How are you doing?"

"Good. I wish I never had to go back to school, though!"

"Why do you say that?" Tom said, pouring himself a mug of steaming hot black coffee.

"It's so nice to be able to play all the time—I wish we had Christmas vacation all year!"

"But wouldn't you miss your friends and your teachers?" he asked his daughter.

"Well, my friends, maybe. But not my teachers!"

"Not even Mrs. Edwards?"

"Well, maybe I'd miss her, but none of the others."

"What about your old first grade teacher, Mrs. Burke?"

Kelli gave him a pained look. "Oh, Daddy! Is this gonna be one of your teacher lectures, again?"

Tom chuckled. "Nah, I'm just trying to give you a hard time. Where are your mom and brother?"

"In the family room. Tyler's watching cartoons and Mom's cleaning, I think."

"Put your dishes away when you're finished there, okay?"

"I will, Daddy."

"Love you."

"Love you, too."

Tom carried his coffee into the family room. Peg was dusting the furniture and Tyler was lying on the floor, his eyes glued to the tube.

"Morning, troops," he greeted.

"Hi honey. Are you feeling any better now? I hope I didn't wake you when I got up."

"I don't think a nuclear blast could've woken me. I feel pretty good—just a little tired and groggy."

Tyler got up, ran over to his father and gave him a big hug. "I'm glad you didn't die, daddy!"

Tom held him tight. "Thanks, son, so am I."

"Did you dream any while you were asleep in the Jeep?"

Tom said, "Hmm. That's a very good question. If I did, I don't remember anything."

"The doctor said breathing gasoline fumes can cause hallucinations," Peg said.

Tom let go of his son and went over to give Peg a peck on the lips. "Is that so? I don't remember doing any of that, either."

Peg threw her arms around him. "Tom, I've never been so scared my whole life! Every time I think of how close you came to dying, I realize how much I truly love you—and how I could never make it without you."

Tom hugged her tight. "I'm sure it was pretty frightening for you. But I'm fine, no permanent damage, and I'm afraid you're stuck forever with my naturally deranged mind."

She laughed. "And I wouldn't have it any other way."

Tom went over and sat down on the sofa. "Who found me, anyway?"

"One of the employees—a young man named Justin Spencer. He was collecting shopping carts out in the lot when he noticed you slumped over the steering wheel."

"I'd like to thank him for saving me. Is he a local boy?"

"Yes, a Thomas Worthington High student. His family lives just a few blocks from us, over on Selby."

"I'll call him later today. I'd like to give him something for what he did, too. You know, a reward or something."

"I think that would be a nice gesture, honey."

"Man, what a weird thing to happen! I still can't believe I couldn't smell those fumes."

"Like I've been telling you, you need to get those sinuses looked at."

"I know, I know. I'll make an appointment—I promise. Did the doctor happen to explain why I passed out so quickly?"

"Actually, he never mentioned anything about that. He must have assumed that the fumes were strong enough by the time you got back into the Jeep that a few breaths was all it took to knock you out."

"Hmm, that must have been the case then."

"And how many times have I told me not to keep the car running while it's parked, Tom? That was really a stupid thing to do!"

Tom shook his head from side to side. "I know. It was just so damned cold and I knew I wasn't going to be very long in the store. I guess I really screwed up there."

"You sure did—you're lucky you didn't kill yourself."

"Honey, I admitted I screwed up, okay? I screwed up over my sinuses and I screwed up with keeping the car running in the parking lot. Now, can you just let it drop so we can move on with our lives and not badger me anymore about it?"

Tom realized that he'd raised his voice and could see that Peg was pissed off now. She glared at him, glanced down at Tyler lying on the floor staring at the two of them then turned her back to Tom. She resumed her dusting without a word.

"Sorry," he said.

"No you're not," she replied.

Screw this! he thought. He decided to change the subject. "I wonder when the Jeep will be ready."

"Not today, it's Sunday," Peg replied with enough edge to remind him he was skating on thin ice. "Why do you ask?"

"I need to go down to the school and catch up on some work. Mind if I take your car?"

"Of course not. When do you think you'll be home?"

"Maybe a couple of hours or so."

"Eat some breakfast, first."

"I will."

With that, Tom stood up and returned to the kitchen. Kelli was putting her dishes in the sink when he entered.

"Good girl," he said.

"I know," she replied before heading out.

Tom fixed himself a bowl of cereal, some toast and warmed up his coffee. When he was finished, he took a shower, shaved and got dressed. He kissed Peg goodbye on his way out the door.

During his shower, Tom had come to the conclusion that he simply couldn't take any more of this any longer. He backed Peg's Accord out of the driveway, booted up his cell phone and punched in Frank Warren's number resolutely.

17

After filling Frank in with the details since regaining consciousness at the hospital the night before, Tom asked him to meet him at the *Panera* on High Street in fifteen minutes and not to tell Julie of their meeting. He said he would explain later. Frank, obviously intrigued by this unusual request, agreed and told his wife he was going to run a couple of errands.

Tom was tired of the guilt he was feeling for not reporting the incident he and Tracy had witnessed on that fateful night. He wanted to—no, *needed* to get this off of his chest. He wasn't sure yet if he was going to tell Frank the whole story—about Tracy being pregnant—he figured he would play that part by ear.

After Tom went inside the popular cafe, he hung out near the entrance to await Frank's arrival. Five minutes later, he saw his friend come through the door.

"Thanks for coming," Tom greeted him.

"No problem. I'm dying to know what all of this mystery is about! I don't suppose it has anything to do with your near-death experience, does it?"

Tom led the way to the counter. "Indirectly, I guess you could say. What would you like—I'm buying."

"Just coffee. I've already had breakfast."

Tom ordered two coffees and the pair made their way to a table near the fireplace in the center of the shop.

Frank took a sip and looked over at Tom. "So what's up?"

Tom wasn't sure exactly where to start. All of a sudden, he wasn't sure that this was such a good idea after all and nearly changed his mind about confiding in his friend. Then he realized it was too simply too late to turn back now.

"First, let me ask you a theoretical question: if someone witnessed a crime and wanted to report it, could he do so anonymously?"

Frank was clearly taken aback by the question and Tom knew that he was already itching to know what this was leading up to.

"Well, yes. Of course he could. A lot of the tips the police get are from anonymous callers responding to public pleas for information on various crimes. Why do you ask?"

"But what if the police wanted the anonymous caller to pick out a potential suspect from a lineup or a mug sheet? How could he do that without getting involved with any litigation that may eventually come up?"

The attorney was clearly mystified about this line of questioning. "What in the hell has happened, Tom? And why do I have the sneaky feeling that *you* are this theoretical anonymous caller?"

Tom smiled uncomfortably. "Okay, so I'm asking on my own behalf. Now, what about the question?"

"It's difficult to say, really. I guess realistically, the police would plead with you to come to the station with the info and to testify in the case if it became necessary. It really all depends on the conditions of the particular crime in question. So level with me, Tom. Tell me what you are referring to here."

"In strict confidence, as my friend?"

"Of course. Shoot."

Tom knew there was no going back now. He could only hope that Frank was leveling with him as well. "Well, remember the girl that was raped and dumped out of a car about a month ago?"

"Yes, of course. They're still working that case."

"I saw the guy do it."

Frank's eyes widened. "No shit?"

"No shit. I not only saw him dump off her body but I got a good look at his car, too."

"That's great news. But tell me, why in the holy hell have you waited this long to tell anybody?"

"Hell, Frank. I can't tell you that. All I can say is that it certainly hasn't been pleasant not coming forward with this before now, but unfortunately there are some, uh, complications that have made me hesitant to do so."

"What do you mean?"

"Can't tell you. Let's just say that there have been some personal reasons not to, and now that I have, I'll probably regret it."

"I don't understand. I don't see how reporting that you eye-witnessed a crime in progress can be anything but a *good* thing. I'm sure the victim will attest to that after they nail the guy."

"Can't we just drop the reasons why and go from there, Frank? I really just want to do my civic duty because it has gotten on my conscience. The rest is irrelevant to the case, anyway. Believe me."

"Okay, okay. I'll back off. But if you change your mind, I'll be all ears, okay?"

"Yeah, I'll keep that in mind. So where should I go from here?"

"Well, if you really don't want to get involved, I'd just go ahead and call the police, anonymously, and tell them whatever it is you want to tell them. Describe the vehicle—make, model, year, color. As for the suspect's appearance, give them a clear description—approximate height, weight, build and so on. Tell them what you saw; be as thorough as you can. They will be forever grateful to you, I'm sure. They don't have squat on this case from what I've heard. Your info will no doubt give them the break they've been hoping for."

"That's great to hear. I feel better already," Tom said.

"Have you told Peg any of this?"

Damn! Tom thought. Why can't Frank just let it go?

"No, of course not. Why else would I be meeting you covertly like this?"

Frank grinned knowingly. "Aha! Now I'm starting to get the picture."

"What do you mean?"

"Tom, it's more than obvious what's happening here. And I don't know why you're so worried talking to me of all people about it. The reason you don't want anyone to know about your witnessing this incident is because you were somewhere where you weren't supposed to be! Am I right?"

Screw it. "You got me there, Frank."

Frank chuckled. "Gotta admit, I didn't know you had it in you! Peg's no slouch and you guys seem to be really tight for an old married couple. This gal must really be something special."

"She is, or I should say, was. So now that the cat's out of the bag, can we just move on and never mention this again?"

"Mum's the word."

"Good. Well, I'm going down to the school and catch up on some work I put off before the break. Thanks for everything, friend."

"No problem. And don't worry about any of this—things always have a way of working themselves out."

"Yeah, I know."

Tom killed the last of his coffee and stood up. The two left and Tom thanked Frank again for his advice before heading to campus.

Alone in his office, Tom debated whether or not to call Tracy and tell her that she wouldn't have to talk to the police after all. He could at least spare her that inconvenience—not that she would have followed through with it, anyway.

He picked up the phone and punched the first four numbers to her apartment then promptly hung up.

What am I doing, here? he thought. All he would do is stir everything up again. Tracy had decided to let him off the hook for getting her knocked up and told him to go fly a kite. Why couldn't he just be content with that and be thankful that he could still have his life?

Could this have come out any better, you nitwit?

With a smug grin on his face, Tom decided to make a call after all, but not to Tracy. He opened his cell phone, pressed "send" and scrolled down to his home number. Kelli answered.

"Hi, kiddo. Is your mother around?"

"Hi Daddy. Guess what I did," his daughter said.

"What?"

"I cleaned up my room all by myself!"

"That's awesome, sweetie! I'll bet your mom is very proud of you."

"She is—she's gonna let me have my own birthday party next month!"

"That's really great, Kelli."

"Well, I'll go get Mom now," she said.

"Thanks."

"Yes, dear, what is it?" Peg said.

"Just letting you know that I'm on my way home. You want me to pick up anything on the way?"

"Yes, now that you mention it. We're almost out of milk and if you want any beer tonight, you'd better pick some up as well."

"Christ, I'm glad you remembered the beer! Anything else?'

"That should do it for now. I'm going to go to the store tomorrow and will get the rest of what we need."

"Okay. I'll swing by the market and be home in about fifteen minutes or so."

"See you then."

Tom cranked up the volume on the Accord's CD player. As he listened to *New Year's Day* by U2, he was reminded of the party that he and Peg were going to on New Year's Eve. One of Peg's friends was having a fairly good-sized get-together at their house and he was dreading the very prospect of it. He would be much more content drinking beer at home and watching the ball drop in Time's Square with Dick Clark than facing an evening of socializing with a bunch of yuppie Bush lovers. Peg sure knew how to pick 'em, he thought.

Five minutes later, he pulled into the parking lot of the supermarket. He avoided parking anywhere near where he had parked the day before, still reeling from the fact that he had almost lost his life in this very place. He found a spot near the entrance, shut the car off, got out and entered the store.

After he'd picked up the milk and a twelve pack of Michelob Ultra, he got into the express line. As he placed his items on the counter, he took one look at the cashier and did a double-take.

The young girl looked oddly familiar. She was about eighteen or so, had brown hair and was quite pretty. He glanced at her name tag, which had *Erin* written in black Sharpie on it—

Erin, he thought. *Why did he feel like he knew this girl?*

"Sir?" she said, staring at him expectantly.

Tom wondered how long he'd been staring at her.

"Oh, sorry! Yes," he stammered, still trying to place the girl in his mind.

"Paper or plastic?" she asked as she scanned the milk.

"Um, neither, really. I'll just carry them."

"That will be $13.79, sir."

Tom fumbled for his wallet and got out his credit card. He swiped it through the machine. Erin handed him a receipt and he signed it then returned it to her.

"Thanks, have a nice day," Erin told him as she handed him another receipt.

"Uh, thank you. Can I ask you something, Erin?"

"Sure."

"Have we ever met?"

She smiled sweetly. "No. But I think I've seen you here before. In fact, I believe I waited on you yesterday afternoon."

Tom thought back to the day before, gazed at Erin and recalled that she had indeed been the one who had waited on him.

"Oh, yeah, you did! Well, thanks for waiting on me again," he said stupidly.

Erin giggled. "No problem."

"Goodbye, Erin."

"Bye."

Tom placed the beer and milk back into his grocery cart and headed for the exit. Once he reached Peg's car, he opened the trunk and unloaded the cart, his thoughts still on the checkout girl.

He knew the girl better than that, he thought. In fact, he knew her quite well . . .

But how? When?

Slamming the trunk lid, Tom walked around the car and got in, his mind lost in thought. He started the car, threw it into reverse and backed out of the spot. He felt like he was moving in slow motion as he headed for the street.

Her name was Erin. Why did that name seem just as familiar to him as her face did? He *knew* that girl, somehow.

But she apparently didn't know him. She had basically denied knowing him beyond having waited on him the day before. She had not shown the slightest shred of recognition while he had been standing there before her all that time.

So he must be wrong, he decided. He must be confusing her with someone else.

Trying desperately to dismiss it from his mind, Tom turned on the radio just as the Beatle's *Hey Jude* was beginning to fade out. The song helped him put Erin out of his mind, but not for long.

He recalled driving on a snow-laden highway in total darkness, a young girl sitting in the passenger seat. She was telling him her life story—how she had been orphaned and run off to New York with Kyle—

"Jesus Christ!" he cried aloud.

Erin was Erin Myers. The girl he had rescued from those delinquents at the Waldorf Astoria!

Tom nearly drove over the curb as the events came back to him in jumbled bits and pieces: The drive to New York in search of Erin and Kyle. The total desolation of New York City. Being assaulted and manhandled out of his Jeep in front of Macy's by those lowlife assholes, Chappy, Hoops, and what the hell was his name? *Bummer!* That was it.

His heart pounded furiously as Tom tried to negotiate a turn along Hartford Road. He realized that he was going to have to pull over before he had an accident. He made a right onto the next street and parked halfway down the block.

Heaving a huge sigh, Tom killed the engine.

What in the holy hell had he just been thinking about?

Where were these memories coming from? Why did they seem as real as this street he was now parked on?

Have to think this through, he resolved.

He had been awakened in his Jeep by those three hoodlums in front of Macy's, he recalled. One of them, the Brit, was going to shoot him. He'd made a break for it and ran like hell—could barely see a thing, it was so dark. He'd ducked into a store that had been looted and hid, but they found him. They had led him back to Macy's and forced him into a goddamn *hearse* of all things!

The subsequent events raced through his mind. Being locked in a room at the Waldorf where the maimed and tortured body of Erin's old boyfriend Kyle was hanging from the ceiling, his escape to the elevator, his confrontation with Bummer (had he actually *killed* someone?), finding Erin in the room tied to the bed, their escape . . .

Tom's head was swimming. Why did these events seem so real—as though they had actually taken place the day before? How could they seem so real when in fact he knew they couldn't be. He hadn't gone anywhere yesterday but to the supermarket—

Then it hit him.

Like a ton of bricks.

Of course none of this had really happened. *He had been dreaming it had happened—*

He must have dreamed all of this shit while he'd been under the influence of raw gasoline and carbon monoxide!

Tom drew in a deep breath and stared straight ahead.

More accurately, he had probably been hallucinating, as well. The doctor had said that hallucinations were a possibility . . .

Whatever it was, it hadn't been real, thank god. It had just been the worse nightmare he'd ever had.

And the *longest* one by far, he suddenly realized.

But why was he recalling it only now?

Of course, it had to be from seeing Erin and recognizing her. Seeing her at the checkout line had triggered his memory and made it all come back to him.

He wondered now how much of the dream he could recall. He knew there had been more to it. Much more. What had happened leading him up to his being in New York in the first place? He knew he had been looking for Erin, who had been abducted by Kyle from his home, of all places. Why had she been in his house?

Of course—the power outage! He had come home from the supermarket to discover that the power was out everywhere and that his family and friends had totally disappeared. In fact, *everybody everywhere had mysteriously disappeared!*

Tom recalled the beginning of the dream now, from the moment he'd discovered his family was missing to the wild chase in pursuit of Erin in his stolen Jeep on I-270 to the sudden unwanted appearance of Kyle at his home the next morning. As he recalled the events, he sat in utter fascination of the clarity of everything, how real and vivid it all seemed now instead of being some sort of vague, random recollection.

Something special in those lethal gas fumes? he thought dryly.

But the ten thousand dollar question was *why?* Why had he dreamt this absurd dream in the first place? Did it have some purpose? Was it some kind of spiritual sign from the heavens? Or had it simply been a random gas fume-induced, hallucinatory trip from hell?

And why would he even sport the notion that it could have some real purpose in the first place? Dreams basically had no purpose, other than to help relieve stress. That was a scientifically proven fact, wasn't it?

Tom sat back in his seat and recollected the entire dream from beginning to end, astonished at the fact that he could actually do it. He recalled the drive back from New York to Columbus with Erin and what he had learned about her past: her being an orphan, the foster father who had molested her as a child, her troubled teen life at school and her running off with Kyle to New York City. Tom grew increasingly angry recalling how Kyle had not only emotionally and physically abused the girl but pimped her into doing kiddie porn movies so that he could sell them on the internet. Then he recalled how she had managed her escape from the lowlife prick down the fire escape and made it back to Ohio by the skin of her teeth.

When Tom reached the part when he and Erin had returned to Columbus and discovered a suspicious car parked in his driveway, his heart began to race—

Donnie Shortridge! Now what in the hell had that been all about?

Tom recalled how he had entered his home and found this strange hillbilly redneck sitting at the kitchen table with a gun pointed at him. Like a blast from the past, this character claimed to have been married to a girl Tom had knocked up and now blamed Tom for his being sent to prison for assaulting his poor wife in a blind rage.

And that he intended to pay Tom back by robbing him blind and then killing him.

How crazy had that been? He hadn't even known a Donnie Shortridge, much less gone out with his wife—

Jesus Christ—he had gone out with his wife!

Mindy Conkel!

Mindy Conkel, he did know. And not only had he gone out with her, he had gone to bed with her. Just once.

And that one time had been enough to get her pregnant!

And now suddenly Tom was beginning to understand why he had had this crazy dream. He had felt guilty for blowing off Mindy when she had called him in New York to let him know that she was pregnant with his child. He hadn't given the news much thought at the time—he had been way too wrapped up in his new life in the Big Apple to give a shit. In a nutshell, he had basically told her "too bad, so sad—"

Wait a minute here!

Erin had shown him a picture—

Tom recalled the very end of the dream. And like a bolt of lightening from out of nowhere, he was struck with why he had dreamed this dream and what he now had to do about it.

Erin had shown him a photo of her birth mother holding her as an infant before she had been put up for adoption. The woman in the picture had been none other than Mindy Conkel!

Was it really possible that he was Erin's father? And that was why he had dreamed all of this?

It had to be! As crazy and impossible as it seemed, this whole dream must have occurred so that he would discover he had a child running around in this world that he never knew he had. It was one of those weird, unexplained psychic phenomena like he'd seen on *Unsolved Mysteries!*

He had to talk to Erin, he resolved. He had to find out if she really was his daughter.

On impulse, he fired up the engine and pulled away from the curb. He circled the block and headed back toward the supermarket, trying to decide what he was going to say once he approached Erin with this. He realized it wasn't going to be easy. *"Hi again, Erin. I was just driving home with my groceries and started wondering if perhaps you are my daughter. I know it sounds a little weird, but you see, I had this dream yesterday and I—"*

Tom laughed out loud. Yeah, right—she's going to think I'm a blithering idiot!

As he drove through the intersection at Dublin Granville Road, Tom realized he would have to ease gracefully into this when he spoke to the girl. Maybe just start up a casual conversation and then ask if he could perhaps up meet with her when she got off work—that he had a couple of questions to ask her.

And of course she would look at him oddly, no doubt wondering why this strange man old enough to be her father was basically asking her out on an impromptu date—

Frick it! he sighed. This would be more difficult than he'd thought.

He reached the Jubilee Supermarket parking lot and pulled in. As he searched for a space, he spotted Erin getting into her car at the far end of the lot. She was probably just getting off work and heading home.

Tom glanced at the clock in the dash: 4:05. That had to be it.

He pulled into a spot and watched Erin start up her car and back out of the parking space. He waited until she drove past him and stopped at the exit before pulling out behind her. She turned left and was stuck at a red light on High Street. Tom pulled out and stopped behind her at the intersection.

When the light changed, she turned left onto High Street and drove south several blocks before turning into a gas station and pulling up to a pump. Tom also turned into the station but parked beside the mini mart. He looked at his rearview mirror and saw Erin get out, swipe her credit card through the machine and reach for the pump handle.

As he sat there, Tom wondered if it was such a good idea following her like this. He almost felt like he was stalking her. After all, he was a virtual stranger and when he approached her, she was going to feel intimidated if not downright threatened by him. Perhaps he should wait until he could speak to her at the supermarket another day.

Erin placed the pump handle back into its slot and got into her car. Tom backed out and followed her. She continued south on High until she entered Clintonville and took a right onto a street just north of North Broadway. Tom followed behind, trying to keep as much distance between the cars as possible.

Erin drove another block or so, then pulled into the driveway of a gray two-story house. Tom recalled that she had lived in an apartment building in Worthington in his dream. This was a house large enough for an average sized family to live in.

He pulled up to the curb a couple of houses before Erin's and parked. He watched her as she got out of the car and headed for the front porch.

It was now or never, he thought.

He jumped out and walked swiftly toward her.

"Hey Erin!" he shouted.

She glanced back at him. At first it looked as if she was going to ignore him as she continued up the steps to the porch. But she came to a halt on the porch and turned around.

As Tom drew closer, she stared at him with a confused look on her face and said, "Hi. What do you want?"

Tom caught up to her and smiled idiotically. "Um, I just wanted to ask you a few questions, if you don't mind. It will just take a minute."

Erin eyed him suspiciously and Tom could tell that she was more than a little put off.

"About what?" she said.

"Well, it's difficult to say, really. Is there any chance I could buy you a soft drink or a coffee somewhere so we could talk? I'm afraid it may take a while to explain."

Erin suddenly lightened up a bit and smiled. "Okay, I guess that would be all right. Let me just run inside to let my brother know I'm home then we can go."

"Great. I'll just wait here."

Tom stood by as she unlocked the door and went inside. When he realized that the teenager lived in this house with her family, he questioned how in the world he could ever fathom that she was his long lost daughter. He considered the absurdity of it all and was about to abandon the whole thing before he made an utter fool of himself when Erin suddenly came out the door.

"Let's go," she said sweetly, joining him at the bottom of the porch stairs. "Where are we going?"

Tom said, "How does Starbucks sound?"

"Awesome—I'm in the mood for a great big café mocha!"

"You've got it."

Tom led the way to Peg's car, held the door open for Erin, went over to the driver's side and got in. He started the engine, noticing out of the corner of his eye that she was staring at him.

"I feel sort of weird doing this," she confessed.

Tom fastened his seat belt. "I don't blame you at all for that. I realize this must seem very odd, but I want to assure you that I my intentions are good. If it would make you feel more comfortable, we could just talk here in the car or on your porch," he added.

She chuckled. "Oh, no—I would much rather be treated to Starbucks! And I'm not afraid of going with you, Mr. Grayson. My brother told me he's seen you at Capital and that you teach there."

"Smart girl—you had him case me out while I was waiting, didn't you?"

"Yeah—one can never be too careful nowadays," she said with a knowing grin.

Tom pulled out and headed back toward High Street. As he tried to think of a good way to lead into what he wanted to say, Erin cleared the way for him.

"Aren't you the man they found unconscious in the supermarket parking lot yesterday afternoon?"

"Yes I am, as a matter of fact. I was overcome by gas fumes and carbon monoxide."

"Wow, I *thought* you were the same guy when I saw you earlier at the store, but I wasn't sure. I sort of doubted it since it seemed unlikely that you would be out of the hospital so soon. You looked awfully bad when they pulled you out and wheeled you into the ambulance."

"You were there when they did that?"

"I watched from the store. It was snowing really hard so I couldn't see what was going on very well. One of the customers came in who had seen everything and said you looked like you were dead!"

"Thank god they were off on that call!"

"So are you going to be alright? I mean, was there any permanent damage or anything from the fumes?" Erin asked.

"No, I'm going to be fine. Just as crazy as I've always been, so they tell me."

"I'll bet that was scary."

"Oh, it was very scary. I was fortunate that someone found me when they did. Otherwise, that customer would have been dead right."

Erin fell silent as Tom pulled into the Starbucks on North High Street.

"Actually, the whole experience was scary for other reasons, too," Tom said.

"What do you mean?"

I'll tell you when we get inside."

Tom bought them both a café mocha and led the way to a table.

"This is really good—thanks," Erin said after taking a sip of her espresso-laced hot cocoa.

"You are more than welcome."

"Okay, so tell me what you meant a minute ago."

Tom hesitated a moment before beginning. It was so strange sitting there with this girl! The feeling of déjà vu was both surreal and overwhelming as he flashed back to the times that he and she had sat together just like this, in the Jeep, in his house, at the Waldorf Astoria, sharing their thoughts and fears, running for their lives in a lonely, frightening world.

"I warn you, this is going to sound really strange."

"Okay."

"Well, while I was unconscious in the Jeep, I apparently had a dream—a very *long* dream. And you were in it."

Erin gazed at him with a combination of shock and fascination as Tom proceeded to recount the dream in its entirety. When he was finished, he explained to Erin that he had asked to speak to her because he wanted to be absolutely certain that she couldn't possibly be his daughter, as crazy and far out as that may sound.

When she replied to this, Erin stared at him with eyes that expressed great compassion.

"I'm sorry," she said.

"Why are you sorry?"

"That I'm not your daughter."

Her blunt, unexpected comment hurt Tom more than he could easily conceal from the girl. Although he hadn't really expected her to be his daughter, he hadn't given himself time to prepare for the reality of the fact.

"How can you be so sure?" he asked weakly, his voice nearly cracking.

"I just know I'm not. First of all, my last name isn't Myers, it's Landry. But since this was just a dream, my last name could probably have been anything. But you will see that I am obviously my father's daughter once you take a look at this."

She opened her purse, took out her wallet and showed him the first picture on the top. Tom realized what she meant when he saw the tall smiling man in the Landry family portrait, who no doubt was her father. She was a spitting image of him.

Tom forced a laugh. "I see what you mean. Your brother resembles your dad quite a bit, too."

"Yes, he does. My mom is always joking that she is on the short end of the gene pool when it comes to her kids."

Tom gazed at Erin's mother in the portrait and had to agree. She was blonde, blue-eyed and very short, quite unlike her husband and children.

So Erin Landry wasn't his daughter after all. No real surprise there, so why was he so damn disappointed?

Partly, because he was now back to wondering why he had had the dream in the first place. And partly because deep down inside he *wanted* her to be his daughter.

He wondered why that was so but couldn't come up with an answer. Not now, anyway.

"You look sad, Mr. Grayson. I'm sorry this didn't turn out the way you wanted it to."

The girl's insight was remarkable, Tom thought. She seemed able to read him like a book.

Just as Erin Myers had . . .

"I'm okay, Erin. And I appreciate your giving me the opportunity to present you with this rather strange situation."

"No problem. I have enjoyed talking to you, Mr. Grayson."

"Please, call me Tom."

"Okay, Tom. If I tell you something, will you promise me that you won't get mad?"

"Of course. I couldn't possibly get angry at you."

"Well, I sort of have a theory on why you had your dream, if you'd like to hear it."

"I'd love to."

"Well, it's sort of obvious why the girl in your dream looked like me, since I was the last girl you saw before you went back to your car yesterday. You also no doubt saw my name tag, so you gave her my name."

"That's a fair enough theory," Tom agreed.

"You said that this Mindy woman had called to tell you she was pregnant, right?"

"Yes, that's right."

"And in your dream, you realized that Erin could have been the child that Mindy had been pregnant with after you saw the picture of the two of them together."

Tom nodded.

"Well, Erin had been an orphan and apparently had had a pretty horrible life, it sounds like. I think you wanted Erin to be your daughter in the dream so you could finally be assured that your child was alive and safe, now that you had found her. "

Tom wasn't sure what she was getting at. "You sort of lost me there."

"I'm not sure how to put this," she said, hesitating a moment. Her eyes looked past Tom then refocused on him. "Maybe after all of these years you felt sort of guilty about this child you never knew and if Erin had ended up *not* being your daughter, that meant that your child could possibly be, uh, gone forever."

Now he knew what she was driving at.

And he realized that this young girl had just hit the nail on the head.

Because now that he knew beyond the shadow of a doubt that Erin Landry wasn't his daughter in real life, he had no idea what had ever happened to the child Mindy Conkel had given birth to. And since Donnie Shortridge had been only a figment of his imagination, he couldn't even be certain that the child had been put up for adoption—

He was going to have to find out what had ever happened to his child. For all he knew, his child could still be living in Smithtown, Ohio.

Tom said, "Your theory is quite sound, Erin."

She blushed. "Well, I've sort of always wanted to be a psychologist. In fact, I'm majoring in psych at Ohio State."

"I think you've made the right career choice."

"I hope so—thanks for your encouragement."

Tom glanced at his watch. "I've kept you long enough. I am so grateful to you for letting me unload all of this on you. You've been most kind and helpful, Erin."

"No problem. And thanks for the treat."

"It's the least I could do. Ready to go?"

"Yeah."

They arose from the table and left the coffee shop. When Tom pulled into Erin's driveway to drop her off, she leaned over and gave him a heartfelt hug. Then she faced him with her expressive brown eyes and said softly, "I hope you find her."

"Thanks, Erin. So do I."

18

Tom had just pulled away from Erin's house when his cell phone rang. He glanced at the LCD, saw that it was Peg calling and cursed out loud. She was going to ream him a new one!

He flipped the phone open, brought it to his ear and said. "I'm sorry, honey. I'm on my way now."

"You have got to be kidding, Tom! Do you realize that you were supposed to be home an hour ago? What have you been doing all this time?"

Her question caught completely off guard as he floundered for some kind of excuse. He realized that he couldn't come up with one quick enough.

"Are you still there?" Peg snapped, absolutely livid now.

He finally said, "Yes, dear. I decided to stop off at the library and look for something decent to read. I guess I lost track of the time."

"You are kidding, aren't you? You are a horrible liar, Tom, and I don't believe that for a second! Not only have you screwed up dinner but you've probably ruined the milk, too. That is if you even remembered to get it!"

"I got the milk and it will be fine, Peg. I'll be home in five minutes."

"Your cold, over-cooked dinner will be awaiting you—"

Click.

Tom flipped the phone closed and stepped down hard on the accelerator. He couldn't blame Peg for being angry—he had gotten so caught up with Erin and his dream that he had totally lost track of the time.

It was scary how compulsive he'd become lately. The last thing in the world he wanted to do was screw up his relationship with Peg. They had had plenty of scrapes through the years but had always managed to keep it together and mend things if they ever got broken. Sometimes he wondered how she put up with him as long as she had, considering his absent-minded ways and crispy-fried memory. He meant well most of the time, but the old gourd just wasn't quite as sharp as it used be.

A little too much partying in his former, single life?

Duh!

He nearly broadsided a car as he sped around a corner, prompting him to slow down his speed. What he didn't need now was a car accident.

After he got home and cooled Peg down, he was going to have to come up with an excuse for driving down to Smithtown tomorrow. This was not going to be easy, especially on such short notice and with the New Year's Eve party happening the following day. Whatever he came up with was going to have to be really good.

Should he invite her and the kids along? No, that wouldn't work at all. There would be no way he could track down Mindy Conkel with his family there with him.

Whatever he schemed to do, he knew that Peg was going to be suspicious. After all, he no longer had any family in Smithtown since his parents had migrated south to bask in the Florida sun. So what on god's green earth could prompt him to suddenly have to make the two-hour drive to his former hometown?

All of a sudden, he had an idea.

Frank!

Instead of making up an excuse for driving to Smithtown, he would pretend to be going somewhere with Frank for the day. He would ask his friend to cover for him so that he could take a very important out of town trip. Frank would no doubt assume that this had something to do the secret affair he had alluded to, which would be fine—he had almost seemed to think it was *cool* that Tom had played around on his wife.

So what could he tell Peg that he and Frank were going to do for an entire day? Then he remembered Frank suggesting that they drive up to Cleveland sometime and check out the Rock and Roll Hall of Fame and Museum.

Perfect.

Later on tonight, he would call Frank to see if he would be game for this scheme. The hardest part would be how to deal with Frank's wife, Julie. Frank would have to make himself scarce for the day in case Julie and Peg touched base with each other—there was no way he could have him tagging along while he looked for Mindy Conkel in Smithtown. Maybe Frank would be willing to go to Cleveland by himself.

Tom realized that this would be asking an awful lot of his friend. Frank was as true-blue a friend as could be, but this just might be a bit more than he'd be willing to do. Lying was one thing; having to find a way to spend an entire day incognito was really pushing it.

But luckily for Tom, Frank Warren owed him a favor. A *big* favor. Earlier that year, Frank had run into some financial problems and covertly asked Tom to loan him a fairly large sum of money. Frank had a weakness for gambling and had lost a bundle in a real estate investment scheme that his wife didn't know about. One day, the Warrens needed money for an emergency situation but Frank had all but drained their savings account dry. So Tom had saved the day, and Frank's ass, by loaning him the money under the table.

Frank had only paid a fraction of the loan off so far. He had promised Tom that he would pay off the balance before the year's end.

And the year was all but over.

Tom smiled to himself. If Frank was hesitant about helping him out with his plot, he would simply remind him of the debt he still owed him.

When Tom pulled into his driveway, more than the wheels on Peg's car were spinning.

19

It was a beautiful winter morning—cold and crisp with a cloud-less blue sky. Tom walked out of the service department at the Jeep/Chrysler auto mall, spotted his beloved vehicle parked on the other side of the lot and walked briskly toward it.

After he slid into the driver's seat and fired up the engine, memories of the longest dream in history returned with a venge-ance. It dawned on Tom that he hadn't been in this car since the day that the paramedics had pulled him out and rushed him to the hospital. The familiar feel of the soft leather seats and his grip on the steering wheel triggered the vibe like taking hold of a live elec-tric wire. He glanced over at the passenger seat, half expecting to see Erin Myers telling him about her grim, unhappy life as an or-phan. But the seat was of course unoccupied.

Tom dismissed his disappointment and focused on getting out of the tight parking space. He pulled out onto the street and checked the fuel gauge, elated to see that he had a full tank. He turned on the CD player, selected the third disk and pressed 'play.' Steely Dan's *Hey Nineteen* shot out of the speakers and into his head like a jolt of strong coffee.

Tom's thoughts were a mishmash of hurtling fragments. In the back of his mind was the huge lie he was living by driving to Smithtown. He had never been comfortable with lying and for that reason was a notoriously lousy liar. But the present situation forced him to go against his better judgment and spin an incredibly lame alibi to cover what could only be considered a compulsive, irra-tional shot in the dark—or just plain madness.

Here he was, a grown adult with a fairly intact grip on reality, embarking on a two-hour road trip in order to track down a woman he had only seen once in his life nearly twenty years ago. And why was he undertaking this ill-conceived mission? Because he had finally decided after all this time to find out what had ever happened to the child this woman had told him was his.

Maybe not exactly grounds for institutionalization, but certainly a valid argument for OCPD.

Because in the midst of all of this deceit and irrationality, Tom was still asking himself the same thing over and over: *Why?*

Why was he doing this in the first place? What did he expect would come from all of this in the unlikely event that he did locate Mindy Conkel and she in turn granted him what he sought? The peace of mind in knowing once and for all that he had an illegitimate kid running around somewhere? A kid who would be a young adult by now and probably didn't give two shits who his or her father was—the father who had not only abandoned him or her but hadn't even been willing to admit paternity?

What *good* could possibly come from this?

Tom couldn't think of any, really.

But he could certainly think of plenty of *bad* things that could come from this—one being that if Peg were to catch him sneaking around like this, he might as well pack his bags and leave town. There was no doubt that she would throw him out of the house—he was certain of that. He and his wife had based their entire marriage on mutual trust and honesty. Not only had he failed to mention this "blemish" in this former life, he had gone a step further and lied to her about this whole ridiculous mission.

Peg would ream him a new asshole and file for divorce all in the same breath.

Tom considered calling the whole thing off as he drove west toward I-71 south. He could call Frank on his cell phone and catch him before he drove all the way to Cleveland by himself. Then he could either join him or they could both simply go back to their respective homes and tell the wives they had changed their minds about going to the Rock and Roll Museum.

But Tom knew he wouldn't do this. Because something deep inside was telling him that he must follow through this. It was the same thing that had told him to track down Erin Landry.

He needed to know the truth.

He pulled onto the I-71 south ramp, cranked up the volume on the CD player and sat back comfortably in his seat. In a couple of hours, he would get to the bottom of what this was all about.

20

As he neared the Smithtown city limits, Tom was barraged with childhood memories. It had been nearly six years since he'd visited his hometown and he wondered how much of the small southern Ohio burg had changed. He didn't expect much since the town of 20,000 always seemed to be standing still in the grand scheme of things. Smithtown had been under economical duress for as long as he could remember and suffered from the same ills as the other small towns in Appalachia: high unemployment rates, low wages, sub-par health care and an alarming rate of poverty. The few friends he knew of that still lived in the area were either doctors or drunks—there seemed to be little else in between.

He passed by the several gas stations that greeted him and continued south until he spotted a phone booth in a small strip mall. He pulled into the parking lot, went into the booth and began thumbing through the white pages.

He looked under the C's and wasn't particularly surprised to discover that there was no listing for a Mindy Conkel. There was an M. Conkel, however, so he dug into his pocket for his cell phone and keyed in the number. After a few rings, a man answered.

"Hello?"

"Uh, hi. I'm trying to locate a Mindy Conkel and was wondering if this was her number."

"No Mindy here," the man replied in a thick hillbilly drawl.

"Oh, I'm sorry. Do you by any chance know a Mindy Conkel?"

"Nope. Never heard of her."

"Okay. Well thanks, anyway."

"Uh-huh."

Click.

Time for Plan Two, Tom thought. He thumbed through the pages until he reached the S's and found a few Shortridges but no Donny nor any D. or M. Shortridges. This came as no surprise either, but it was at least worth a shot.

Plan Three was to track down his old friend, Alan Hughes, and see if he could help him locate Mindy. Although he had doubts that Alan knew her, he figured that his friend might at least give him some ideas of where to start looking. Smithtown was, after all, not a very big place.

He looked up Alan's number and gave him a ring, only to get a recording that the number had been disconnected. No forwarding number was given so Tom snapped the phone shut in disappointment.

Already, he was losing faith in this whole insane idea. Besides the fact that he felt depressed every time he came to this miserable hellhole of a town, it was beginning to look like he might have driven all this way for nothing. He was so out of touch with everybody here that at the moment, he wasn't sure what to do next. He tried thinking of anybody else he knew who might be able to help him locate Mindy but came up empty. Desperately, he picked up the telephone book and starting with the A's, flipped through the names randomly, hoping to spot a name he recognized.

He'd gotten to the F's when he noticed the name of the same bar where he had met Mindy all those years ago. He decided that Frankenstein's Pub was as good a place as any to begin his search.

Hopping back into the Jeep, he proceeded south toward the downtown section of Smithtown. As he entered the business section, he couldn't help but notice that most of the old stores he'd known as a child were shut down. In fact, the whole town seemed eerily ghost-like, save for the occasional pedestrian walking down the street.

He spotted Frankenstein's and parked a few doors down. When he entered the place, Tom noticed that very little had changed over the years as he walked past the pool table toward the bar.

He sat down and waited for the bartender to come over, noting that there were only four persons other than himself in the whole place.

"Whatcha need?" a gruff looking man in his mid-sixties with greasy gray hair asked.

"Mick Ultra, please."

The man turned and headed toward the cooler. Tom watched him pull out a longneck bottle, pop the top and return with it.

"Two fifty," he said as he set the beer down on the weathered wood bar.

Tom pulled out three ones and slapped them down.

He took a long slug of the ice-cold lager, relishing the feel of it going down. He wasn't much of a daytime drinker, but this beer was as welcome as it was required under the circumstances.

He fixed his eyes on the two guys playing pool, trying to determine if he recognized either of them. He had seen the tall one before, but had no idea what his name was. The other one drew a total blank.

There were a couple more men standing toward the back of the bar playing a video game. The bar was rather dark so it was hard to make out their faces. Tom got up and sauntered toward them.

As he drew closer to the pair, he realized that he knew one of them fairly well. It was one of the friends he used to hang out with when he was in high school. Brad Thompson looked almost the same as he did nearly twenty years ago except for the fifty or sixty pounds he had tacked on since then. Tom hadn't seen him since graduation.

Brad glanced over and recognized Tom before he could open his mouth.

"Jesus Christ, if it isn't Tom Grayson! How the hell are ya?" Brad said, extending his hand.

Tom shook and said, "Great! How have you been, Brad?"

"Can't complain—still stuck in this shit hole trying to make a livin.'"

The other man finished his game and turned around.

"Tom, this is my cousin, Lenny. He's visitin' from KY." He said to Lenny, "Tom is an old high school friend I haven't seen in over twenty years."

Tom shook the man's hand. "Nice to meet you, Lenny."

"So where are you livin' now, Tom? Last I heard, you'd moved to New York City. You still there?"

"Not anymore. I moved to Columbus a while back. Got married and have a couple of kids, in fact."

"Hey, that's great! So what are ya doing up there?"

"Teach at Capital State."

"Don't tell me—some kind of art course, right? You always were the artistic type."

"Yeah. Art history."

"I knew it! So what the hell brings you down here?"

Tom wasn't sure how to answer that at the moment. "Well, I'm sort of looking for somebody I haven't seen in a while."

Brad looked at him suspiciously. "Not some old girlfriend, I hope. Your old lady wouldn't be too happy with you if that's the case!"

Tom realized that Brad was trying to be funny—if he only knew that he was on the right track.

"No, just an old friend of mine. You don't know Mindy Conkel, do you?"

"Hmm. Mindy Conkel. Charlie Gossett's old lady was named Mindy, but I'm not sure what her maiden name was. Do you remember Charlie?"

Tom tried to hide his shock. Charlie Gossett was a hillbilly redneck that was always getting into bar fights.

And if he had to think of someone who reminded him of Charlie Gossett, it would be a certain character that didn't exist in real life—

Donnie Shortridge: the stuff that bad dreams were made of.

Tom recovered enough to say, "Yeah, I remember Charlie. He was one of the scariest guys in high school. Always carried a knife looking for trouble."

Brad nodded. "Yep, that was Charlie all right. He finally got sent up the creek quite a while back. Beat up his wife so bad that he nearly killed her. Like I said, her name was Mindy. Never knew the chick before she married Charlie, though."

Holy hell! Tom thought. *This can't really be happening!*

"What did this Mindy look like?" Tom inquired.

"Well, I only saw her a couple of times. She used to come here every now and then without Charlie. No one would ever go near her though because they knew that Charlie was the jealous type and would probably murder anyone who tried to pick her up. Anyway, she was a freakin' beauty, no doubt about that. Really blonde hair, kinda tall with great tits. Had one hell of an ass, too."

That had to be Mindy Conkel, Tom thought. He couldn't have described her better himself.

"You don't happen to know where she lives now, do you? She sounds like the same girl I'm looking for."

Brad Thompson shook his head. "Nope. I haven't seen her in a few years. She may have left town after Charlie got sent to prison."

"Hmm, maybe you're right. Oh well, it's not the end of the world if I don't find her. She used to have an uncle that owned a home improvement business somewhere near Columbus and I was trying to find out how to reach him. He supposedly does great work for reasonable rates but I can't remember his name or the name of his business to save my life. We want to add a family room to our house."

Tom knew this fabricated story sounded lame, but Brad didn't catch on to it.

"Sorry I can't help you more. Hey, you want to play some cut-throat?"

"Nah, I'd better get going. I've got to get back to Columbus before the wife reams me a new one."

"I hear ya! I heard there's supposed to be a big snowstorm coming sometime this evening. You sure as hell don't want to get stuck in that."

"For sure," Tom replied. He killed the last of his Ultra and offered his hand to Brad.

"Hey, take care of yourself, man. It was great seeing you again."

"You, too. Give me a call next time you're in town and we'll tie on a good one."

"Will do. Nice meeting you, Lenny. See you around."

Tom headed for the door, dropping his beer bottle off at the bar on the way. He noticed that the wind was picking up as he stepped outside, reminding him of what Brad had said about an approaching winter storm. He checked his watch: half past noon. He still had an hour or so before he should start heading back home.

Back in his Jeep, Tom was still reeling from what Brad Thompson had told him about Mindy and Charlie Gossett. He was absolutely numbed by the eerie coincidence. Not only had Mindy married a redneck hillbilly just like the fictitious Donnie Shortridge in his dream, her husband had ended up being a wife-beater and sent to prison for assault to boot!

What in the hell was that all about?

He hadn't been prepared for this. Although his dream had had a certain ominous quality to it, he never expected to see a direct connection between what had happened in the dream and reality. The girl named Erin in the dream had nothing whatsoever to do with the Erin in the real world—he had simply assigned Erin Landry's face to a fabricated character named Erin Myers, a by-product of his poison fume-fueled imagination.

But now, the more he thought about Mindy Conkel and her real life crazy, violent husband, or ex-husband, the more nervous he got.

Would he be better off leaving well enough alone? Get out of Dodge City before he got himself into *REAL* trouble?

Tom now wished that he hadn't drank that beer. Because he wouldn't mind having a few more right this moment.

He pulled up to the traffic light on the corner of Second Street and waited for it to turn green, staring across the street at the bridge crossing the Ohio River into Kentucky. Something about all of this crazy shit had some kind of hold on him. That much he knew. And he would never know what it was if he backed down now.

The light changed and Tom hung a right. Two blocks later he spotted a convenience store and pulled into the parking lot. He got out and entered the store, glancing around for a pay phone. He spotted one near the coffee machine and headed for it. He picked up the phone book and shuffled through the pages.

He found the G's and looked for any listing that could be Mindy's. There was only one Gossett listed: a Floyd Gossett with a West Smithtown exchange. His only hope now was that Floyd was a relative of Charlie's and willing to tell him where Charlie's estranged wife lived.

He was hoping for a miracle, he realized.

The store employee was staring at him so Tom decided to use the pay phone to call Floyd instead of pulling out his cell phone. He found a quarter in his pocket, dropped it in the slot and dialed the number.

Six rings later, a thin raspy voice said, "Yellow."

"Is this the Gossett residence?"

"Uh huh."

"Hi, I'm trying to locate Mindy Gossett and was wondering if you by any chance know her whereabouts," Tom said, crossing his fingers.

"What's that you say?" the man said, apparently hard of hearing.

Tom upped the volume to his voice. "I said I'm looking for Mindy Gossett and wondered if you might know how I can reach her."

"Mindy, you say? Now what would you be a-wantin' with her?"

"I would just like to talk to her about something. Do you know how I could contact her?"

"Who is this?" the man asked suspiciously. "This ain't one of Charlie's friends, is it?"

"No, sir. I'm an old friend of Mindy's. I haven't seen her in a long time and would like to talk to her if I may."

"And what would be your name?"

"Tom. Tom Grayson."

"Well Tim, I'm not so sure that's such a good idea. You see, I don't want nobody botherin' that poor gal and since I don't know you from the man in the moon, I'm not gonna give you no help. That goddamn son of mine has done screwed up her life already and I ain't gonna let another Gossett screw her over again."

Jesus, Tom thought, it was Charlie's father! And he had just given him his name like an idiot—Charlie will probably want to kill him when he gets out of prison!

Or maybe not. Charlie's father didn't exactly sound like he was particularly pleased with his son—in fact, quite the contrary.

"Mr. Gossett, I can assure you that I mean no harm to Mindy. If it would make you feel any better, maybe you could let her know I was looking for her and ask her if she would be opposed to meeting with me. Then, if it's all right with her, I could call you back and you could tell me how to find her."

There was a moment of silence before the man spoke again.

"I reckon that would be okay, long as it's okay with the girl. I'll give her a call and tell her you're wantin' to talk to her. What was that name again? Tim Anderson?"

"No, Tom Grayson."

"Okay, I'll pass that on to her."

"When should I call you back?"

"Give me ten minutes, son."

"Thanks, Mr. Gossett. I'll call you back then."

Tom was ecstatic as he hung up the phone. He had finally found her!

He went over to one of the coolers and took out a bottle of Ice Mountain, paid for it and left the store. After he was back in the Jeep, he realized that he'd forgotten Gossett's telephone number. He grabbed a pencil and paper from the dash compartment, ran back into the store, located the number in the phone book and jotted it down. As he returned to the Jeep, he hoped that Mr. Gossett got his name right when he spoke to Mindy and that she would be willing to see him, or at least allow him to talk to her.

Screwing off the cap, Tom took a huge gulp of cold water and looked out ahead, noticing that it was clouding up. He started thinking about Peg and how she would react if she knew that he was in Smithtown hunting down some chick from his past instead of at the Rock and Roll Hall of Fame in Cleveland with Frank.

He felt faint as he realized just how absurd this whole situation had gotten and how much deeper he was getting into it by the minute. What was driving him to *do* all of this, running around like a madman trying to make sense of something that seemed so utterly *senseless?* Was it worth the risks he was taking with his marriage and his family, the most important things in his life?

The cell phone rang and simultaneously danced around like a hooked catfish on the Jeep's console, causing him to spill his water on his lap. He picked it up and read the caller ID—

It was Peg!

In a panic, he debated whether or not to take the call. At first he wasn't going to—Peg would just assume that he didn't hear the phone or had forgotten to turn it on. Then he changed his mind. What if something bad had happened?

He took a deep breath and flipped the phone open.

"Hello, babe," he said, trying to sound as normal as he could.

"Tom, I'm so glad I reached you! You'll never guess in a million years who just blew into town!" she said excitedly.

He breathed a silent sigh and wondered who it could be. "Who?"

"Maggie! Can you believe it?"

Maggie Tolman was Peg's best friend who had moved to Colorado a few years ago. The two were as close as two friends could be. "That's great, Peg. How long will she be in town?"

"Not very long, I'm afraid. She has a two-hour stopover in Columbus on her way to New York—apparently her flight is all messed up. Anyway, I'm going to drive out to the airport and have lunch with her."

"Sounds like fun. Be sure to tell her I said hi," Tom said.

"I will. How's the museum?"

Tom thought he took too long to answer. "Great! Lots of cool stuff here."

"And are you and Frank behaving yourselves?"

"Of course."

"Well, you may want to consider coming back soon. They're forecasting another snowstorm heading our way."

Peg's voice was starting to cut out. Tom looked at the signal strength indicator on his cell: two bars. His battery strength was down to a single bar, and it dawned on him that he'd forgotten to charge the thing before heading out of the house.

"I'm sorry, dear. What did you say about a storm?"

"It's going to snow again. They're predicting three to four inches by late evening."

Shit, he thought, he was going to have to get a move on with this and get back on the road ASAP.

"That's not good news at all," he said. "We'll probably head back in an hour or so."

"Okay. Well, be careful on the highway. I should be home when you get here."

"I'll see you then, Peg. And have a nice time with Maggie."

"See you later."

Tom disconnected and continued staring out the windshield. He noticed that the wind was really picking up and dark gray clouds were blowing in from the west. He glanced at the phone in his hand, wondering if it had been ten minutes yet. Deciding it had been long enough, he tapped in Floyd Gossett's number.

"Hi, Mr. Gossett, it's Tom Grayson again. Were you able to reach Mindy?"

"Yep, sure did."

"What did she say?"

"Well, can't say as she was real thrilled with the idear of meeting up with you. In fact, she didn't seem to know who you were when I mentioned yer name. But then I repeated it for her and a light bulb lit up, I reckon."

"Will she let me see her?" Tom asked, wondering how much Floyd Gossett had butchered his name before Mindy finally realized who he was talking about.

"I reckon she's okay with it. She told me to give you her phone number so you could call her."

"That's great—what is it, Mr. Gossett?"

He read the number to Tom, who in turn punched it into his cell.

"I can't thank you enough, Mr. Gossett," Tom said sincerely.

"No problem, boy. Just don't let me hear that you've done anything wrong by Mindy or I'll personally see that you regret it!" the old man growled.

"Oh, don't worry about that—I just want a few words with her."

"All right then. I reckon I'll be going now."

"Thanks again, Mr. Gossett."

"Uh-huh."

Click.

Tom stared at the number Floyd Gossett had given him and realized that the exchange was the one used for the west side—way out in the boonies. He took a deep breath and a swig of water then pushed the "send" button.

Mindy Conkel answered after two rings.

"Hello."

"Hi, is this Mindy?" Tom asked, trying to sound as relaxed as he could despite the fact that the last time he'd talked to this woman was nearly twenty years ago and his nerves were frayed.

"Yes, and who might this be?"

"It's Tom Grayson. Long time no see, eh?"

"I don't believe it! When my ex-father-in-law called and told me you were trying to find me, I about flipped out. So what have you been up to?"

Tom was both surprised and pleased that she seemed so receptive. This was a good thing.

"Oh, where do I begin? I lived in New York for a few years then moved to Columbus. I'm teaching art history at Capital State, married with a wife and two kids and that's basically it in a nutshell. What about yourself?"

"My life hasn't been quite as exciting or glamorous as yours, I'm afraid. Just doing hair at a salon and living in this crappy town. That's really about it."

"C'mon, there's got to be more than that! You make it sound like this is the most boring place on earth!

"And you would disagree?"

Tom chuckled. "You got me there, I have to admit. Anyway, I was wondering if we could get together for a drink or something. I know it sounds sort of weird and on short notice but it's really important."

"Sure. But I can't leave home—my kids are here and I can't trust them by themselves. Why don't you just come out to my home?"

"Great!" Tom said. "How do I get there?"

"Just take Route 52 west until you're almost to the Adams County line then take a right on Slow Possum Hollow. I'm about three miles from the highway in a white mobile home. You can't miss it."

"That sounds easy enough. Is it okay if I come now? There's supposed to be a storm blowing in and I have to get back to Columbus soon."

"Sure. I'm not doing anything but the laundry."

"Great. I'll see you soon."

"See you, Tom."

Tom was thrilled—it had almost been *too* easy. He was surprised that Mindy would be so willing to see him after all these years. Especially after what had happened so long ago.

He closed the phone and started the engine. He was already headed in the direction of the west side so he pulled out and proceeded along Second Street until he reached the bridge crossing the

Scioto River. Glancing at the dashboard clock, he estimated that he would reach the Adams County line in about thirty minutes. That would make it around 2:40. Hopefully he wouldn't have to stay long to get his answers. That storm wasn't going to hold out forever.

As he drove, Tom flashed back to Mindy Conkel and his one-night stand with her twenty years ago. She would have been around twenty or so at the time, making her about forty now. He wondered how much she had aged since then. She would probably be overweight with an outrageously outdated hairstyle, he thought, like the majority of the women around this hillbilly town. There was a unique quality of Smithtown that set it apart from any place he'd ever seen: the place was in an eternal time warp. Whatever was happening in the rest of the country would be about ten years ahead of where Smithtown was at that time, socially and politically. It was as though the little river town was an eternal time capsule, reflecting the way the world had been ten years past.

Tom spotted the first flurry about ten miles from the Adams County line. In another five minutes, it began spitting snow. He checked the clock nervously, realizing that this would indeed have to be a brief encounter with Mindy Conkel Gossett. Not only did he want to avoid driving in a snowstorm, he didn't want Peg to be calling him endlessly, worrying about his making it home safely.

He sped up to sixty-five, hoping the highway patrol hadn't set any speed traps up ahead. In another few minutes, he spotted the sign for Slow Possum Road as he whizzed by the tiny two-lane road. Cursing, he continued until he reached the first driveway he could find, pulled into it, backed out and backtracked to Slow Possum.

The road was incredibly rough—a mixture of dirt, gravel and decaying asphalt. Dodging crater-sized potholes, he carefully negotiated the winding road that ran parallel to a swift running creek. He realized that he was actually in Shawnee State Forest when he spotted one of the familiar wooden marker signs along the way, indicating a specific trail. He passed a two-room shack that blatantly reminded him that he was on the fringe of Appalachia, where the ugliness of poverty still prevailed amidst the enchanting beauty of the forest.

Just as he was about to glance at his odometer, he spotted a white mobile home on his right. It was at the end of a dirt road that forked off then ran over a small, ramshackle bridge before dead-ending ten yards to the east of the trailer.

Tom pulled onto the road and held his breath as he crossed over the bridge. He could feel the thing sway sickeningly from side to side as the Jeep deposited its full weight upon its fragile rotting boards. On the other side, he saw a ten-year-old blue Honda Civic parked around the back of the trailer and pulled up beside it.

Tom got out and strode toward the small covered patio, aware of a face peering through one of the windows. It was a young boy, about eight or nine, with longish blonde, unkempt hair. Tom had just stepped onto the patio when the inside door opened. The boy stared at him from behind the door curiously, making no effort to open the storm door. Tom smiled at the boy, who suddenly turned around to look behind him. He heard Mindy say, "Let the man in, Jason, for crying out loud!"

The boy grasped the handle and opened the door about a foot. Tom stood there awkwardly, not sure whether to go on in or not.

"Come on in, Tom. My son doesn't seem to understand English."

Jason turned and ran away as Tom took hold of the door. He stepped inside, noticing the beige shag carpet and smell of laundry detergent at the same time.

"I'm loading the drier, Tom. Make yourself comfortable and I'll be there in a minute," he heard Mindy holler from a room to his right.

"Okay," Tom replied. He headed across the living room to a sofa and sat down.

The mobile home seemed twice as large as it looked from the outside. The living room was good sized with a couple of vinyl upholstered chairs, a coffee table, an end table and a big flat screen television set. To his left was a spacious kitchen, spotlessly clean and equipped with slightly dated appliances.

He noticed several framed photos hanging on the wall above the television, stood up and went over to examine them. There was one small black and white picture of an elderly couple, perhaps Mindy's grandparents, hanging beside a much larger framed family photo. Tom drew closer and saw Mindy and a middle-aged man standing directly behind two children sitting in matching chairs: Jason and a girl who apparently was Jason's older sister of around twelve or thirteen. Mindy herself looked damn good—much better than Tom would ever have guessed. The man standing beside her seemed camera shy and awkward, forcing himself to smile as if he would be elbowed if he didn't.

Mindy's father? Tom wondered.

He looked at the remaining pair of photographs on the wall, which were both 8x10 portraits of the two children.

There were no other photos on the wall.

Tom looked around, anxiously hoping to spot a photo of an older child somewhere—an older son or daughter who would be around nineteen by now . . .

He saw no more family photos.

Mindy suddenly entered the room. Tom was barely able to repress a gasp when he saw her. She looked even better than she did in the photo. She wore tight jeans and a white oversized oxford shirt, unbuttoned a third of the way down from the top. Her hair was tied in a rather loose ponytail, long strands of blonde falling randomly onto her shoulders. Her eyes were large and blue, her skin radiant with just enough age lines to complement her mature good looks. And her full lips were just as pouty and sensuous as they had been on that fateful night.

Mindy was still in fact, a frigging knockout—

"Hi, Tom," she smiled, approaching him and throwing her arms around him.

Tom felt her soft, firm breasts press against his chest as he held her close.

"Hi, Mindy."

They held each other a bit longer than necessary, and Tom felt himself actually regret letting go of her. She stood back and looked him over from head to toe.

"You look damn good, Tom. In fact, you look about the same as you did twenty years ago!"

"Right," he replied. "Except for this large growth above my belt, which seems to have taken on a life of its own. You look absolutely awesome, Mindy. And I must say, even *better* than you did twenty years ago!"

She smiled warmly. "Why thanks, Tom. I haven't been complimented like that in a long time."

"You've got to be kidding!" Tom said in genuine disbelief.

"I shit you not. Anyway, have a seat. Would you like something to drink? Coffee, a beer?"

"Coffee would be great if you have some handy."

"I just brewed a fresh pot a few minutes ago. How do you take it?"

"Black."

"I'll be back in a flash."

Tom stared at her beautiful ass as Mindy made her way over to the kitchen. He was mesmerized by her looks and wondered why he hadn't taken this girl a little more seriously all those years ago. Then he recalled the fact that Mindy Conkel really hadn't been his type. At least not personality-wise. She was much too extraverted if not downright *slutty* for him to have considered any kind of lasting relationship with her. Yes, she had been drunk and no doubt more forward than usual, but her drink-fueled behavior and blind lust had left Tom feeling zero emotional attachment and little respect for her after that crazy night.

Mindy Conkel had been just what he needed and nothing more: an easy one-night stand.

She returned to the living room, set a mug of steaming coffee on the coffee table in front of him then sat down on the sofa. She leaned back against the arm of the sofa and swung her long legs up, encircling them with an arm at the knees. After taking a sip of coffee, she motioned toward the rear of the mobile home and cast him a conspiratorial smile.

"My son is incredibly shy around strangers. That's why he hesitated to let you in. He'll make the scene though soon enough and you then you can meet him properly. He's as curious as he is shy and literally can't stand still for over five minutes at a time."

"I see. He's a good-looking boy," Tom said. "Looks a lot like his mother."

"Thanks. Some people think he looks more like Charlie. I think he looks a bit like us both."

"I noticed a girl in the picture over there. Your daughter, I presume?"

"Yeah, that's Josie. She'll be showing up pretty soon, actually. She's been over at a friends but just called to say that she was getting ready to head home."

"What grade are your kids in?"

"Jason's in fourth; Josie's in seventh."

"Well they sure seem to be nice kids," Tom said, not sure what else to say.

"Thanks, they are. How old are your kids?"

"My girl, Kelli, is seven and Tyler is five."

"That's great—isn't having children a wonderful gift?" she said, eying him oddly.

"Yes, it is." Tom paused a moment then said, "Um, I've been wondering, Mindy, what ever happened to—"

"Our baby?" she interjected.

Tom's heart skipped a beat as he stared at Mindy, trying hard to read what she was thinking behind those blue eyes. He detected a note of sadness—or was it remorse? He wasn't sure. All he knew was that in a moment he was going to discover the fate of his child. The one he had forsaken so long ago.

Mindy looked away a moment, then turned back and gazed at him intently.

"I had an abortion," she declared flatly.

Tom was stunned. She may as well have slapped his face.

The child in his dream, his *Erin*, had never existed. She had never even had a chance . . .

"You mean, you never had the baby?" he asked lamely.

"Yes, Tom. That's exactly what I mean."

"But why not?"

She stared at him reproachfully and Tom realized how stupid his question must have sounded to her.

"You have to be kidding, right, Tom? It's not like you made any indication that you wanted me to keep the child back then. In fact, if I remember correctly, you didn't even give it a second thought."

She was right, of course. He had blown off the matter like batting away an annoying fly. But he had never considered for a moment that she would abort the child. In fact he had—

Tom looked away from Mindy, trying his damnedest not to let his emotions show. The cold, hard truth reared its ugly head: he had in fact not given *any* of this any thought back then! He had simply told Mindy to go away and not to bother him with it, not considering the possible consequences for even a moment of his precious time.

Could he really blame her for not having the child?

"I'm sorry, Mindy. I understand why you did what you did. I was a total asshole about it. I just wish that—"

"That I would have told you I was having an abortion? And what good do you suppose that would have done?"

She had taken the words right out of his mouth. And again, she was dead right. Had Mindy called back to tell him that she was going to have an abortion, he would have simply told her it was fine with him, to go ahead and do it. He may have actually had the decency to offer to pay for it. But he would not have wanted her to have the child—that much he knew. He had been much too busy with his life in the Big Apple to even give that the slightest consideration.

But still . . . Didn't he at least have *some* say in the matter? She could have at least given him the option to oppose the abortion, for chrissakes! After all, it had taken both of them to make the baby.

"I think you should have called me first, at least," he finally said.

"Why? So you could tell me that I had your permission to murder our child? Because you know as well as I do that you would not have wanted to be a father to that baby. Nor would you have offered to help pay any of the expenses in raising it. C'mon Tom, admit it!"

Tom lowered his head and replied, "You're probably right."

He looked into her eyes again. He saw a single tear stream down her cheek and drop off of her chin. He scooted over on the sofa and put his arms around her. He held her close.

"God Mindy, I'm so sorry. I was such a jerk back then. It's just that I didn't want to believe I had gotten you pregnant in the first place. I mean, look at the odds! We'd only been together that one night and surely you were—"

She pushed him away. "Screwing other guys? Is that what you were going to say, Tom?"

Tom felt as low as he could go.

"Screw you, Tom! Just for your information, you were the first guy I had gone to bed with in over six months! That is how far off you were in your brilliant deduction of the situation. Granted, I was drunk and aggressive that night in the bar—it's not like I don't like to go out and have a good time once in a while—but that doesn't make me a slut. Which is apparently what you thought I was."

Her words stung. And as he considered the intensity with which she argued her case, he knew that it was all probably true. He had unfairly misjudged this girl—big time.

And had he known then what he knew now . . .

"All I can say is that I'm sorry, Mindy. I obviously was wrong about a lot of things back then."

"Listen, Tom. You have no idea how many times I've thought back to the day I had the abortion. I think of how my life could have been different if I wouldn't have done it. Had I kept the child, maybe I would never have made the mistake of hooking up with Charlie. Don't get me wrong, I love my kids and have no regrets whatsoever about the beautiful children Charlie and I made together. But that man has ruined my life. He abused me in ways I can't even begin to explain. I'm afraid of him every time I get up in the morning— terrified that he is going to get out of prison and murder me and the children. The man is a maniac! And he *is* going to get out of prison one of these days—he only got five years. And then he's going to find me and kill all of us. I just know it!"

Tom winced. It now hit home just how much his actions twenty years ago had changed this woman's entire life. He felt weak and sick to his stomach.

What a selfish prick he'd been!

He was momentarily speechless. He wanted nothing more than to explain to Mindy that he had changed since then, and if he had it all to do again, he would never have left her in the lurch like that. He would have offered to support the child and do the responsible thing. . .

But all of this would just sound like so much drivel to Mindy Conkel Gossett. Even if she believed him, which he doubted she would, what difference would it make? What had happened had happened—there was no turning back the hands of time.

"I'm so sorry, Mindy," he said again.

"It's okay, Tom. I've long since learned how to live with it and get on with my life. We were both young and foolish back then and

I probably got what I deserved. The Lord saw to it that I paid for my mistakes."

Tom wanted to protest, but didn't. At that moment, he wanted to take Mindy in his arms and apologize a hundred times over for ruining her life. And tell her that he didn't deserve her forgiveness, for what he had done simply wasn't forgivable. And that she was wrong in thinking that she deserved the miserable life she had been living thanks to Charlie Gossett.

In fact, he wanted to tell her that if anyone deserved to be punished for all of this, it would be his own lame ass . . .

But Tom kept these thoughts and words to himself. Instead, he decided that he would simply thank Mindy for seeing him on such short notice, wish her well, then get back on road before the storm hit.

And that is just what he did.

21

There was a good four inches of snow on the ground by the time he approached the Columbus city limits. Tom was thankful for the lack of heavy traffic on I-71 as he proceeded north on the slick freeway at forty-five miles an hour.

He tried Tracy's home number and got her voicemail again. *Shit!* he thought. Why hadn't he ever stored her cell phone number into his contacts? The battery strength indicator was showing a single flickering bar. His power was all but shot.

He cursed again and flipped the phone shut, feeling like Captain Kirk unable to reach the Enterprise.

"We are in grave need of some dilithium crystals here, Scotty," he murmured to the Jeep's vacant interior.

Tom planned on going directly to Tracy's apartment whether he reached her or not. He was about to crawl out of his skin. He needed to talk to her—to let her know how he felt about things.

He pulled onto the Hudson Street exit and headed west at the light. When he reached Summit Street, he hung a left and noted that none of the streets had been plowed or salted yet. It looked like a ghost town.

And it was really dark. *Too dark*, in fact . . .

Tom slowed down and glanced at the windows of the houses he passed by. No lights on. The streetlights weren't even lit.

The frigging power was off!

Déjà vu swept over him and Tom began to panic. Suddenly, he felt like he was re-living his dream. Deep snow, no traffic and no power. The sudden impulse to scream was strong, but his curiosity was even stronger.

He flipped opened the cell phone.

It was as dead as a doornail.

The battery had totally died.

With his heart in his throat, he slowed down to a crawl and began looking for Tracy's apartment building. It should have been easy enough to find, but the street was shrouded in darkness and the houses were set back far from the street. He finally reached the intersection of Holmes Road and spotted Tracy's apartment building on the corner. He pulled onto Holmes to access the building's parking lot located behind in the ally.

As he was about to pull into the ally, a car suddenly sped out in front of him and fishtailed wildly before straightening out and flying down Holmes. Tom hit the brakes hard to avoid smacking into the careening car, sending the Jeep into a slide before it came to rest against the curb.

Tom's first reaction to the near-collision car was shock, which gave way to momentary relief—

It meant he wasn't the only person alive, which was a good thing.

Tom backed away from the curb and drove the short distance to the parking lot. He noticed Tracy's car parked near the end and pulled up beside it.

She must be home now! he thought triumphantly.

Grabbing his coat, he stepped out onto the virgin snow. In the weak light, he noticed that Tracy's car was cleared of snow and the windshield was wiped clean, indicating that she had arrived home quite recently. He stepped past her car and headed for the rear stairway of the apartment building, then froze in his tracks—

There were no footprints leading away from Tracy's car. Nor were there any prints leading to the stairway from the parking lot.

Tom turned and backtracked to Tracy's car. When he reached the driver's side, he saw what appeared to be two sets of footprints outside the door. But the tracks appeared to begin and end there, which was impossible.

Tom tried Tracy's car door handle and was surprised to find it unlocked. He opened the door and felt heat escape from inside. It couldn't have been more than a few minutes since she had gotten out—

A cold jolt of fear hit Tom like a sledgehammer. He whirled around, slung open the passenger side door of the Jeep and reached inside the glove compartment for the flashlight. He switched it on and trained the beam on the ground between the two vehicles. He suddenly realized why the footprints appeared to lead nowhere when he spotted the second set of car tracks running parallel to the Jeep's.

Another car had been parked beside Tracy's just before he had arrived here. And Tracy had gotten into that car.

By her own will, or had she been forced?

The two sets of footprints implied the latter—

That car he had just seen fly out of the ally—he had seen it be-fore!

He hadn't realized it at the time, but Tom was now certain that it was the same car that had dumped the raped girl into the ally that night!

Shit! And now the bastard has snatched Tracy right out of her car!

Tom ran around the Jeep to the driver's side and got in, started it up and spun out of the parking lot in reverse. Switching on his high beams, he followed the tire tracks of the car onto Holmes Road and drove east.

Tom's mind was racing as he followed the trail to the intersection of North Fourth Street. How had this happened? How had the rapist found Tracy in the first place? For that matter, did he even know that she had witnessed his dumping of the girl's body? Tom was certain that the man hadn't seen either of them that night. Or at least it had seemed that way.

But even if the man had spotted Tracy and Tom watching him from the shadows, why would he wait until now to abduct Tracy? Hell, how did he know that she lived here—that she would be at this particular place on this particular night? It didn't make sense—

Unless . . .

Tom pulled north onto Fourth Street. He realized that there was at least a half-dozen sets of tire tracks running along the well traveled street as he headed toward the light on Hudson. When he reached the intersection, he strained his eyes to see where the maze of tracks led.

The thought returned as he mulled over which way to turn at the light . . .

What if the man had been shadowing Tracy all this time since that night, just waiting for the perfect time to nab her? And now he was going to see to it that she never told the police what she had witnessed?

Tom grimaced. In the true spirit of his unabashed selfishness, he had essentially allowed Tracy Adams to become an open target to a brutal rapist. By going his merry way to avoid the muck and mire of any potential life-ruining consequences, he had left the poor girl alone and vulnerable to one uber-scary son of a bitch.

Nice going, Tom, you lowlife prick . . .

And now there wasn't a goddamn thing he could do about it.

There were crisscrossing sets of tracks leading in all three directions beyond the light: straight-ahead, to the left and to the right.

Got a coin? he asked himself in desperation.

Aware that the odds were against his catching up with Tracy's abductor, he resolved to do what he should have done in the first place.

Call the cops.

He reached for his cell phone, flipped it open and saw that it was still as dead as it was before. Swearing to himself, he turned left and headed toward Summit Street again. He drove too fast and nearly rear-ended a car as he pulled up to the same pay phone he had used to call 911 the night of the crime. He jumped out and fumbled in his pocket for a quarter, grabbed the handset and dropped in the coin. There was no dial tone, just utter silence.

Shit!

Tom slammed the phone down onto the hook so violently that his whole arm hurt. Then a weak smile came to his face as an idea came to him. He headed back to Tracy's apartment building, got out and ran up the rear stairway. Outside her door, he knelt down and ran his fingers along the bottom of the threshold until he felt a seam in the siding. He pulled out on the seam and groped around until he felt the key wedged between the siding and the wood. He withdrew the key and plunged it into the keyhole.

Tom had learned about Tracy's secret hiding place for the spare key the night they had gotten drunk at a local club. They had returned to her apartment only to discover that she had locked herself

out. He could still see the sly grin on her lovely face as she pro-
duced the key and giggled so hard that she could hardly get it into
the keyhole.

Tom opened the door and stepped inside. He cursed to himself
as he realized he should have brought his flashlight. He headed
blindly toward the kitchen in the darkness, picking his way from
memory. He reached the kitchen, located the gas stove and turned
on one of the burners. In the pale blue light, he fished though all of
the drawers until he found a flashlight.

He turned on the light and saw the wall phone mounted near the
doorway. He picked up the phone and started to dial 911, glancing
at the "things to do" dry erase board mounted beside the phone.
Tom's heart skipped a beat as he read Tracy's even handwriting:

Columbus P.D. 4:30. Detective Collins.

So that's what had happened, Tom thought. Tracy must have
made an appointment with the cops to give her statement on the
crime earlier today. And somehow the perp found out and came
after her!

Tom pressed in the three numbers. The phone was dead.

Of course.

He replaced the phone and debated what to do. He could drive
to the nearest police station, but wasn't even sure where it was located. Then another idea came to him.

He recalled that Tracy had a second cell phone that she had
planned on giving her grandmother the next time she visited her.
He could only hope she hadn't yet made the trip to the nursing
home in Toledo. If he could find that phone and it was charged up,
he would be in luck.

Tom dashed out of the kitchen and entered the living room. The
last time he had seen the phone, it was plugged into the wall near
the entertainment center. He walked over and shone the flashlight
around but didn't see it. He opened one of the drawers and spotted
the phone lying on top of the clutter. He nearly cried out in joy.

He pulled it out and pressed the power button. There was a brief
pause before he heard the welcome chime and saw the LCD screen
glow brightly.

After it booted up, he observed the battery status bar. Fully
charged. And he had three bars of reception.

Tom punched in 911 and held his breath. After two rings, there was a connection.

"What is your emergency?" a woman's voice said.

" I want to report an abduction."

"When did this abduction occur and who was abducted?"

"It was just a few minutes ago," Tom replied. He hesitated before continuing, realizing that he was about to spill all of the beans. He no longer cared.

"Tracy Adams."

"And what is your relationship to the victim?"

Tom nearly hung up, but knew he couldn't. He was just going to have to go all the way with this. "I am a friend of hers."

"And your name, sir?"

"Tom. Tom Grayson."

"Where did the crime occur?"

"Just outside Tracy's apartment. It's on Summit Street. Please, you have to send a cop before it's too late!"

"I will, sir—just a few more questions. Do you know the make and model of the abductor's vehicle?"

"Yes, it was a late model gold-colored Ford Taurus. It had Ohio plates."

"Did you happen to get the plate number?"

"I'm afraid not."

"Can you give me a description of Ms. Adam's abductor?

Tom recalled the man he had seen the night of the original crime. "White, tall and lanky. About 6 feet. Medium build."

"Hair and clothing?"

"He had really short dark hair, like a burr cut. I didn't see what he was wearing. Please hurry and get the cops over here!"

"I've already radioed the police and they are on their way. You are at 2342 Summit Street, correct?"

"Yes, that's right."

"Did you see which way the vehicle was headed when it fled?"

"East toward North Fourth on Holmes. Then it had to go north on Fourth since it's a one-way street. I'm not sure where it went from there."

"Fine, sir. Please stay where you are until the police arrive."

"Okay. But please hurry!"

The operator disconnected and Tom started to shut down the phone. Then a thought occurred to him.

He clicked on the button for contacts and saw that there was one solitary listing . . .

Tracy's cell phone number!

Excitedly, he pressed the send button. He brought the phone to his ear and heard it ring once. Then twice. A third time—

Suddenly, he heard Tracy's hushed voice, muffled and weak.

"The campus bee—"

There was a rustling noise and what sounded like a struggle as the line suddenly went deadly silent.

"Tracy! Can you hear me? It's Tom!"

No reply. Suddenly a message appeared on the tiny screen: "call disconnected."

Tom hit "send" again. After a single ring, he got Tracy's voice-mail.

Shit!

Tom closed the phone and repeated her words. *"The campus bee"*

What the hell had she started to say? Bee-fricking what? She was apparently giving her location. But what started with "bee?"

The other mystery was which campus she was referring to. Ohio State University was almost exclusively the college referred to whenever the term "campus" was used in Columbus. But there was also the slim possibility that she could have meant the Capital State College campus. After all, she was a student there and he taught there. It was one of the few things they had in common, in fact.

Tom strained to think of any bars, restaurants or other popular venues that began with *"bee"* on either campus. He couldn't come up with much—in fact, he couldn't come up with anything at all. It was frustrating because every second he sat there doing nothing, Tracy was getting closer to god only knew what kind of trouble—

He had to go now. Screw the cops. There was no way he was going to just sit here with his finger up his ass while Tracy was clearly in imminent danger.

Especially now that he had something to go on.

He stuffed the phone into his coat pocket and headed for the door.

22

As Tom drove along High Street, he was relieved to see that there were some lights on in the businesses lining Columbus's main artery. This was little solace, though, because he still felt as desperate and alone as he had in his dream. He actually considered calling Peg just to hear her voice, but immediately dismissed the idea. That would only compound his problems.

Since Ohio State University was nearest Tracy's apartment, he had decided to begin his search there. Cruising south along the snow-covered thoroughfare, he kept his eyes peeled for any businesses beginning with "bee" on either side of the road. The snow had tapered off to flurries and traffic was understandably light.

He went as far south as Fifth Avenue and turned east, opting to make a sweep up Fourth Street until he was at Lane again. There were only a few businesses along the way—much of this area was comprised of off-campus apartment rentals.

He reached Lane, took a left and headed south on Summit Street. There were a few more businesses among the rental properties but nothing that started with "bee." He checked the dashboard clock and realized that he had been cruising the streets for nearly fifteen minutes. He wondered what might have happened to Tracy in all of this time—if she were even alive now. The feelings of frustration and remorse were palpable as he determined to wrap up his search on OSU's west campus before heading downtown to Capital State.

He checked his fuel gauge and realized he would have to refuel soon if he was going to keep this up any longer. He spotted a BP station, pulled up beside a pump and fished through his wallet for a credit card.

As he watched the pump's numbers flicker by at a staggering speed, he questioned whether he had made the right decision leaving Tracy's apartment instead of waiting for the police. There probably would have been a much better chance of finding her with the cops on his side, he conceded with regret. His sudden impulse to go on this fishing expedition by himself had been a foolish move.

Screw this, he thought. He needed to get back to Tracy's apartment pronto and let the cops do their job.

He jammed the fuel nozzle back into the pump, screwed on the gas cap and tore off his receipt. Then something on the pump caught his attention.

BP.

This was a campus *Bee-Pee* gas station. The *only* campus BP gas station he knew of.

Could this be what Tracy had referred to?

Tom looked around at the rundown housing in the area and hopped back into the Jeep. He sped out onto Summit Street and peeled his eyes for a gold colored Taurus along the street and in the driveways.

He didn't have to look very far.

He spotted the old Ford just a few houses down from the station, parked in front of a two-story house in poor repair.

Tracy is in there right now! he thought.

His heart pumping hard, he drove past the house until he found a parking space a few doors down and parked the Jeep. He killed the engine and sat for a moment, wondering what to do next. He considered calling the cops, but refrained—he needed to act now, and the sooner the better.

He grabbed the flashlight, got out and walked swiftly down the sidewalk toward the house. As he neared the Taurus, he shone the light on the front bumper, noting that the car had Ohio plates. He slowed down his pace until he came to a narrow walk leading up to the house. He could see a light in one of the second floor windows but the first floor looked dark as pitch.

Not a good sign.

Tom stood there in the darkness a full thirty seconds, not sure what to do next. He could create a distraction of some kind, which might force Tracy's abductor to think twice about what he was doing or was about to do at least for a moment or two. And then what? Bust into the house like Dog the Bounty Hunter and force the guy to surrender wielding a mini-flashlight as a weapon?

Not.

The cops. He simply had to call them in on this. And pronto.

Tom pulled Tracy's cell phone out of his coat pocket and punched in 911. Before the operator had time to answer, he heard a scream.

Tracy's scream—

He crammed the phone back into his pocket and ran along the side of the house, looking for a possible side entrance to the place. There was none. He sprinted to the rear of the house, jumped the three-foot wire fence and approached the back porch. He saw light coming through a small window in the door. Then he heard Tracy scream again, more faintly this time.

She must be on the second floor, he thought. Facing the street.

Without thinking, Tom threw open the storm door and frantically tried the inner door handle. It was locked. Without hesitation, he held the flashlight like a knife and stabbed at the small windowpane in the door. The glass shattered but barely made a sound. Poking his hand through the opening, Tom groped around until he located the deadbolt and turned it. He used his other hand to turn the doorknob and pushed the door open with his shoulder.

He stepped into a dimly lit kitchen and began looking around for a weapon of some kind. Suddenly, a wall phone rang and his heart nearly burst out of his chest. He heard a loud thump come from upstairs as the phone rang a second time then ceased.

A man's voice, muffled and barely audible, came from the direction of the front of the house. Tom continued searching for a weapon, relieved that Tracy's captor apparently considered the call important enough to stop whatever he had been doing at that moment.

Having rifled through a couple of drawers and finding nothing but silverware and kitchen items, Tom crept through the tiny dining room into the living room, the floor boards creaking loudly with nearly every step he took. He shone the flashlight around the room. With the exception of a big flat screen TV, an enormous stereo system and a cheap sofa, the living room was void of furnishings.

Tom spotted the stairs across the room in a foyer and crept toward them, stopping dead in his tracks each time the floor creaked, half expecting the voice on the phone to stop mid-sentence after realizing there was an intruder downstairs.

As he neared the staircase, Tom could make out the voice more clearly. He noticed that the stairs were carpeted and felt grateful for the dampening effect the carpet would have on the inevitably creaky wooden stairs.

Tom ascended the staircase as quietly as possible. As he neared the top, he could clearly make out what the man was saying.

"I don't think we have anything to worry about."

Tom reached the top and stopped, then carefully peered around the corner down the hallway. He saw three rooms, two with their doors closed. The man was in a room adjacent to the one furthest away. Judging by the sound of his voice reverberating off the walls, he was in a bathroom.

"We'll be holding down the fort until then."

Tom noticed that the furthest door was barely ajar. His guess was that Tracy was inside and the man had left her there long enough to answer the phone and take a leak. He wondered why Tracy wasn't making any sound now as his heart filled with dread.

Was she unconscious? Or had he already killed her?

Something had silenced her—that much was sure.

Tom knew he had to move quickly if he was to have any chance of saving Tracy. The man could walk out into the hall any moment and head for the stairs. Then Tom would be screwed.

He took a deep breath, peeked around the corner again and stepped quietly toward the nearest room. He put his ear to the door and didn't hear a sound. He opened the door quietly, stepped inside then heard a beep as the man ended his call.

Tom stood frozen just inside the doorway, half expecting the man to pass by the room and see him there. Then he heard the sound of a creaky door open.

He had gone back in with Tracy!

Nervously, Tom shone the light around the room and saw what appeared to be a second bedroom. There was an unmade twin bed, a beat-up chest of drawers and a mismatched nightstand beside the bed.

No potential weapons in sight—

Except for a brass lamp.

Tom went over, snatched up the lamp and tore off the plastic shade. Grasping the heavy lamp by its base, he turned around and headed toward the door.

With his heart nearly bursting out of his chest, he stepped into the hall and headed directly toward the room where Tracy and the man were. He was just about to reach for the knob when the door suddenly swung open and revealed a man standing in the doorway, staring at him in utter surprise and disbelief.

"Who the hell—"

With all of his strength, Tom swung the lamp and hit the man square in his face, making a sickening dull thud sound. The man's eyes were wide-open in absolute shock and pain as his body slumped down to the floor, blood gushing out of his smashed-in nose.

Tom stepped over the body when a second man suddenly appeared in the doorway, aiming a pistol directly at Tom's head. It was the same man he and Tracy had seen dumping off the body of the black woman.

"Hold it right there, asshole!" the man commanded.

Tom froze in his tracks.

"Drop it or I'll make mincemeat out of that pretty-boy face of yours."

Tom dropped the lamp.

"Back up."

Tom took a few steps backward, certain that the next thing he heard would be the sound of a gunshot that would signal the end.

"Keep moving. Into that room," the man ordered, motioning toward the second bedroom with his gun.

Tom turned around, stumbled across the hall to the room and lurched inside.

"On the bed," he barked.

Tom hesitated a moment before stepping over and standing beside the bed

"Now, sit down and close your eyes."

"What are you going to do?" Tom asked fearfully.

"You'll see in a minute. Just fucking *do it!*"

Tom sat down slowly. He stared anxiously at the man who was now standing directly over him, feeling a cold sweat break out on his brow, trying to accept the grim reality that he was about to be executed.

"Sweet dreams," the man said.

And the next thing Tom knew, the whole world turned black.

23

As he regained consciousness, Tom couldn't make out where he was in the darkness or how he had gotten there. He was in a room that was cold and damp, possibly a basement, lying flat on his back on a concrete floor, his head feeling like it might explode from the excruciating pain. Instinctively, he tried to touch where it hurt and discovered that his hands were bound together. They weren't tied behind his back though, so he raised up his arms far enough to feel his head with his wrists. There was a lump not quite the size of a golf ball.

He tried to stand up but his legs were also bound together. He reached down and felt several layers of duct tape wrapped tightly around his ankles.

It was at that moment that he recalled what had happened. He had been knocked unconscious by the man with the gun and was apparently being held captive somewhere in the house. He gazed at the luminous dial of his wristwatch, wondering how long ago he'd been out. To his surprise, it hadn't been for much more than an hour.

Then it hit him: *Tracy! He had to find Tracy!*

Tom's eyes adjusted to the darkness as he looked around at his surroundings. To his right, he made out a rectangle of dim light in the wall near the ceiling. There was another rectangle on the opposite wall.

Basement windows, he thought.

He rolled himself over in an effort to get onto his feet. After several head-splitting twists and turns, he was finally able to get up onto his knees. He was certain he'd given himself a hernia in the process. In a sudden surge of sheer determination, he managed to get to his feet and stand upright—very wobbly at first, then steadier once he backed himself up against a wall for support.

Luckily for him, his captor had apparently assumed he would be knocked out much longer than he actually had been—otherwise he would have been more thorough restraining him. Another thought occurred to him. Maybe he had been in too much of a hurry to finish Tracy off at the time to bother doing a better job on him . . .

Tom liked the first option much better.

The only thing he was sure of was that too much time had already gone by since he'd been whacked out and he needed to get moving instead of standing there reminiscing.

He eyed the nearer window and hopped over to it, fighting to keep his balance. He peered out and could see light in the windows of the adjacent house. But the tiny casement window was simply too small for him to fit through.

He peeled his eyes across the room and could just make out fine slits of light forming an L-shape along the ceiling—the outline of a door, perhaps.

He hopped in that direction a few feet then suddenly felt a jolt of pain as his left knee smacked into something hard and sharp. Tom grimaced in agony as he groped around to feel what he had run into. It was a table, probably a workbench.

Excitedly, Tom skimmed his bound hands along the surface of the table, hoping to locate a tool of some kind. He nudged a large tin can and before he could stop himself, knocked it to the floor. The sound was absolutely deafening in the darkness. Swearing at his klutziness, Tom stood still and held his breath, praying that no one had heard.

A moment later, he moved to his right, continuing to scour the tabletop. He came across a variety of objects: a block of wood, a paper booklet, a pair of work gloves and a yardstick. He needed something sharp enough to cut duct tape and none of these items fit the bill.

He reached the end of the table and skirted around the corner to continue his search on the other side. He ran across a jar full of what sounded like nails or screws and decided to tip the jar over in order to examine its contents. In the process, he bumped into something that would work much better than a nail—

An electric grinding wheel.

Tom brought his wrists to the wheel and began running them back and forth along the edge of the coarse wheel. The wheel cut into his flesh but he knew that it was doing the same job on the duct tape. After several minutes of slicing, Tom felt blood trickle down his arm but continued slicing until he was finally down to a single thickness of duct tape. He pulled his wrists apart with all his strength. The ripping sound of the fatigued tape was music to his ears.

His hands now free, he groped around on the table until he found a utility knife under a pile of work cloths. He bent down and sliced at the duct tape binding his ankles until he was free.

He grinned victoriously. Then, without thinking, he broke into a run and tripped over a box, causing him to fall hard onto the concrete floor. The only thing that hurt more than his elbow was the fact that his fall created more racket than the tin can had. He rose to his feet painfully, held his breath and prayed that no one had heard him. When it was safe to continue, he headed toward the door at a more cautious pace.

As he drew closer, he could see the steps of the stairway leading up to the door in the dim light shining through the cracks. He grasped the railing and ascended the stairs two at a time. Reaching the top, he brought his ear to the door and listened. He heard nothing.

Tom turned the handle and pushed, but the door wouldn't budge. It was locked. His captor hadn't done so poorly a job after all.

He stood there for a minute, contemplating his next move. He could try to kick the door open, but the noise would most certainly alert his abductors. Could he somehow squeeze through one of those casement windows now that he was freed? No, they were definitely too small. His only option was to find a tool he could use to pry the door open.

A thought suddenly occurred to him as he started back down the stairs: there just might be a light switch somewhere. He ran his hand along the wall until he located a switch plate, flipped the switch and the basement was instantly bathed in light.

That will certainly help.

Tom descended the stairs and took a quick look around. The basement was larger than he had imagined and littered with all kinds of clutter. Amidst the old rusted lawn tools, cardboard boxes and tattered furniture stood the workbench he had run into. He went over and began searching for a screwdriver or similar tool he could use to pry the door open with.

Finding nothing there, he glanced around the room and saw another table pushed against the wall on the other side of the furnace. He headed toward it, sidestepping a threadbare sofa along the way. As he passed the sofa, he saw what he thought was a pile of old clothes.

Then he realized that someone was wearing the clothes.

Bewildered, Tom moved cautiously toward the body and saw a young girl of about eleven or twelve. She was wearing faded denim jeans and a red nylon coat. The girl's eyes were closed and he thought at first that she was dead. He drew nearer and crouched down, placed his hand on the girl's forehead. It was warm and she was breathing regularly.

Thank god, he thought.

But what in the hell was she doing here?

He examined the girl more closely and saw that her ankles and wrists were bound in duct tape.

What in the hell is going on here?

The discovery of the girl prompted Tom to recall something he had forgotten until now: the other man—the one he had whacked with the lamp. There were *two* men involved in all of this, not just one. Had the pair abducted Tracy and the other girls as part of some kind of crime spree? If so, what was their motive? To simply rape the victims then drop them off in an alley?

The concept of two men working in collaboration to abduct and rape women seemed very unlikely. Then he recalled the Hillside Stranglers, who tortured and murdered girls in Los Angeles in the late 70's and realized that it was plausible.

Tom placed his hands on the girl's shoulders and gently shook her.

"Hey, wake up!" he spoke in a hushed voice. "Can you hear me?"

The girl made no response.

He tried again. "Wake up, girl! We've got to get out of here. Can you hear me? You've got to wake up so we can get out of here!"

She made a moaning sound and mumbled something.

"That's it, snap out of it! I'm not going to hurt you!"

The girl moaned again and her eyes fluttered open for a moment. Then she immediately shut them.

"No! Please don't hurt me!" she cried.

"Don't worry, I'm not going to hurt you. I want to help you. What's your name? My name is Tom."

She opened her eyes reluctantly and stared at Tom. Her expression showed fear and suspicion.

"How do I know that you won't hurt me? Those other men scared me really bad!"

Tom tried to comfort her by gently taking hold of her hands.

"Those men are the bad guys and they have locked us down here for some reason. I came here to find someone they kidnapped but they caught me. You have to believe me, I'm not making this up."

"Promise?" the girl said with pleading eyes.

"Scout's honor," Tom replied with an encouraging smile.

"Okay, I think I believe you. You seem too nice to be bad."

"We have to move fast, uh—what's your name?"

"Molly. Molly Barnes."

"Okay, Molly, let's get you untied so we can get out of this place."

Tom helped her to sit up and said, "Did they hurt you any?"

She shook her head. "No, not really. Just when they pulled me into their car."

"What exactly happened?" Tom asked, pulling the utility knife out of his pocket.

"I was walking home from Kristi's house earlier this evening and all of a sudden a car pulled up beside me. A man jumped out and pulled me into the front seat. Another man was driving. Then the first man got in next to me and told me not to scream or he would hurt me really bad."

"Had you ever seen either of these men before?" Tom asked as he began cutting the duct tape from Molly's wrists.

She shook her head. "No. I was so scared! I started to cry and the one man yelled at me to shut up then put his hand over my mouth. We drove around for a while until we came to this house. The man driving the car got out and watched while the second man took my hand and told me not to struggle or he'd kill me. Then he pulled me out and led me up to the house."

"There. Now, your ankles," Tom said. "What happened after that?"

"Once we got inside, the men suddenly started acting like, kind of nice to me. They asked me if I wanted anything to eat or drink and I said no, and that all I wanted was to go home. They told me that I could go home in a little while, after they got done doing what they had to do. I asked them what that would be and one of them laughed and said that I'd find out soon enough. That really scared me, the way he said that, and I started crying again."

"You're free now," Tom said, making the final slice of the duct tape.

The girl smiled at him. "Thanks, Tom."

"You're welcome. So what happened after that?"

"They both got really mad again when I started crying. One of them told me to sit down and be quiet while the other one went into the kitchen. He came back with a glass of Coke and offered it to me. I told him I wasn't thirsty and he told me to drink it anyway, or else he'd force it down my throat. So I took a drink.

"I thought it tasted funny and I asked him what was in it. He said nothing but good old Coca Cola. I didn't believe him, though. Then the other man turned on the television and we all just sat there for a while. Then . . ."

Molly looked confused as she struggled to recall.

"And then I—I don't really remember what happened after that."

Tom saw a red flag. "You can't remember anything at all? Are you sure?"

The girl looked past Tom with a vacant look in her eyes. "I can't remember! I guess I just fell asleep then."

"And you don't remember anything else that happened until I woke you up?"

"No, nothing," she said uncertainly. "It was like, a big blur. I mean, I think I was awake on the sofa but I don't remember what I was doing. It was sort of like a dream that I can't remember."

This disturbed Tom and had dire implications. He hoped that what he was thinking wasn't true. That the men had drugged her with something and that was why she couldn't recall anything.

But now was not the time to be worrying about this. He had to find a way to get them out of this basement and find Tracy.

"Can you stand up?" he asked.

"I think so."

Tom put his arm around the girl's waist and helped her up onto her feet.

"How do you feel?"

"A little wobbly," she replied. "But not too bad."

"Good, let's see if you can walk."

Molly took one step then suddenly froze.

"Shit!" she cried.

"What's wrong?"

"I think I'm bleeding—I must have started my period."

"Are you sure—I mean, that it's just that?"

She gave Tom a troubled look, realizing what he may be getting at. She shook her head slowly. "I don't know for sure. The time is about right, though."

"Listen, Molly. You need to check yourself out. I'll go to the other side of the basement and wait for you, okay?"

"I'm scared, Tom! What if those men did something to me?"

Tom faced her and gently held one of her small hands in his. "Try to calm down, Molly. I don't know how to say this but what ever happened has happened and there isn't much we can do about it now. The important thing is that you're still alive and that we get out of this place ASAP. Do you understand?"

She nodded slowly. "Go away and I'll look."

Tom headed across the basement to the other side of the stairwell and waited nervously. He wondered what this poor child may have gone through at the hands of these two assholes. His pity turned to anger as he thought about them upstairs now and how he would love nothing more than to shoot them both in the balls.

His thoughts shifted to Tracy. What in the hell has happened to her? Had she been drugged and raped? Was she still alive or unconscious?

"Okay, Tom," he heard Molly call.

Tom emerged from around the stairwell and went over to Molly.

"I think everything is all right," she said with an embarrassed smile.

Tom couldn't hide his relief. "That is the best news I've heard all day."

"But my mother is going to kill me! She told me never to walk alone at night and I disobeyed her."

"This isn't your fault, Molly—and I'm sure your mother will just be happy to see you again. What do you say we get out of this place?"

"Let's do it."

"Help me find a screwdriver and we'll be on our way."

24

The door leading out of the basement was old and warped. Molly held the flashlight while Tom wedged a screwdriver between the door and the jamb, its tip pressed firmly against the metal latch bolt. After several attempts, he finally managed to create a space great enough for the latch to clear the hole in the jamb, allowing him to push the door open.

They were free.

Molly smiled when Tom gave her a thumbs-up and then motioned for her to wait while he checked out the situation. He inched the door open just enough for him to slip through and enter the kitchen.

Tom's first task was to grab the phone and dial 911, but his heart sank when he discovered that the wireless kitchen phone had been removed from its wall cradle. Swearing under his breath, he realized he was going to have to proceed with Plan B. He returned to where Molly was standing on the other side of the door.

"Here's what I want you to do: I'm going to open the backdoor and you are going to run like hell away from this house to the BP station less than a block away. I want you to tell whoever is on duty there that you need to make an emergency 911 call. Tell the operator that you have been kidnapped and that there is an assault in progress at a house on the east side of Summit Street just south of the BP station. Then I want you to call your mother and tell her where you are—she no doubt is worried sick about you. Think you can do all of that, Molly?"

"Yeah, but what will you be doing? You should go with me—these men are dangerous!"

"I've got to see if I can locate the friend I've been looking for. She may not have much time left. I'll be okay, don't worry. Just get yourself out of here and run like the wind!"

"I'm scared, Tom! What if I get lost?"

"You won't get lost, I promise. All you have to do is hop over the fence and run between the houses toward the street. When you reach the street, head right and you'll see the gas station less than a block away."

"Okay, I guess I can do that," Molly said slowly.

"That's my girl! Now, come with me."

He took her by the hand and led her over to the back door, opened it quietly and held the storm door open for her.

"Remember, go to the right, over the fence and head toward the street. Be careful!"

She gave him a quick hug and a peck on the cheek. "Thanks, Tom, for saving me. Please be careful!"

"I will—now go!"

Molly ran outside and out of his sight. He heard a rustling sound as she scaled the old wire fence and then the soft thud of re-treating footsteps in the snow.

Tom moved quietly toward the front of the house, aware that he hadn't heard a single sound since escaping the basement. Could they have already abandoned the place? he wondered. He reached the living room, paused, and listened hard. After a moment, he thought he heard the faint muffled sound of voices coming from upstairs.

He scanned the living room for his flashlight and cell phone but came up empty. Then he tiptoed over to the stairway and ascended the stairs. As he neared the top, he could clearly hear voices. He carefully peered around the corner and saw that all of the doors to the second story rooms were shut. The voices were coming from the same room he had believed Tracy to be in. He slipped around the corner to the nearest room where he'd been whacked and put his ear to the door. He didn't hear anything. Praying that Tracy's cell phone might be there, he inched the door open.

A light was on in the unoccupied room. He closed the door be-hind him and searched around for his gear. After rifling through all of the drawers of the dressing bureau, he checked the closet and found nothing but a few shirts and a vacuum cleaner.

Tom wasn't sure what to do next. He had no phone and no weapon. He was up against two men that were armed and holding all of the aces. What in the holy hell could he do, realistically?

Not much, he realized. But he had to at least try to save Tracy. He had a feeling that she was still alive only because the men hadn't killed anyone as far as he knew. If they were murderers, they would certainly have killed either Molly or himself by now. He could only hope that the same held true for Tracy.

Only one way to find out, Tom thought.

He crept back out into the hallway. Quietly, he walked over to the door where the voices were coming from and held his ear to it.

"Looks like she's out like a light," he heard a voice say.

"She is. We'll give her ten more minutes, then the Versed," a second voice said.

"Why do we have to wait so long to give her the shot, Doc?" another voice said.

Christ! Tom thought. There were *three* of them in there! Who was the third man?

And what in the holy hell were they doing to Tracy?

"Because, Ernie, this is all about timing. The GBH we gave her will knock her out for several hours and make her an easy lay. I've also added something to help control the vomiting, which will make our experience all the more pleasant.

"But the injection should make her forget that anything bad ever happened to her. In fact, if all goes well, she will have amnesia and forget everything that's happened since we picked her up. But we have to delay the injection. Otherwise, it would not only screw up the metabolic process, but probably kill her, too."

"I see." Ernie replied. "But why didn't you give the little girl a shot of that stuff, too?"

"She is too small for us to take the risk with that combination of drugs. The last thing we need is a murder rap."

"But she's going to be able to ID us once we let her go, isn't she?" the first man argued.

The man referred to as "Doc" chuckled. "We haven't let her go yet, now have we? I've got another formula I want to try on the young one before we turn her loose. And if this little concoction works, she won't know any of us from the man in the moon."

"Whoa, that would be awesome! So if all of these drugs of yours work, we could get away with all kinds of shit with any babe we want—and no one will ever know the difference!"

"I'm more interested in the money we're going to make, but yes, that's what we're shooting for. But neither of you are getting a red cent until we perfect the process, so don't get all excited yet."

"I know, Doc. But don't think we aren't enjoying these little experiments, right Billy?"

"That's for sure. God, she's a looker, ain't she? I can't wait to get my hands on those tits! When can we strip her down, Doc?"

Ernie answered instead. "Jesus, Billy, hold your horses! You damn near screwed everything up with that black chick by being so gung-ho, remember? If Doc hadn't saved the day, we'd all be up shit creek by now."

Tom stepped back from the door. His first reaction was absolute shock. Tracy was being forced to act as some kind of lab rat so this "Doc" lunatic could test his street drugs! She had evidently just been given a date rape cocktail and would be shot up with another drug in ten minutes. *Versed*—he'd heard of that drug before. It was a powerful sedative given before surgery to relax you.

So that's what this is all about, he thought. These cretins, led by the doctor, were trying to develop the ultimate date rape drug—one that would not only make the victim more vulnerable to abuse but able to induce total amnesia. This would theoretically make it impossible for the guilty party to get caught since the victim's memory would be completely eradicated.

Tom thought of little Molly Barnes and realized that she was very fortunate to have gotten out of this creepy laboratory when she had. The doctor's plans of future experimentation on the girl would definitely have put her at serious risk.

And the "black chick" Ernie had referred to was most likely the same girl that had been dumped off in the alley. Tom recalled Frank saying that she had been raped and assaulted but had had no recollection of her attacker. She must have been part of these experiments, too, and the drugs had apparently worked.

He simply had to get Tracy out of there before they gave her that shot—

But how?

And why haven't the cops gotten there yet? Had something happened to Molly to keep her from calling 911?

Tom looked at his watch. It had been almost five minutes since Molly had left the house—plenty of time for her to get to the BP and place the call. The cops should be here any minute.

Tom couldn't wait any longer.

He suddenly heard someone walk toward the door. In a flash, he ran down the hall and into the spare bedroom. He stood there holding his breath and heard someone go into the bathroom to take a leak. He waited a little longer then heard the person go back into the bedroom and close the door.

Out of nowhere, Tom had a flashback of his dream. He and Erin had been speeding through the Midtown Tunnel with Chappy and his crony in hot pursuit, gaining on them. They had almost run out of time—

This gave him an idea. And it just might work.

He opened the door and peeked out to make sure the hallway was clear. Then he fled the room and moved silently down the stairs. Heading for the kitchen, he kept his eye out for anything he could find to create a diversion.

He found a Bic lighter in a counter drawer near the stove and considered the white linen curtains covering the window above the sink. Kindling, yes, but not enough fuel to sustain a fire. He peered over at the valence hanging over the window of the kitchen door. That wouldn't work either.

Tom glanced at his watch and estimated they would be giving Tracy the injection in another two or three minutes. He was going to have to hurry or it would be too late.

He ran down the stairs into the basement and looked around. He spotted a cardboard box filled with old clothes near the workbench. He also found an old scuffed up baseball in another box and stuffed it into his pocket. Then he picked up the box of clothes and ran back up the stairs.

Tom closed the basement door and quickly dumped the contents of the box out on the floor. Using his feet, he banked the pile of clothes up against the basement door and ran over to the drawer where he'd seen a can of lighter fluid earlier. He ran back over to the pile of clothes, doused them in lighter fluid then squirted the basement door with the rest of the can. He stooped down, flicked the Bic and ignited the pile of clothes.

There was a huge whoosh as the clothes caught fire and flames ran up the door, licking the ceiling. Tom threw the can on the flames and dashed out of the kitchen.

His heart was nearly busting out of his chest as ran up the stairs as quietly as he could—just long enough to open the door to the spare bedroom. Then he ran back down the stairs halfway and stopped. He took the baseball out of his pocket and took careful aim at the large living room window at the far end of the room. Drawing in a deep breath and holding it, he threw the ball as hard as he could.

Tom saw the window shatter and then retraced his steps up the stairs, entered the spare bedroom and shut the door behind him. He immediately heard the door to the other bedroom burst open and the sound of footsteps running down the hall then down the stairs.

Tom held his breath. Any second now . . .

"Fire!" someone shouted from below.

Seconds later, he heard two more sets of footsteps running down the hallway.

"Where is it?" the doctor shouted.

"In the kitchen—the whole room is engulfed!" someone replied.

This was his only chance.

Tom ran out of the room, down the hall and into the bedroom. He was outraged when he saw Tracy lying on a bed unconscious, stripped down to her bra and panties.

He ran over and started shaking her.

"Tracy! Wake up!"

She was so lifeless that Tom wondered if it was too late. He looked around and saw a syringe lying on the bedside table. It was still full of the drug, thank god.

He held his ear to Tracy's chest. Her heart was beating faintly.

"Tracy, it's Tom! Can you hear me?"

He stared at her closed eyes expectantly but they remained closed.

Tom glanced around the room, knowing that he had precious few seconds before they came back upstairs. He looked around for a gun but didn't see one.

He went over to the window, raised the mini blinds and looked outside. As his eyes adjusted to the darkness, he saw an eave just outside the window that jutted out a few feet. Beyond the overhang he noticed that the roof gently sloped out over the front porch. Tom couldn't believe his good luck.

He unlatched the window and raised it up as far as he could. He then went over and placed his hands under Tracy's armpits and pulled her body gently down to the floor. He dragged her over to the window and set her down, grabbed the blanket off the bed and hastily wrapped it around her half naked body.

He could tell from the shouts of the men downstairs that they were trying to put out the fire that he had started in the kitchen. It wouldn't be much longer before one of them remembered that Tracy was still upstairs and run up to get her. Tom scurried over to the bedroom door, closed and locked it.

He hoisted the unconscious girl up until her back was resting against the wall directly below the windowsill. He then backed his way out through the window, carefully planted his feet in the snow and took hold of Tracy from behind. He was surprised at how light she felt as the adrenalin kicked in. He gingerly pulled her body through the window and out onto the eave of the roof. Tracy's feet had just cleared the windowsill when Tom suddenly lost his footing and nearly fell off the eave. Fortunately, the overhang was only slightly pitched and he was able to regain his balance while still keeping his hold on Tracy.

Tom paused long enough to catch his breath and figure out the best way to move Tracy from the overhang onto the porch roof. Then he heard the sound of someone banging on the bedroom door.

Realizing that it wouldn't take too long for them to break down the door, Tom tightened his grasp on Tracy's body and dragged her toward the area where the overhang met the line of the porch roof. Tom's heart sank when he heard the sound of smashing woodwork and knew that they had just busted the door down.

It would only take a second for them to discover where he was.

Just then, Tom heard the sound of tires screeching below him and saw a blast of light bathe the roof where he stood holding Tracy's limp body.

It was the cops! Tom glanced over and saw one of the abductors appear in the window. It was the one who had dumped off the black girl in the alley. He glanced over at Tom then spotted the cruiser on the street, its spotlight trained on the window. The man spun around and was out of sight in an instant.

Tom heard sirens as another cruiser sped up to the house, followed by a fire truck. One of the cops had gotten out and was pointing a gun at him.

"Hold it right where you are!" he commanded.

"They are going to escape out the back!" Tom shouted. "Three men—they have a gun!"

Tom heard more sirens and saw the paramedics pull up in front of the police cruisers. A second officer got out, drew his gun and headed toward the rear of the house. The first policeman continued pointing his gun at Tom. A pair of firemen jumped from the fire truck and began uncoiling fire hose.

Tom suddenly heard two gunshots ring out from the rear of the house. A third police officer hopped out of one of the cruisers and hustled back toward the action. The first officer still had his gun pointed cleanly on Tom.

"Remain where you are and don't make any sudden moves!" the cop warned.

Tom's arms were numb from holding Tracy's body. "I have an unconscious woman here who needs medical attention—she's been drugged and is barely breathing!"

The cop called the paramedics over and spoke to them. A moment later, he said: "Hold on to her and we'll get someone up there as soon as the scene is cleared."

"Okay, but please hurry!"

Tom saw the three men appear from around the side of the house, followed by the cops. The men were handcuffed.

"Is that everybody?" the cop holding the gun asked the other officers.

"Yeah, I'm pretty sure. Except for the two on the roof," Tom heard a cop reply. "The fire is spreading pretty quick."

On cue, the firemen began moving toward the rear of the house, followed by the paramedics and one of the officers. The cop motioned toward Tom.

"We'll be up to get you in a moment."

Tom watched as the three men were escorted over to the cruisers, frisked and then placed into the rear of the cars. A small crowd had gathered and was looking on curiously.

A cop suddenly stuck his head out the window and aimed his flashlight directly into Tom's eyes.

"Hold it right there and don't make any sudden moves," he commanded.

"Okay," Tom replied.

"Do you have any weapons on you?"

"No, sir."

The cop trained his light on Tracy's face, frowned, then disappeared. A moment later, one of the firemen stuck his head out and surveyed the situation.

"We're going to get a ladder up to you, mister," he called to Tom. "A medic is coming out to take a look at the woman."

Tom nodded. The cop appeared again and managed to climb nimbly out onto the eave, despite his large size. He had his gun drawn and kept his flashlight on Tom as he made his way over. The officer gave him a quick pat-down for weapons then focused his attention on the unconscious Tracy Adams.

"What happened to her?"

"Those bastards drugged her. They gave her some kind of date rape drug."

"And what was your part in all of this?" he asked accusingly.

"I had no part at all in this—I came here to try to save her!"

"We'll continue this interrogation once we get you off this roof," the cop said. He shone his light on Tracy's face. "She doesn't look very good."

The officer stepped over to the window.

"You can come out now," he said to the paramedic on the other side of the window.

Tom watched as the medic climbed out onto the roof then came over and knelt down beside Tracy. He opened each of her eyelids and shone a light into each eye, checked her pulse and took her blood pressure.

"Do you know how long ago she was given the drug?" he asked Tom.

"I'd say about a twenty minutes ago."

"Do you have any idea what drug it was?"

"I heard them say GHB, but there were other drugs too, I think. He said that there was an anti-nausea drug added in."

Tom suddenly heard a clatter and saw the top of a ladder appear at the edge of the roof several feet away. A moment later, a fireman came into view.

The medic said, "I'll hold onto the woman while you go down with the fireman. We're going to have to get her back inside and onto a gurney."

Tom nodded and let the medic take hold of Tracy's arms. The fireman climbed onto the roof, went over to Tom then helped him onto the ladder.

"Is she going to be okay?" Tom asked the medic.

"I think so. She probably just needs to sleep it off."

Relieved, Tom began his descent down the ladder. He glanced down and spotted that the policeman who had kept his gun on him all this time standing there awaiting him.

25

A week later, Tom climbed the stairs up to Tracy's apartment, wondering how this was going to go. The last time he had seen her was when she had been loaded into the ambulance and transported to Riverside Hospital on that horrendous night when the shit had royally hit the fan.

He stood at her door and knocked. A moment later, the door opened and Tracy stood there with a mixture of joy and anxiety on her lovely face.

"Hello, Tom. It's so good to see you."

"Hi Tracy. Nice seeing you, too."

Tom followed her inside.

"You want a beer?" she asked.

"That would be great," he replied. He sat down on the sofa and stared at her as she went into the kitchen. She looked as beautiful as always in her tight jeans and oversized blue Capital State sweatshirt. Every time he saw her, he was reminded of why he had taken the monumental risk of cheating on his wife.

She returned with a Michelob Ultra and an Ice Mountain for herself.

"Thanks," Tom said as she handed him the beer. "Have you missed the booze any?"

She sat down on the sofa a few feet from him and took a swig of her water. "Not really. I tried one of those non-alcoholic beers a couple of days ago but it wasn't quite the same as the real thing. I'm just thankful that all of those drugs they gave me didn't hurt my baby any. My doctor has given us both a clean bill of health and I plan on keeping it that way."

"That's really great to hear, Tracy," Tom said. He paused a moment and then said, "Surprised to see me?"

"I wasn't too awfully surprised when you called me, but I have to admit I was a little shocked when you said you wanted to come over tonight," she replied. "Where did you tell your wife you were going?"

Tom took a huge slug of Ultra, feeling a welcome jolt as the cold brew flowed down his palate. He stared over at Tracy and shook his head slowly from side to side.

"I'm going to level with you, Tracy—I've had more than my share of avoiding confrontations and beating around the bush with everybody."

Tracy gazed at him inquisitively. "What do you mean by that?"

"I mean that I've learned a whole lot about a lot of things lately. I've learned why some things are *not* better left unsaid and that there is a price to pay when you turn your head and look in the other direction when things aren't going quite the way you want them to go."

"Okay, now I'm really confused. What in the world are you talking about, Tom?"

He took another slug, trying to get his courage up, grasping for the right words to say.

"Peg and I have split up."

Tracy was unable to hide her disbelief. "You *what?*"

"We split up. That shouldn't really come as any real surprise to you, taking into account all that has happened."

"Jesus, Tom! I knew she would be pissed at you, but you always told me that you were madly in love with each other and that nothing would ever tear you two apart. Did you try to reason with her?"

"Ha, now that's a laugh! Tracy, there isn't anything reasonable about what has happened—not a damn thing! I've been living a lie with my wife ever since you and I went out on our first date. Now that she knows about us, she has done exactly what I knew she would do. I'm not surprised in the least."

"Oh God, Tom—I'm so sorry! I know how much you love her and the kids. I never wanted this to happen!"

"It's not the end of the world—so don't be too hard on yourself. If I had to sum up the biggest lesson I've learned, it would be 'you can't have your cake and eat it, too.' You can try like hell, but it just doesn't happen."

"But I can't believe that she wants to end your marriage! I mean, it doesn't have to be the end of the world when a partner strays in a marriage. She should at least give you a second chance! You did ask her for a second chance didn't you?"

Tom snickered. "Oh yeah, I was literally down on my knees begging her. But it's one thing having an affair with somebody and another thing making a baby with that somebody."

Tracy gaped at him, aghast. "What do you mean by that? You didn't tell her—"

"Yes, I did. I told her you were pregnant."

"Christ, Tom, *why?* You didn't have to!"

"Yes, I did. I told you I'm sick and tired of living lies all the time. I wanted to tell her the truth, so that's what I did."

Tracy was speechless. She looked away a moment, took a drink of her water and stood up. She went over to the window, parted the blinds and stared outside. Then she turned around and faced him.

"I can't *believe* this! I know what all I said to you awhile back about this, but now I'm not sure what to say. I mean, I told you that I wanted you to be the child's father and to accept responsibility, but I didn't really realize what I was asking you to do at the time. Now I do . . ."

Tom stood up and went over to her. He held her in his arms and looked directly into her eyes.

"Listen, Tracy. The last thing I want now is for you to feel bad about any of this. What you wanted me to do when this first came up was completely fair and reasonable. We went out together, had some great times and in the process you got pregnant. You wanted to keep the baby and you wanted me to accept responsibility and do the right think by being a father to the child. And that is exactly what I intend to do."

Tracy pulled back. *"What?"*

Tom smiled. "I'm going to be a father to our child."

Tears welled up in her eyes. "God, Tom—don't do this if you don't really mean it. I mean, I can't take another—"

Tom kissed her lightly on the lips. "Believe me, I mean it."

He took by the hand and led her over to the sofa. They sat down and Tom faced her.

"I'm going to let you in on something that may help you understand why I have changed my mind about this. But first, I want you to know that I do indeed love my wife and my kids. And I want nothing more than for my family to stay together. In fact, if Peg walked through that door right now and told me to come home, that she forgave me, I'd go with her in a heartbeat.

"But I really don't think that's going to happen. And if she can't ever forgive me, then I guess that's just the way it will have to be. I'll get by—I'll *have* to get by. And I will always be a part of my kids' lives in either case—Peg would never try to alienate them from me; I'll give her that.

"But the bottom line is that I have to—no, I *want* to be a father to this child. I have finally realized that I owe both of you *at least* that much."

As she listened, Tracy's face wore a range of expressions. And right now she looked confounded.

"I'm speechless, Tom."

"I can see why you might be. A lot has happened in the last week or so that you need to know about. And when I'm done telling you, I think you'll understand why I feel the way I do."

Tom proceeded to tell Tracy about the dream from beginning to end, and all of the events leading up to his meeting with Mindy Conkel. It was during his account of that meeting that Tom became uncharacteristically emotional.

"In a nutshell, I visited her and learned that she had two kids, a young boy and a girl. Both were too young to have been the child she had been pregnant with. So I just came right out and asked her what had ever happened to the child that had supposedly been mine. She told me she had aborted it."

Tom realized that his voice had trailed off and he had to force himself to maintain his composure. It wasn't easy.

"Oh, Tom—" Tracy said. "That is so sad."

"Well, I won't sit here and pretend that this news didn't hurt. Not only did it mean that I would never know my child, but I realized that *I* was the reason she had an abortion. I hadn't made any effort to hear her out, or to even consider the possibility that this was my flesh and blood we were talking about. Nope, instead I just basically told her too bad, so sad and went on my merry way. And look what happened. That baby never had a chance."

Tracy placed a hand on Tom's shoulder. "God, Tom. This is horrible. But you can't totally blame yourself for this. *She* made the decision not to keep the child, not you."

"No, I helped her make the decision by default. By not giving a shit or even acting like I gave a shit. That's what iced it."

They both fell silent. Tom took a drink of beer and shifted uncomfortably on the sofa. Tracy stared at the window, lost in thought. A few moments later, Tom spoke.

"When I drove back to Columbus, all I could think of was you and how I was not going to let this happen again. All I wanted to do was tell you that I would be a father to our baby and that I didn't care what happened as a result. I tried to call you several times but only got your voicemail. I went straight to your apartment and that's when I realized that those bastards had taken you."

Tom looked intently into Tracy's eyes. She put her arms around him and they embraced. He could hear her crying softly as her body heaved against his. He resisted his own urge to cry for a moment, then relented. He didn't care. They were tears of relief.

He faced the girl and smiled. "You may not believe this, but I haven't felt this good in a long, long time. For once, I feel complete. I know that I'm doing the right thing for a change. And it feels good."

Tracy said, "You don't know how much this means to me, Tom. I've been so down and beside myself since all of this happened. I blamed myself for much of this—I knew that we should have been more careful, but I didn't do or say anything about it. I started feeling cheap and unworthy of any joy. But right now, I couldn't be any happier. Thank you so much."

"Please don't thank me—I don't deserve it. Do you realize that I almost got you killed by not listening to you in the first place? And Molly Barnes? None of that would have ever happened if we had gone to the cops like we should have. I was an *idiot!* All I thought about was myself and how this was going to ruin me. I still can't believe I was that damn selfish."

"I must confess, I was appalled at how self-centered you were being. It just wasn't right, our playing mute while that man went scot-free after raping some poor girl and dropping her off like she was so much garbage."

"That's what I'm saying—I should burn in hell for being such a heartless bastard!"

"But Tom, you're forgetting something. You have more than atoned for what you've done. As it turns out, you were responsible for busting a drug ring that would have resulted in more violence and god only knows how many more victims."

"That's not necessarily true."

"Come on—give yourself some credit! The paper said that the cops have been trying to nail that doctor on drug charges for a long time. *You* were the reason they were able to finally nab him."

"I'll admit I'm happy about that. But it doesn't lessen the hell I put everyone through by being so damn obstinate. I just wish I'd listened to you in the first place, that's all."

A moment of silence fell. Tracy suddenly took Tom by the hand and placed it over her tummy.

"I think we should call her Erin, if it's a girl," she said.

Tom smiled and replied, "That would be a fitting name."

Tracy said, "More than just fitting. Don't you see, Tom? This little person living inside of me is the Erin you've been looking for since you had your dream. It has just taken you this long to realize it."

Tom considered Tracy's words and experienced an epiphany. Her words rang absolutely true.

He had indeed finally found the elusive Erin.